"I meant to say, men are less romantic than women."

"Perhaps you have known the wrong men."

The breath stilled in her lungs. Heat rushed from deep inside her like hot honey flooding her body. She licked her lips, watched his pupils dilate at the movement. She knew she was playing with fire.

"Is there a right one?" Had she leaned closer to him, or had he leaned closer to her?

"Of course. The key is in knowing him when you see him."

"Perhaps he could carry a calling card," she said, "to make it easier to recognize him."

"You will be able to tell in the way he looks at you," John murmured.

"And how would that be? As if I were the most beautiful woman in the world?"

"Not always. Sometimes he will look at you as if you are a tasty morsel he longs to devour."

"Mr. Ready!" Heat swept her face as his intimate tone sent delicious shivers rippling through her.

"Don't miss Debra Mullins."
Samantha James

Romances by Debra Mullins

Too Wicked to Love
Tempting a Proper Lady
To Ruin a Duke
The Night before the Wedding
Two Weeks with a Stranger
Scandal of the Black Rose
Just One Touch
Three Nights . . .
A Necessary Bride
A Necessary Husband
The Lawman's Surrender
Donovan's Bed
Once a Mistress

Too Wicked To
Love

Debra Mullins

AVON

An Imprint of HarperCollinsPublishers

This is a work of fiction. Names, characters, places, and incidents are products of the author's imagination or are used fictitiously and are not to be construed as real. Any resemblance to actual events, locales, organizations, or persons, living or dead, is entirely coincidental.

AVON BOOKS
An Imprint of HarperCollins*Publishers*
10 East 53rd Street
New York, New York 10022–5299

Copyright © 2011 by Debra Mullins Welch
ISBN 978–0–06–188250–0
www.avonromance.com

First Avon Books mass market printing: June 2011

Avon Trademark Reg. U.S. Pat. Off. and in Other Countries, Marca Registrada, Hecho en U.S.A.
HarperCollins® is a registered trademark of HarperCollins Publishers.

Printed in the U.S.A.

10 9 8 7 6 5 4 3 2 1

To the Plotiquers:
Beth, Brianna, Heather, Lynn, & Susan

Too Wicked To Love

Prologue

March 1872

It was done.

Jack Norman sat alone by the fire in his tiny parlor and lifted a glass in salute to the memory of his daughter and her new husband waving their good-byes from the coach after the wedding. Anne would be happy in the protection of her William, comfortable in her new life on her husband's ranch in Australia.

And safe, now that she was far away from him and the past that haunted him.

"Here's to you, Raventhorpe," he said. "May you rot in hell."

"Now, Jack, is that a nice thing to say? I am crushed."

The silky voice made him jerk in his chair, spilling his precious whisky all over his hand. His heart faltered as a familiar, dreaded figure stepped into the light from the dark hallway. The man was tall, thin, and fair-haired, dressed in black from his hat to his swirling cloak to his trousers and shoes. His light-colored eyes narrowed to slits above his beaky nose.

Raventhorpe.

"My lord!" Jack scrambled to his feet, but Raventhorpe pushed him back into the chair with one gloved hand on his chest.

"Sit. We have much to discuss."

Jack glanced at the unlit hallway leading to the bedroom. "But Alice . . . my wife . . ."

Raventhorpe smiled, a sinister baring of the teeth that chilled Jack's blood. "She will not be interrupting us."

"What have you done to her?" Jack dropped his glass and lunged from the chair.

Raventhorpe produced a wicked-looking blade, freezing Jack in his tracks. "She is sleeping. And I do mean sleeping, Jack, like an innocent babe."

Jack slowly raised his hands in surrender, his gaze fixed on the deadly weapon inches from his face. Raventhorpe was younger and probably faster. It would be suicide to try anything heroic. "She's still alive?"

"So far. Test me further, and that will change."

Jack swallowed hard and took one step back from the blade, then dropped into the chair again. "I am surprised to see you, Lord Raventhorpe."

"I expect you are. You thought you got away with trying to betray me."

He wiped his mouth with one shaking hand. "I don't know what you mean."

"Yes, you do. Last month you had a visit from Lord Phillip St. Giles."

His breath stilled in his lungs. "I did not tell him anything."

"Oh, come now, Jack. Of course you did. Why would you not? You promised to come to London and testify on behalf of his son—after your daughter's wedding, of course."

Dear God. He knew.

"I . . . he . . . he was a very determined man, my lord."

"I am certain he was. Of course, he is dead now."

Jack nodded. "I heard. Drove his phaeton into a frozen lake."

"Yes." Raventhorpe's lips curved ever so slightly. "Such a tragedy."

Jack squeezed his eyes closed, then opened them again. Raventhorpe had killed Lord Phillip. He might have simply said it out loud. But then, Raventhorpe had killed many people.

Including the woman Jack had helped him murder four years ago.

Even now, the shame nearly crippled him. Oh, he had not held the knife or even witnessed the deed. But he had helped cast suspicion on an innocent man. And for that, he would probably burn in Hell.

"You disappoint me, Jack. I want an apology. Right now and in writing."

"Writing?"

"Yes. Come now, be quick about it. I should hate for your wife to awaken early and witness things she should not see."

The implication was clear. Jack scrambled across the room to the chest where his wife kept her precious writing supplies. With a son in the military and now a daughter married and on her way to Australia, writing letters had very nearly become a daily chore.

He got a piece of paper and the pen and ink and sat down next to a tiny table. "I shall begin 'Dear Lord Raventhorpe . . .'"

"No. No names." Raventhorpe came to stand over him. "Or perhaps you would like to write it in blood."

"No, my lord." Jack cleared his throat, though a lump still lodged there. "How would you like this written?"

"Let's keep things simple. Just write 'I am sorry for everything' and sign your name."

Jack did as he was told. He had not had much schooling and couldn't write well, but it was legible. He signed his name.

"Excellent," Raventhorpe said. He took the letter and set it aside. Then he reached into his pocket and pulled out a small bundle wrapped in a handkerchief. "I thought you might be interested in seeing this." As he unfolded the layers of material, Jack noticed splotches of red on the snowy linen. Cold crept through him. Finally the object was revealed. His chest tightened.

"Where . . ." His voice faded as Raventhorpe displayed the bloodstained oval cameo on its dark ribbon resting against the white of the handkerchief. The last place Jack had seen it had been around his daughter's throat as she waved good-bye from the coach. He raised his gaze to meet the earl's.

"Did you really think it would be so easy?" the earl whispered.

"My . . . Anne . . . is she . . . ?"

"Dead. Yes. As I told you she would be if you told anyone about that night." Raventhorpe wrapped up the cameo again and shoved the bundle into his pocket. "You told Lord Phillip. Now he is dead, and so is your daughter and her new husband."

"Dear God." The words slipped from his lips as he fell back in the chair, all his strength gone. He had thought he had been clever enough. Thought Anne would be safe. But now . . . "My daughter is dead," he choked, tears stinging his eyes, trickling down his face.

"Yes, she is. And it is your fault."

Jack narrowed his eyes at Raventhorpe. "You killed her!" He leaped from the chair, reaching for the earl.

Raventhorpe grabbed him, twisted his arm behind his back, and held the knife to his throat. "No, Jack.

You killed her. And yourself." The earl gave one swift yank of the blade.

Blood spewed. Jack grabbed his throat as the life gushed from him, as the world tilted. He hit the floor.

Raventhorpe put the knife in his hand, curling his fingers around the handle. "So sad that you killed yourself. And here is the proof." He set the letter Jack had written nearby, then he stepped over his body and left the room.

The pale page of the note was the last thing Jack saw as the world faded from his senses.

You think you're smart, you bastard. You think you've won. But I suspected this day might come. I made a plan.

Father Holm will not fail me . . .

Chapter 1

London, four years later
June 1876

The girl mesmerized him.

John watched from his post against the wall as Genevieve Wallington-Willis flirted with a young viscount. Her husky laughter carried across the room, and her dark curls, bound by ribbons and flowers, bounced with each toss of her head. The full skirt of her white bridesmaid's dress rippled with her movements, and the fitted bodice accented her generous bosom. Even from yards away, he found himself distracted by her infectious smile and sparkling eyes.

Lured in, just like the young viscount.

He could not blame the lad. Genny Wallington-Willis had it all: beauty, social status, and intelligent wit all in one enticing package. Was she aware of her power over the opposite sex, he wondered? He had been watching her all morning, ever since he and Samuel had arrived at the church where Samuel's wedding to Genny's sister Cilla had taken place. Now that the vows were said and the wedding breakfast devoured, the guests lingered in the reception rooms of Admiral Wallington-Willis's London home, awaiting the cutting of the wedding cake. All the while, Genny flitted from one man to the other like a butterfly in an extensive garden, fascinating all of them but staying with none.

He had seen her do the same at the handful of events that preceded the wedding. At all of them, like now, he had kept himself apart from the other guests, lingering on the sidelines so as not to draw attention to himself. He was not there to dally with the opposite sex, no matter how casual the affair. Yet as he watched her dazzle then abandon yet another besotted suitor, a dangerous notion slipped into his mind, taking hold like the devil's whisper.

She would never walk away from me.

He was no rake, but he'd had a fair amount of success with the ladies in his time. He doubted such skills could be forgotten, even with the monkish existence he had been living these past few years. She laughed again, a siren song that ensnared his hungry libido. What would she do, he wondered, if challenged by a man who could match her?

The urge to try his hand, to stake his claim, silenced the voices murmuring caution in his mind. Surely a few minutes of innocent flirtation would do no harm. After all, he had managed to resist her all these weeks, and he would go back to resisting her again. But something about this day, about watching his best friend pledge to share his life with the woman he loved, awoke an unexpected yearning inside him. What could it hurt to exchange a few words of banter with a pretty girl? After Samuel came back from his honeymoon, John would probably never see her again anyway.

He took a step forward just as someone called her name. She turned, a ready smile on her lips. That smile dimmed as a handsome naval officer approached. Alarm, horror—both flickered across Genny's face in less than an instant at the sight of that gentleman, but then the brighter-than-the-sun smile returned full force. Had John not been studying her so closely, he would never have even realized anything was amiss.

She knew the young man. And she was dismayed to see him.

He halted, watching as she spoke with the naval man for a few moments. As the conversation progressed, all trace of her former flirtatiousness vanished. Her smile disappeared, her lips pressing together in a line. Her fluttering hands settled at her sides in clenched fists, her spine straight as any blade.

The young man, on the other hand, kept his charming smile in place, his posture relaxed. What was he saying to her that put the light of battle in her eyes?

"There you are, John." Samuel Breedlove stepped into his line of vision.

John fixed his gaze on his best friend's face, managing with effort to conceal his irritation that the brawny, dark-haired bridegroom had managed to block his view of Genny. "Samuel. Allow me to offer my congratulations on your marriage."

Samuel laughed and clapped John on the shoulder. "Why so formal? You sound like some stranger, not my most trusted friend."

"Nonetheless, my felicitations are sincere."

Samuel grew serious. "I know they are, as I know that without you, I might never have met Cilla. And for that, I owe you a tremendous debt."

John shrugged and shifted so he could see past Samuel. Genny had vanished, though the naval officer now lingered near the door. "Your friendship is thanks enough. You had best return to your bride, Samuel."

"You're just concerned my presence will draw attention to yours."

John met his friend's gaze. "That, too."

"Very well, let's go into the admiral's study. I need to talk to you."

The gravity of Samuel's tone put John on the alert. "Is everything all right?"

"Just come with me." Samuel started through the

crowd, leaving John no choice but to follow. They left the ballroom, passing Genny's naval officer, and headed for the stairs. As they descended, John noticed the fellow dart from the ballroom, down the hall, and into a nearby sitting room.

John hesitated on the stairs. First Genny had disappeared, and now this fellow had slipped from the party as well. She had not seemed to want the man's company—or had that been a ploy to distract anyone watching from noticing a secret assignation? Such things were not unheard of with a coquette like her.

"John, are you coming?"

"Yes." Turning away, John took the rest of the stairs at speed and followed Samuel into the admiral's study.

Genny ducked into the small sitting room and closed the door behind her. Folding her arms around herself, she wandered to the window and looked out on the street below without actually seeing any of it.

"You will not cry," she whispered to herself, even as the betraying tears stung. "Just because Mama and Papa did not warn you that Bradley would be here, in your own house . . ." She clenched her eyes closed. "He must have come with his parents. Of course he did. But I did not even know he was back from India." She took a deep breath, straightened. "You can handle this, Genevieve. You learned your lesson. You are strong."

The door to the sitting room opened. She whirled around as Midshipman Bradley Overton filled the doorway. "Hello, Genny."

He dared follow her in here?

"This room is for private family use only, Bradley. Please rejoin the guests."

"There was a time I was considered family." He ignored her request and closed the door behind him. "I've missed you, Genny."

His tender tone irritated rather than soothed. "Do not insult either of us with more lies."

"It is not a lie." He took a step closer to her. "Ever since we—"

"Stop." She held up a hand. "You told me you loved me when all you wanted was to marry the admiral's daughter. That constitutes a lie."

"You misunderstood."

"No," she snapped. "I did not. It is quite difficult to misunderstand one's own fiancé laughing about her gullibility with his shipmates. You courted me for your naval career. Not because you loved me as you claimed."

He tilted his head as he regarded her. "You have become quite hard-hearted, Genny. I can hardly credit it."

"Perhaps you should consider yourself lucky that we did not wed after all."

"I hoped our time apart might have made you see reason." He gave her a slow, lingering study that would once have sent shivers of delight through her. "I miss you, Genny."

"I certainly do not share your sentiment." She eyed the distance to the door. The only problem was, he stood between her and escape. "I should return to the reception. My family will be looking for me." She started forward. Perhaps if she moved quickly enough, she could slip by him.

"Wait a moment." He took her arm before she could pass him.

She halted, finding herself staring into the blue eyes that had once made her weak at the knees. *You are stronger than this. Walk away.*

"Do you remember the last time we were alone together?" he murmured, tracing her cheek with his fingers.

God help her, but she did. She closed her eyes as longing swept through her, challenging her hard-won confidence. Why couldn't he have been the man she had thought he was? She had wanted so desperately for it all to be real. To be married and have a family. To have someone who would finally love her, completely and unconditionally.

His deception had left her feeling foolish. Unwanted. Naïve.

Not anymore. She would not accept his imitation of love, no matter how blue his eyes or how pretty his words. She had made that mistake once, had allowed herself to be lured into the fantasy and to throw caution to the winds. Living with the consequences of that fateful night had taught her a hard lesson.

One she would never forget.

John closed the door to the study behind him. "What happened, Samuel? This should be a happy day for you."

"It is a happy day. Cilla is my world. I only hope that you, too, will someday experience such happiness."

"Dear God! Never tell me that you are married for mere hours and already seeking to see your friends join you in matrimony." John grinned, trying to stave off another odd pang of envy.

Samuel chuckled and perched a hip on the admiral's desk. "No, not at all. I know you intend to stay in England until Cilla and I get back from our wedding trip, then you'll head back to America with us. What are your plans while we're gone? Are you going to visit family?"

"No." John's heart clenched as he said it, and he turned to peruse the admiral's globe so his expression would not betray him.

"You have no plans at all? London is a fascinating city."

"I know." John gave the globe a spin. "I spent much of my youth here."

"Was that before or after you eloped to Scotland?"

"Both." The edge to the word spoke volumes.

"I'm sorry, John. I have marriage on my mind, I suppose. I know your past is not something you tend to discuss."

"Correct."

"So let's talk about my past then."

John looked over at him. "Raventhorpe?"

"Raventhorpe," Samuel confirmed.

John turned to face him, frowning. "Has our mutual enemy resurfaced already? I thought he was in France, waiting out the scandal from trying to abscond with your ex-fiancée."

"He is, as far as I know. But this is the bastard who left me for dead on a deserted island, then tried to steal Annabelle away from me. And that's only a short list of his numerous offenses."

"I do not know how that snake always manages to slither away," John said. "The people he has killed, the women he has sold into sexual slavery . . . How does he keep escaping punishment for his crimes?"

"The devil watches after his own," Samuel said.

"Apparently so. At least Miss Bailey was smart enough to jilt the blackguard."

"And that's the problem. Annabelle did jilt Raventhorpe, and he won't forget that. But she also freed me from my betrothal to her so I could marry Cilla, something *I* can't forget. She allowed me my heart's desire, John, at personal sacrifice to herself."

"A noble act," John agreed. "But you are correct. Raventhorpe will not allow her rejection of him and the ensuing scandal to go unpunished."

"That was my thought, as well. I think he might see my absence as an opportunity to strike back at her. He'll think she is unprotected."

"Agreed."

"Which is why I need you to watch over her until I get back. He doesn't know about you."

"True."

"And you did such a good job of staying out of sight—posing as my coachman, for God's sake—that he has no idea you're back in England."

"I did not pose. I *was* your coachman."

"As if anyone with eyes could not tell that you were born to be more."

"Leave it be, Samuel."

"Leave it?" Samuel stood. "Even though you never confided in me, I know you are more than the humble man you seem. Something happened that made you flee England, and you only came back here to help me stop Annabelle from marrying Raventhorpe."

"The past is done and gone, Samuel. Let us move forward into the future."

"Look, I'm grateful for everything you've done for me, and I want to respect your desire to stay in the shadows, but bloody hell, John, you wouldn't even stand up for me at my wedding!"

"Virgil Bailey did a good enough job of it." Seeing Samuel's impatience, John shook his head. They had been over this before. "It would have been my honor to stand up with you, Samuel, but it is better if no one notices me, especially those in positions of authority. And the front of a crowded church is hardly the best place to stay out of sight."

"I know that, blast you! But—"

"Look, you asked me to guard Miss Bailey while you're gone. Consider it done."

"I . . . oh. Well. Excellent then." Samuel nodded and let the other matter drop, though not permanently if the stubborn set of his jaw was any indication. "I know I'm asking a lot, John. I wish I could think of another way." He paused. "I could hire a security detail, I suppose—"

"Except that Miss Bailey is an heiress. You need someone you can trust."

"Exactly. I trust you, John. Not only do you have a fortune of your own, but I don't think Annabelle appeals to you that way."

"God, no. She's a pretty girl, but I see her more as your little sister, not to mention your former fiancée. And as for the fortune—"

Samuel scowled and folded his arms. "Don't you dare tell me again that you don't want the money, John. You spent your own savings to come and find me when Raventhorpe left me for dead. Fate was kind enough to hand us a pirate's treasure in return, and you deserve half of it."

"As I started to say, I would be grateful for my share once we get back to America."

Samuel blinked. "Well, hell. What's gotten into you today? I thought I would have to tie you down and shove the money down your throat."

"Maybe weddings make me sentimental."

"Oh, right. Certainly that must be it." Samuel fixed him with blatant look of disbelief.

"Leave off, Samuel," John said, heading for the door. "You're not my captain any longer. Or my employer for that matter since you no longer need a coachman."

"Then what the hell am I?"

John stopped with his hand on the doorknob and met Samuel's gaze. "My one true friend."

The anger fled Samuel's expression like steam escaping a boiling pot. "I just want to help you," he said.

"I know. But some things are better left alone."

Samuel nodded. "All right. Thank you for protecting Annabelle while we're gone."

"You are welcome." John opened the door.

"If it helps," Samuel said, making John pause at his

words, "the Baileys intend to leave London for Nevarton Chase tomorrow. So you'll be out of the city and sequestered in happy obscurity in the country."

"Good news indeed." John hesitated, then said, "Be happy Samuel. Enough for both of us."

He left the study, shutting the door before his friend could respond.

Genny jerked free of Bradley's hold and backed up a step, shaking off the nostalgia of the past. Bradley Overton did not like to lose, and she had bested him by breaking off their courtship last year. And as for the last time they had been alone together. . .

She preferred not to relive the crowning jewel of her humiliation. That was the past. She was a different woman now. "Let me pass, Bradley. My parents will be missing me."

Bradley did not budge, his gaze intent like a spider with its prey. "Come now, Genny. Let's not part in anger."

"Too late for that." She tried to pass him again, but this time when he reached for her, she snatched up one of her mother's cherub figurines from a nearby table and raised it like a weapon. "Touch me again, and your head will be ringing for weeks."

He slowly drew back his hand. "I suppose you are still overset about what happened between us."

"Overset!" Her voice ended on a squeak of outrage,

and she forced herself to take a breath. "I am not over-set. Overset would indicate that I cared anything for you or what you think. And that is just not true."

"Then why did you just threaten me with Cupid?" He narrowed his eyes at her. "Perhaps you have heard my name recently linked with Miss Fitzwarren's?"

"Certainly not."

"Maybe you are jealous. I know she is your friend."

"Hardly jealous," Genny said, "but perhaps I should warn her of your talent for spinning falsehoods."

"The rumors are not true, you know. You are the only woman I have ever wanted to wed."

The knowledge that such an utterance would once have filled her heart with joy only added to the bitter taste of shame at her own naïveté. How could she have been so easily fooled by a charismatic smile and a few well-chosen words? Was she truly so gullible? So hungry for someone to love her that she would accept even this sham of the real thing?

"Do you miss us, what we had?" He lowered his voice as he came closer, backing her into the corner between the door and the table. The scent of the cigars he favored filled the air between them. "I cannot forget, Genny, not any of it."

"I already have," she lied.

Anger flared in his eyes, and he grabbed her free

arm, hauling her against him. "Now who is 'spinning falsehoods'?"

She swung the Cupid at his head, but he caught her wrist and squeezed. The figurine crashed to the floor.

The door opened. Genny closed her eyes for a moment and imagined how it looked—her caught in a man's arms, however unwillingly—and anticipated the social doom that was about to descend.

"Miss Wallington-Willis," a male voice said, "they are preparing to cut the cake."

She opened her eyes and found John Ready standing in the doorway like calmness personified. Tall, dark-haired, dark-eyed, and bearded, his very stillness should have acted as balm to her fractured composure, but those enigmatic eyes had always given her the impression they saw more than she would have liked. At that moment, his steady gaze fell on Bradley, who suddenly released her and stepped back, as if commanded by John's look alone.

She could not help but be impressed by this silent show of male power. John Ready was a mystery. He worked as a coachman but talked like a gentleman and held an odd place in Samuel's household, more friend than employee. And had it been anyone else who had walked through that door, she would have been effusive in expressing her thanks. Yet all she could think as she moved away from her former suitor was *why did it have to be* him *who stumbled upon them*?

"Thank you, Mr. Ready," she said, seeking comfort in protocol.

He swung that unwavering, condemning gaze on her, chilling the warmth of any gratitude she harbored.

"I will escort you back to the ballroom," John said.

Censure underscored the words, and she stiffened, stung by his quick judgment. "That would be lovely, thank you." She arched her eyebrows at Bradley, who stepped aside so she could join John at the door.

John swept his arm toward the hallway.

She eased past him, so close that the tang of his cologne tingled her senses, her skirts brushing against his long legs. Dear Lord, she had never realized how very *tall* he was!

Bradley apparently realized he had lost control of the situation. "Hold a moment! I said hold, Mister . . . er—"

John stopped in the doorway and looked back at Bradley. "Do not leave this room for five minutes. There will be no scandal at this wedding."

Bradley opened his mouth to respond, but one hard look from John had him closing it again and nodding.

John shut the door behind them as he and Genny left the sitting room.

"Your timing was excellent," Genny murmured, as John guided her back toward the reception.

"I did this for your sister," John said. "She does not deserve the scandal that would result if it got out her sister was consorting with a lover during her wedding breakfast."

She sucked in a sharp breath. "You are quite blunt, Mr. Ready."

"I just try to tell the truth."

"Then add this to your truth: I have no lover."

He slanted her an unreadable look. "Based on what I just witnessed, I find that hard to believe."

"Try," she gritted through her teeth.

"If that young man was not your lover, then why did I find you in his arms? Why did you not cry out for help?"

Heat crept into her cheeks. "When you say it like that, it certainly sounds terrible. I was hiding *from* Bradley, not *with* him. He followed me."

"Perhaps it was prearranged."

She bit back a rude retort and tried for a reasonable tone. "I was almost engaged to Bradley, but our association ended last season. However, he apparently has not accepted our parting as well as I thought."

John stopped. "Is he making a nuisance of himself? "

She halted as well, noting the warning tone of his voice, the tension of his stance. Here stood a man ready for battle. A tingle swept through her. Clearly, if he thought Bradley was bothering her, he would do something about it. Part of her wished she could allow him to defend her honor, but it would only make matters worse.

She was wise enough now to handle her own problems. And she had no desire to be indebted to *him,* of all people. Not with his obviously poor opinion of her.

"I have not seen him in nearly a year, and I did not know he was going to be here today. No one told me." She pressed her lips together, still angry at the oversight.

"I apologize for my conclusions. I thought this was an assignation." He cast a narrow-eyed gaze down the hall. "I will go back and have a word with him."

"No." She grabbed his arm, then dropped her hand when he raised his brows. "As I said, I have not seen him in over a year. I do not understand what he wants from me when our association has clearly ended."

John gave a hard chuckle and smoothed his sleeve. "He wants what every man wants."

She cast him a sharp glance. "What do you mean by that?"

"You know what I mean, Miss Wallington-Willis." He gave her a quick assessment from head to toe that made her breath catch. She was still trying to calm her racing heart when he placed her hand on his arm and led her to the doors to the ballroom. "You are a beautiful woman, but you cannot play with men's hearts like toys. One day you will flirt with the wrong gentleman and discover you have bitten off more than you can chew."

Genny stiffened, her cordial feelings toward him

evaporating. "Are you saying I somehow gave Bradley the impression his attentions would be welcome?"

"Men are easily dazzled by beautiful women. Perhaps you should be more conservative in your behavior toward the male sex."

She jerked her hand away from his arm. "You are very rude, John Ready. How dare you accuse me of being a . . . a . . ."

"A flirt? Fast?"

"And now you insult me. Well, thank you for your assistance, Mr. Ready, but I believe I can see myself back to the festivities." She turned on her heel and marched back into the ballroom.

John watched her go, a hint of her scent lingering in her wake. She was a handful, that one. Beautiful and spirited. At least he would soon be leaving for Nevarton Chase with the Baileys to watch over Annabelle. He would no longer have to associate with—or fight his attraction to—the distracting Genny Wallington-Willis.

It wasn't that he didn't want a woman in his life. Quite the contrary. But not someone like Genny. Not a woman with connections to the very life he'd abandoned, especially a flirt who appeared oblivious to the broken hearts she left in her wake.

He could not help but wonder, had she been telling the truth about the young naval officer, or had she said that because she had been caught? If the fellow's attentions had truly been unwelcome, why hadn't she let John have a word with him?

The entire situation brought back old memories he had managed to keep at bay until then. He knew well the games these coquettes played, and Genny Wallington-Willis seemed no different than any other. Better for all of them if he kept his distance from her and focused on what was important.

With Samuel married to Cilla and Raventhorpe in retreat for the moment, he felt he was ready, for the first time in years, to pursue his own goals—but not in England. He would claim his half of the fortune he had discovered with Samuel and start a new life in America. He could have a wife, children. A home. Everything he had always dreamed about.

No one was ever going to take that away from him again.

"Oh, John, here you are."

He glanced down, surprised to see that the new Mrs. Breedlove had approached while he was watching her sister and was now standing in the doorway in front of him. The petite brunette looked stunning in white silk and lace with a wreath of orange blossoms in her dark hair. She smiled, and he caught the flash of a quick dimple in the corner of her mouth, a trait she shared with her sister, Genny.

He gave a brief bow. "How may I be of service, Mrs. Breedlove?"

She laughed. "Do be certain to call me that a few more times, John, so I can become accustomed to it!" She stepped out into the hall with him and waved her hand to indicate he should join her out of sight of the doorway.

He followed her, puzzled. "Is something wrong?"

"I only have a moment. We are getting ready to cut the cake, and once that happens, Samuel and I will be rushing off on our honeymoon. So this is the only time I can approach you to ask a terribly important favor."

"Of course. Anything I can do."

She clasped her hands together, her brown eyes full of apprehension. "I feel somewhat selfish asking this of you. After all, we are not family, though I know Samuel considers you closer than a brother. That would make you akin to my brother-in-law, correct? Family. And I am just so worried about her, John. Someone needs to look out for her while I am gone."

"Is this about—"

"She is just so young, John," Cilla plowed on, "and she thinks she knows the ways of the world, but she does not. I have tried to talk to her, but we have all been at sixes and sevens over the wedding preparations."

"I know. Samuel already—"

"She is just so headstrong. So certain she knows how things work. But that is just not true, even if she refuses to believe it. And I simply cannot go off to my wedding trip without making certain someone will be watching over her, especially way off in the country at Nevarton Chase. She could get into all sorts of mischief there."

"Mrs. Breedlove." John held up a hand when she paused for breath. "Have no fear. I have already discussed this with Samuel."

"You have?" She beamed, relief lighting her eyes. "I did not even share my concerns with him."

"He thought of it himself."

"Dear God, I have married the best man in the world." She clapped her hands together. "Except for you, of course, John."

"Of course, except for me." He grinned.

"I cannot thank you enough!" A servant came into the hallway, caught her eye, and waved her back toward the ballroom. "I must go. You must have some cake, John. Say that you will."

"I will."

"Wonderful." She reached out and squeezed his hand. "Thank you so much, John. I cannot tell you how much easier I will rest knowing that you are looking out for my sister." She turned and hurried toward the ballroom.

Sister? Not Miss Bailey?

"What . . . wait! I am to leave with the Baileys for Nevarton Chase right after the wedding."

"Yes, I know." She flashed him an impossibly happy smile. "Genny is going, too. They are having a house party." She gave him a little wave as the servant hustled her back into the ballroom, leaving him alone in the hallway.

"Ah, hell."

Miles away, in the small village of Elford-by-the-Sea, the Reverend Father Cornelius Holm crossed off the next item on his list. That was the last of the locations in London. Now he would begin searching the places outside the city. But not this week. No, his tiny parish needed him. There had been three deaths and one birth. Funerals and christenings. His task would have to wait until next week, when he had more time.

It had been years already. What was a few more days?

Chapter 2

Nevarton Chase
Three days later

Genny marched through the woods, shoving aside the branches blocking her way. She followed a path so faint that had she not known better, she would have thought no one had come this way in years. But she did know better. She had seen Annabelle and John Ready disappear this way only minutes ago from the window of her bedchamber at Nevarton Chase.

Naturally, when she had discovered that the former coachman had joined their house party as Annabelle's bodyguard, her first reaction had been annoyance. She had expected to be rid of the man once her sister had spoken the vows, yet now she was trapped with him for the next fortnight out in the middle of the country, where it was harder to avoid him. But she reminded herself (again) that she was strong. If he proved irksome, she could just ignore him.

But she could not ignore what he was doing now.

She noticed that Annabelle tended to disappear during the same occasions when John was also missing. Observation over the last day or so had led her to believe they were going off together. She had never been able to catch them in one of their secret meetings . . . until today, when she had spotted them vanishing into the trees from her bedroom window.

What respectable reason could John have for whisking Annabelle off to the middle of the woods?

She tried to be fair. Yes, the man had basically accused her of conducting an affair at her sister's wedding and made it clear he thought very little of her, which pinched at her ego. But that was hardly reason to think him dishonorable.

Yet she could not overlook that he was a good-looking man of the working class who had somehow managed to ingratiate himself with the upper echelon of society—specifically a certain American coal heiress. A man might be tempted to use his position as bodyguard to get close to a lady like Annabelle, perhaps court her in hopes of bettering his own social status.

She scowled, unhappy with the direction her thoughts were taking. Was this Bradley's legacy, to leave her distrustful of all men? She did not want to turn into a bitter spinster based on the dishonorable actions of one man. But also, she could not pretend to be ignorant of the male capacity for deception. She could not think of a single, acceptable reason why John should be leading Annabelle into the woods alone, and that itself led her to more unsavory possibilities.

Whatever his scheme, poor Annabelle would surely fall quite readily for it. She was entirely too trusting, especially considering that John was the good friend of a man Annabelle's parents thought of as a son. The young American heiress had become wealthy practically overnight only a couple of years ago when her father had discovered coal beneath their farm. She was a bit naïve and fairly unaware of the dangers of fortune hunters.

Just as Genny had been, only a year ago. Which was why she could not stand idly by and let Annabelle get caught in the same trap.

Catching the echo of a female laugh up ahead, Genny increased her pace. The laughter led her to a sunny clearing. She stopped and stayed hidden behind some bushes to assess the situation. John crouched on the ground with his back to her, a sack open at his feet. Annabelle strolled over to examine a cluster of wildflowers, blond hair gleaming in the sunlight. John rose, a blanket in his hands. Genny expected him to spread the coverlet on the ground in preparation for some romantic interlude. Instead he came up behind Annabelle, threw the blanket over her head and grabbed her around the middle with both arms.

Annabelle cried out and began to thrash as John hauled her struggling form across the grassy glade.

She stared in shock. Dear God, this was worse than she had imagined. The bounder intended to abduct her!

Fear and anger twisted in her belly, then settled into a hard core of determination. She looked around, grabbed a stout branch from the ground, then charged into the clearing, brandishing it like a club. "Leave her alone, you brute!"

John's head whipped around, shock flickering across his face. Annabelle's body suddenly sagged, jerking him off balance. Genny swung her stick, connecting with his shoulder blade. Annabelle fell. He stumbled, tripped over Annabelle's squirming form, and crashed facedown on the ground.

Genny stepped over to him and raised her weapon again. "If you even think of getting up, you will regret it."

"What the devil are you doing?" John rolled onto his back and sat up, his dark gaze promising retribution. Genny swung the branch again, but he caught it one-handed, then jerked it from her grasp with an easy strength that surprised her.

She backed out of his reach. "What the devil were *you* doing? Kidnapping an heiress perhaps?"

"Fine language for a lady." He hurled the makeshift club into the woods.

"What's happening?" Annabelle had managed to

free herself from the blanket and sat up as well, looking from Genny to John.

"This miscreant," Genny said with a wave of her hand toward John, "was trying to abduct you. Or something worse."

John rose, making Genny realize at close range just how much bigger he was. There was nothing of the lower classes about him, just several feet of irritated, powerful male. Something about that potent masculinity made her breath catch in her throat, and the low rumble of his voice vibrated through her as he spoke. "Miss Wallington-Willis, I believe you are suffering from a misconception."

"Oh, am I?" She did not want to meet those hot, dark eyes, but she made herself do it—and only because she did not want him to think her afraid, not because her insides fluttered when he looked at her. "What other explanation could there be for a man throwing a blanket over a woman's head?"

"What explanation is there for you to come charging at me with a stick?"

"You were carrying her off against her will." Genny went over and helped Annabelle to her feet. This had the happy coincidence of putting more distance between herself and the unsettling man. "I think Annabelle and I should return to the house, and you, Mr. Ready, should prepare yourself to be ejected from Nevarton Chase."

"Miss Wallington-Willis, if I *were* the type of man to abuse a woman, you yourself would be in danger right now. It was foolish to charge in like that, especially when you do not comprehend the circumstances."

Genny raised her chin, linking her arm with Annabelle's. "I comprehend well enough, thank you. If you think to kidnap Annabelle, you will have to contend with both of us."

"Genny, what are you talking about?" Annabelle unhooked their arms. "John meant me no harm."

"Annabelle, surely you cannot misinterpret what he did." Genny sent a hard look at John that was intended to cow him, but he only glared right back.

"No, I didn't misinterpret, but perhaps you did." Annabelle beamed at John. "How did I do?"

To Genny's surprise, he gave Annabelle a wide smile. "Perfectly. You notice how when you became dead weight in my arms, it was much more difficult to drag you off."

"You even fell over!" Annabelle giggled.

"As much as I would like to give you credit for that, it was Miss Wallington-Willis and her bludgeon that felled me. But you did make abducting you more difficult, so points to you, Miss Bailey."

Miss Bailey? Confused, Genny looked from one to the other. Would a lover refer to his sweetheart by so formal a title? Or was this an act for her benefit? "Annabelle, are you trying to tell me that you knew he intended to try and carry you off?"

"Of course I did. John would never do anything so terrible for real. He's teaching me to protect myself. If Richard comes back to England and tries something, I want to be ready." She scowled. "Not like last time."

"I see." The pieces began to fall together in her mind, and she looked at John. "I take it you did not want anyone to know that Annabelle can defend herself? That is why you are meeting secretly in the woods?"

"That's right." His tone offered no apology.

"Don't scold him; he didn't do anything wrong. Having John guard me was Samuel's idea." Annabelle narrowed her eyes at Genny. "Maybe if you talked to your sister more, you would have known that."

The mild rebuke hit home. Annabelle was right; she had deliberately avoided her prodigal sister despite having no contact with her for the past four years. She had done her duty and stood up as a bride's maid at the wedding, but she considered her strained relationship with Cilla to be a private matter. The fact that people had noticed it, that Annabelle had commented on it, brought hot embarrassment flooding to her face.

"Well, what was I supposed to think when I saw him throw a blanket over your head?" Genny demanded, hiding her chagrin in anger. "I knew you had sneaked off with him several times over the past couple of days.

I had no idea what the two of you were about."

"Sneaked off? You think that we . . ." Annabelle glanced at John, then burst out laughing. "Land sakes, no! John is way too bossy for me to think of him *that* way!"

John frowned at Genny. "You have a poor opinion of Miss Bailey, Miss Wallington-Willis, if you think she would dally so indiscriminately."

"You would not be the first man who tried to better his life by taking up with a woman above his station," Genny snapped. "Annabelle is a wealthy heiress. What else was I to think?"

"Why didn't you just ask me?" Annabelle said.

"I did not have time to ask. I thought he was abducting you! Besides, it is quite easy for a young lady to fall prey to a handsome man who says the right things and does the right things. You might not have listened." She stopped herself and sucked in a breath. Was she talking about Annabelle, or herself?

Annabelle propped her hands on her hips. "You don't give me much credit, do you? Do you really think that after what Richard did to me I would fall so easy for a charming smile and a way with words? What sort of ninny do you take me for?"

Genny stiffened. "I apologize if I was mistaken. I feared for your safety."

"I'm perfectly safe with John."

"Nonetheless, perhaps I should stay and observe the rest of the lessons." She slid a meaningful look at John. "To chaperone."

She had thought her suggestion would anger him, but he just nodded and addressed Annabelle. "Not a bad idea. Your reputation is already suffering, Miss Bailey. I do not want to add to any unfavorable speculation, however unwittingly."

"That's fine with me." Clearly still displeased with Genny, Annabelle gave a jerk of her head. "You can sit on that fallen tree over there."

Genny nodded and made her way to the makeshift bench. Clearly, she had been wrong about their relationship. He really was just trying to help Annabelle stay safe until her family returned to America in a few weeks. Once again her misinterpretation of a man's motives left her cheeks burning.

Fuming, she sat down on the bench, determined to keep silent. She refused to give him further opportunity to rattle her. She had sworn once that no man would ever make her feel like a fool again.

But this one just had.

John watched Genny take her seat on the tree trunk, her spine stiffer than a ship's mast, then returned his attention to Annabelle's instruction. Though he tried to ignore their audience, his back itched with the weight of their chaperone's stare. He managed to cast a glance or two her way to gauge her mood during the lesson in fighting off an opponent. He could tell she was angry, but at him or herself?

A knot clenched in his gut. Her accusations had stung, and it had been all he could do to remember his current social class and not challenge her further. Knowing Genny was forbidden fruit only added fuel to the fire. Given the situation, he could not fault her for thinking the worst, but he'd been misjudged before, and it had ruined his life.

Maybe it was being back in England that had shaken his normal calm. It had been nearly seven years now, and the simple things, like the sound of crisp English pronunciations instead of the nasal American twang to which he had become accustomed, brought a pang of bitterness for what he could not have.

He had been banished from his homeland against his will, forced to flee or else suffer punishment for a crime he had not committed. To be home again now, so close to his old haunts and his old acquaintances, made him realize how dearly he had missed his native land, even though no one who had known him before would recognize him now.

He would be leaving again in a few weeks, this time never to return.

He glanced over at Genny again. She threatened his

ability to stay away from anything connected to his old life. In his current circumstances he could never approach her, yet he was strongly tempted to pursue her anyway, consequences be damned.

If this were seven years ago, he could have had her, no questions asked.

He tormented himself by allowing his gaze to linger a bit longer this time, his churning emotions simmering in a dangerous broth of frustration and sexual attraction. Despite her lack of height, she had a voluptuous figure that exceeded anything in his most heated fantasies. He itched to touch her, to see if her skin was as soft as it looked. To feel those lush dark curls sweeping against his flesh. To look into those cat green eyes as he kissed that pouting mouth and buried himself inside that sweet, inviting body.

With other men she flirted, but around him she walked as if her spine were an iron poker and spoke as if words were arrows. If he had been free to be himself, he could have helped her channel all that unreleased passion into something more satisfying for both of them.

The hard bone of Annabelle's elbow slammed into his solar plexus, knocking the breath from him. He staggered back a step, fighting for air, jerked from his distraction.

"Oh, John, I'm so sorry!" Annabelle came over to him, hovering like a young girl over a broken doll. "Are you all right? You usually catch my arm."

"You slipped one past me." He inhaled deeply, then glanced at Genny, who looked entirely too amused. "Pleased to see me bested, Miss Wallington-Willis?"

"Pleased to see that Annabelle is such an adept student," she replied. "If she can take you, John Ready, then a true assailant will have little chance against her."

"Do you think so?" Annabelle clapped her hands. "Am I ready, John?"

"Not yet." He glanced at Genny. That superior smile of hers grated against his wounded male pride. "You will need several more lessons before I will feel completely confident that you can defend yourself unaided, so we must continue our meetings."

"John . . ." Annabelle whined.

"For now, we had best return to the house. Your mother has given strict instructions that you are not to be late to dinner again."

Annabelle scowled. "Can't we stay a little longer? This is more fun."

"I am afraid we must get back. We cannot have anyone gossiping about you."

"Fine." Annabelle spun on her heel and flounced into the woods.

"Annabelle!" He took up his sack, grabbed the blanket from the ground, and stuffed it inside. "Blast that chit!"

Genny rose from her perch. "A word, Mr. Ready."

"Another one, Miss Wallington-Willis?"

As expected, she stiffened. "I simply wanted to apologize for my assumptions earlier."

He searched her face. She looked like she wanted to chew nails, but he could tell at least part of her was sincere. "Apology accepted."

"I also want you to know I will be watching you, John Ready. And I will not hesitate to speak my mind at any questionable word or deed."

Impatience flared. "You extend one hand in apology only to strike with the other?"

"I am simply saying—"

"I know what you are saying. You doubt my character, even though your own brother-in-law requested my services." He closed up the sack with swift efficiency.

"Not every man can be taken at his word, as you witnessed at the wedding." Her green eyes hardened like shards of glass. "I will be monitoring these lessons of yours to assure no impropriety occurs. It is best for Annabelle."

"What makes you qualified to make such a decision? You are neither her mother nor her guardian."

"I am a concerned friend."

"A friend who takes it upon herself to make decisions for a woman two years her senior."

"A person's age makes no difference in the face of experience."

"Experience? Whose?" He guessed her meaning by the look on her face. "Yours?" He chuckled. "You have some arrogance, Miss Wallington-Willis, to think that Annabelle cannot make up her own mind."

"Me? Arrogant?" If she were a cat, she would have been spitting. "I cannot help but notice that *you,* my good man, have become very defensive at my very reasonable proposition. And as for Annabelle's making up her own mind . . . well, the girl could not decide which fiancé she wanted to marry only three weeks ago!"

"Are you so much more qualified than she is to make decisions about her own life? Tell me, what great life experiences have made you qualified for such a post? Have you been married? No. Are you a world traveler? No. Have you been in battle, survived a great illness, studied under the great minds of Europe? *No.* What you are, Miss Wallington-Willis, is jealous."

"Jealous!" Her eyes widened, then narrowed, sparks flickering behind thick lashes. If speech were a weapon, the words that came next would have skewered him like a scimitar. "Do you consider yourself such a good catch that I would be jealous of your relationship with Annabelle?" she hissed. "Perhaps you are nothing more than a man who apes the manners and style of his betters in hopes of charming a woman of the upper class so that he can improve his own social standing!"

He studied the purse of her lips, the stiffness of her

spine, the passion in her eyes. Only one thing, in his experience, got a woman agitated like that.

"I assume Mr. Overton is to blame for this outburst?" he asked. "Is he the man who tried to *charm* you to improve his social standing?"

She sucked in a sharp breath. Panic flickered across her face before she controlled her expression. "We are not discussing me."

"Yes, we are. You are assigning yourself as Annabelle's chaperone to guard her from my nefarious ways. While I have no objection to the idea itself, it is the spirit in which you suggested it that irritates me. From where I stand, Genny Wallington-Willis, I think that fellow's carelessness with your heart has made you into the prickly, stiff-rumped young lady I see before me."

She gasped, her mouth falling open in obvious shock. "How dare you!"

"Someone has to dare, Genny girl, or else you're going to find yourself an old maid living in your father's house, dandling Cilla's children on your knee and wishing you had had the courage to take a risk when you were still young enough to take it."

"You overstep yourself, John Ready! How dare you speak to me in so common a manner! And . . . and I did not give you leave to address me by my Christian name. You will show me some respect."

"Respect?" He blatantly sized her up with a swift

glance from face to toes and back again. "You're a pretty woman, Genny, but that attitude of yours is not going to win you a husband anytime soon. You truly are going to end up a lonely spinster if you do not learn how to control that anger of yours. Now if you will excuse me, I have to catch up with Annabelle."

He strode past her into the woods, leaving her floundering and alone in the empty clearing.

Chapter 3

Fury burned in John's gut as he strode after Annabelle. He supposed he should be grateful that Genny cared enough about the girl to come charging to her rescue. There was something admirable in that. But he could not help the way his temper simmered at being accused—again—of being dishonorable. In all the years he had lived in America, no one had ever questioned his motives. Only when he returned to England did such things happen. It was like a curse.

And his carnal reaction to Genny did not help matters.

He caught up to Annabelle where the woods let out into the meadow. "Hold a moment, young lady."

She whirled around at that, clenching her fists at her sides. "Don't speak to me like I'm a child, John."

"Then perhaps you should not sulk like one."

"Sulk!"

"What else would you call marching off in a cloud of drama just now?"

She stiffened, then sighed and relaxed her shoulders. "I suppose you're right. I apologize."

A crashing of brush behind them reminded him of their uninvited chaperone. "I expect you will have to apologize to Miss Wallington-Willis, too. I do think she honestly had your best interests at heart when she came after us."

"She thought we were having some sort of romantic interlude." Annabelle laughed. "Truth is, I bet you can't wait for the day you're free of me."

Genny broke through the trees at that moment, her expression tight with displeasure. John sighed. He regretted his harsh words now though he knew much of her attitude had to do with her past with Bradley Overton. "Will you walk with us, Miss Wallington-Willis?"

"No, thank you," she said, her tone icy. "I will make my way on my own."

"I cannot allow that," John said. "It would not be right."

"You might as well just do as he says," Annabelle said. "He won't be talked out of his duty."

"He has no duty to *me*." Genny marched forward, leaving the two of them standing there.

It took only two long strides for John to catch up with her. "On the contrary, Miss Wallington-Willis, I cannot in good conscience allow you to go off by yourself. You must allow me to see to your safety."

She stopped and turned to face him, hands on her hips. "And were you seeing to my safety just now when you said those terrible things to me? When you left me alone in the woods?"

"I apologize for walking away from you, but I had to catch up to Annabelle."

"John!" Annabelle scolded as she reached them. "Goodness, what did you say that got her so riled?"

"It does not bear repeating," Genny said.

Annabelle sent John a disapproving look. "John, tell me."

"It was a private conversation."

"Private? As if I know the meaning of the word with someone always following me about! I can't wait until Samuel and Cilla return, and you are free of your guard duty. And neither can you, I bet."

"My duty ends when your family leaves for America. Or when you marry."

"Ugh! Don't even mention that word." She wrinkled her nose and gave a shudder. "There's nothing like a forced elopement to discourage a girl from marrying."

"Agreed," Genny said. "But your marriageable years will not last forever. Do not cast them away because of one bad experience."

John raised a brow. An interesting statement from one who apparently was doing that very thing. "All men are not like Raventhorpe," he said to Annabelle.

"You *will* marry, probably sooner than you think."

"Leave it to a man to say that. I might get married, yes. But not for a good long time."

He barked a laugh before he could smother it.

Anger darkened her face. "I'm serious. Before I hitch my wagon to a man's mules, I'm going to find out what I'm made of first."

"A wise idea," Genny said. "A woman should always know her own mind, especially before marrying."

John shook his head. "You say that now, Miss Bailey, but I expect that you will change your tune when you meet the right man."

"And what makes you so knowledgeable on the subject?" Annabelle demanded.

"Instinct. And years of experience."

"Years of experience," Genny repeated. "At what, being a coachman?"

He shot her a wary glance. "Of living."

"I find it hard to understand how a man of your station can understand the subtleties of society courtship," Genny said with a dismissive shrug. But the look she gave him contained dangerous speculation.

"Oh, he wasn't always a coachman," Annabelle said.

Genny narrowed her eyes. "Indeed? Who were you before, then?"

His defenses slammed into place. "It does not signify."

"So secretive," Genny mused.

"Doesn't matter who he was before, it's who he is now that matters," Annabelle said.

"And who might that be?" Genny asked.

"Samuel's friend," Annabelle replied. "And my protector, though truth be told, Samuel didn't have to send him here to look after me."

"He cares about you," John said, his tense muscles relaxing.

"Only because we used to be engaged." Annabelle looked at Genny. "Not that I begrudge Samuel for marrying your sister. He was honest about his feelings for her. I was the one who broke the engagement, but it was the best thing all around. I think after all these years of us knowing each other, he sees me more as a little sister than anything, so it was best I didn't marry him. I just wanted you to know."

"Thank you," Genny said, then looked at John. "So my brother-in-law is the one paying you to watch over his ex-fiancée?"

John stiffened. "It is a favor, not a paid position. When he and Cilla return, all of us, including the Baileys, are going back to America." He turned his attention to Annabelle. "Now, let us return to the house so you are not late for dinner."

"Fine." Huffing out a breath, Annabelle turned and trudged toward the manor.

"After you, Miss Wallington-Willis." John waved a hand for Genny to precede him.

"I see you have not forgotten everything about civilized behavior in the wilds of America." She lifted her chin and swept past him with the regality of a queen.

He bit back the remark he would like to have made, and instead he let out a slow breath and fell into step behind her, enjoying the view of her pretty back end and bouncing curls. Just a couple of weeks more, and Samuel and Cilla would return from their honeymoon. Then they could all return to America and leave the temptations of England behind.

An hour later, Genny smoothed her hands over the silk skirt of her favorite evening dress as she regarded her reflection. She frowned, tugging down the edge of the bodice to show a hint more bosom. Then she pinched her cheeks for color and smiled.

Tiny lines appeared at the edges of her lips and eyes. Alarmed, she leaned closer to the mirror, smoothing the infinitesimal creases that had appeared. She was only eighteen. Surely the marks of old age were not setting in already? She tried for a less sunny grin, and the little wrinkles disappeared. She would have to be careful about how she smiled so no one would realize how life had already begun to ravage her face. Otherwise, she looked every inch the lady she was—and tempting enough to attract a gentleman's attention, no matter what John Ready said.

The man was insufferable. Arrogant. Entirely too brash for his station. Though he spoke like an Englishman, clearly he had spent too much time in America and forgotten his proper place in society. How dare he imply that she was too hidebound to attract a husband? He knew nothing about her!

Well, except what he had seen at the wedding.

The discomfort of that moment when he had discovered her in Bradley's arms still lingered. He had seemed to believe her when she had told him she had been an unwilling partner in that embrace, but apparently he had exchanged one bad opinion of her for another. Now he no longer regarded her as a tease, but instead he had marked her as a difficult woman doomed for spinsterhood.

She met her own gaze in the mirror. At least she had found out the truth about Bradley before she had wed him. How horrible would her life have been had she said the vows, only to realize that her husband's undying love extended to her father's position as a Navy admiral and no further? She had escaped a bad situation by a hairsbreadth and was grateful the truth had been revealed in time.

But though she had walked away from the battlefield victorious, some injuries never seemed to heal.

And now here was John Ready, scratching at the wounds she thought so well guarded. She needed to find out more about him, to uncover the secrets he hid. Only then would she have the upper hand.

Setting aside the memories of the past, she made her way downstairs to the drawing room, where everyone awaited the summons to dinner. Near the fireplace, their host, Virgil Bailey, held a low-voiced private conversation with Genny's father, the admiral. Everyone else clustered around their hostess, Annabelle's mother, Dolly Bailey, where she held court from her wheeled chair.

John normally joined them for dinner, but he was nowhere to be seen.

"Genny, dear! There you are!" Dolly, blond, buxom, and perpetually cheerful, waved Genny over. "We have the most marvelous afternoon planned for tomorrow."

Genny joined the group surrounding Dolly, careful to avoid her blanket-covered leg, which was elevated in an extended position by the adjustable footrest of the chair. Dolly had broken her leg nearly a month ago, but like any lady of a fashionable bent, she sought to keep her infirmity from sight at all times. Seated around her were Annabelle, Genny's mother Helen, and an eligible bachelor Dolly had invited to balance out the party, Sir Harry Archer.

Sir Harry was a baronet with a small holding nearby. Genny did not know him particularly well. Brown-haired and hazel-eyed, he wore spectacles and had a jovial personality that never seemed to dim. He did not appear particularly old, in his thirties perhaps, but he walked with a cane due to a leg injured in a hunting accident.

"It is the most wonderful thing," Helen said after Genny had greeted everyone and taken a seat on the settee beside her. "Sir Harry has written a play for us to perform. Won't that be amusing?"

"He has?" Genny fixed the baronet with what she hoped was a polite smile even as she groaned inside. "How clever, Sir Harry!"

"Not at all, not at all." He smiled, pushing up his spectacles. "I have written roles for all of you, even Mrs. Bailey. I shall direct."

"Me?" Dolly exclaimed. "Well, I'm afraid I can't do much with this leg of mine, Sir Harry. But wasn't that sweet of you?"

Like the gentleman he was, Sir Harry ignored the American's scandalous use of the word "leg." "Now, Mrs. Bailey, I have considered the situation of your mobility and taken that into account. You will be playing the queen of the fairies and only need to sit on your throne. So you see? No problem at all."

"The queen of the fairies? Oh how lovely!" Dolly clapped her hands.

"Naturally your husband will play the king," Sir Harry continued.

"Who am I going to play?" Annabelle asked, leaning forward in her chair.

"You are Bella, daughter of the queen, who has found her true love despite the jealous plotting of her evil sister."

"Oh, my! And who is my true love?"

"That will be played by Mr. Ready." Sir Harry adjusted his spectacles again and looked around. "Will he be joining us this evening?"

"Our head groom asked him to look at a horse's leg," Dolly said. "Something about a poultice. I don't think he'll be dining with us tonight."

"Ah, yes. I suppose a man who used to be a coachman would know a bit about horses. Very well." Sir Harry frowned down at the small list in his hand. "Well, I have him set to play Frederick, a farm lad who is secretly a prince and has fallen in love with the beautiful Bella."

"I'm sure he'll be tickled at the part," Dolly said.

"The admiral and Mrs. Wallington-Willis play Prince Frederick's real parents, the king and queen, who hid him with a farmer's family to protect him from the fairies."

"Sounds like they found him anyway," Annabelle said.

"You are correct, Miss Bailey."

"Annabelle," she insisted with a sweet smile.

Sir Harry fumbled his list, appearing a bit undone by

Annabelle's flirtatious tone. Then he cleared his throat, straightened his spectacles (again), and returned his focus with visible effort to the piece of paper. "The . . . that is, Malevita, the other daughter of the queen of the fairies, has found Frederick and wants him for herself. She is quite envious of Bella and will stop at nothing to prevent him from marrying her."

"So that means Genny plays Malevita," Annabelle said. "Since she's the only girl left."

"Yes, that is also correct." Sir Harry gave Genny an anxious look. "Does that meet with your approval, Miss Wallington-Willis?"

Stunned, she could not speak for a moment. A childlike protest rose inside her, but she held it back. She would have to play a jealous, evil wretch to Annabelle's sweet heroine? And with John Ready as her love interest? "Me?" she finally squeaked.

"I wrote the role especially for you," Sir Harry continued. "Malevita hates her sister Bella and is determined to win Fredrick for herself so they can take over Fairyland together."

"She sounds awful," Genny said.

"There is no play without Malevita. I think you will be most compelling."

"Come now, Genny. You know you are perfect for the part," Annabelle said.

"What does that mean?" Genny asked. "Are you saying I would not make a convincing Bella?"

Dolly laughed. "That would mean Annabelle would play Malevita, and that would just not work, would it?"

"I agree," Genny's mother said. "Annabelle has the look of a romantic heroine. You are such a strong personality, Genny, that I believe Sir Harry has the right of it. You will make an excellent Malevita."

She was certain they didn't realize the blow they had just dealt her. Was this how everyone saw her? When they said "strong personality," did they really mean "difficult"? Or, heaven help her, "stiff-rumped"?

Dear God, had that odious man been right?

Since there was no escaping the production, she would have to accept the role they had assigned her. She was nothing like the character of Malevita, but perhaps if she performed poorly enough—for clearly she was incapable of playing anyone truly evil—they would all realize their mistake in casting her as the villain.

"I tire so easily these days that we can't start tonight," Dolly declared. "We should begin tomorrow afternoon. If we can all learn our lines, maybe we can perform the play at the picnic next week to celebrate Samuel and Cilla returning from their honeymoon. Won't that be a wonderful surprise?"

"Perform? In front of an audience?" Annabelle

clapped her hands to her cheeks with a little squeal.

"Of course! It will be marvelous," Dolly said.

"A splendid idea, Dolly," Genny's mother said. "Sir Harry, thank you so much for writing the play."

"My pleasure," Sir Harry said. He fixed Genny with a look that gave her the strange impression his bright hazel eyes saw everything, whether she wanted him to or not. "Thank you for agreeing to play the villainess, Miss Wallington-Willis. I am sure you will not find the part difficult."

She forced a smile. "I am certain you are right."

At this hour of the evening, the stables were nearly deserted. John lingered at the stall where the mare, Melody, was stabled. He stroked his hand along her neck as Sam Webb, the head groom, checked the poultice on her leg again.

"How is it looking?" John asked.

"Smells like something died." The older man rose from his crouch, patting the mare's flank. "But in my experience, those are usually the best ones. What the devil is in that stuff?"

John shook his head, grinning as the mare nudged his shoulder with her nose, no doubt looking for the chunks of carrot he had been known to carry with him. "Old family recipe. If I tell anyone about it, I will be disowned."

Sam rubbed his chin, peering at John in the dim light. "Any chance your pa could adopt me?"

John laughed. "Sorry, no."

"That's a shame." The short, stocky groom stretched, then exited the stall, latching it behind him. "It's getting late. I'm going to the kitchen to see if I can flatter the cook into feeding me."

"That should not be too hard, seeing as she is your wife."

Sam chuckled. "You'd be surprised. You coming?"

"No, thank you. I am not hungry." Melody nudged him again, and he dug a chunk of carrot out of his coat pocket. "Here you go, Greedy."

Sam laughed as the horse lapped the carrot from John's hand. "Females. Always want what's in your pockets."

John grinned. "I will be certain to tell Mrs. Webb you said that."

"Only if you promise to say my eulogy after she kills me." Sam gave the mare one last rub on her neck. "You'll douse the lamps?"

"I will."

"Fair enough. Good night, John."

"Good night, Sam."

Sam's footsteps echoed through the empty stables, followed by the creak of the door as he left the building. John lingered with Melody a few moments longer, then stepped away and began to go through the building, extinguishing the lamps. The music of the stables followed him: the swish of tails, the shuffle of large bodies, the occasional equine whuff. And the smells: sweet hay, the musk of horses, leather. By the time he had put out the last lamp, emotion clogged his throat.

Bittersweet memories flooded into his mind, flashes of a life that no longer existed. He gripped the door of a stall for a moment, trying to forget the feel of fine horseflesh beneath him, the power of the animal surging forward as the landscape swept past him in a blur, the stinging wind whipping at his face . . . There was a time when he'd had his own stables of pedigreed horseflesh and a small estate where he'd trained some of them. He'd had dreams of breeding champions.

But everything had changed after Elizabeth.

The recollections haunted him, as alive now as the events that had created them. And as painful. After Elizabeth's death, he had left England, intending never to return. Yet now he was back, and he could not help but remember with longing a different time, a different life.

A life he wished he could get back.

But there was no sense in wishing for what could not be. His old life was gone, and so was the man he used to be. He was already risking a lot by staying in England this long. It was only pure luck that someone had not recognized him before now. Or perhaps the passage of years had changed his appearance enough that no one would see his former self in the guise of the humble coachman, John Ready.

No one except Genny Wallington-Willis, that is.

What had she called him? *A man who apes the manners and style of his betters . . . so he could improve his own social standing.* Ah, if she only knew. He would have to keep a sharp eye on that perceptive young lady. Smart, beautiful—she was exactly the kind of woman he liked, even with her prickly exterior. But if she got it into her head to ask questions, she could ruin everything.

Most people did not look past the picture he presented to the world. Here, in England, he was a humble coachman. At home in America, he was simply one more crewman, one more pair of hands on board ship.

Once they returned to America, with his half of Samuel's treasure in his pockets, he would finally make a home of his own even though that home would not be the one he had always dreamed about in his youth. No, that life would be far from England and the past that sought to trap him. But it would be his. And that would have to be enough.

Genny escaped after dinner as soon as she was able. Claiming a headache, she excused herself from the company, who had returned to the drawing room and were even now eagerly discussing Sir Harry's play. She trudged up the stairs, grateful to leave the aspiring thespians to their fervent discussions. After all, none of them were playing the villain.

What had possessed Sir Harry? An evil fairy who was jealous of Annabelle? And for that matter, a stiff-rumped spinster who would dandle her sister's children on her knee? A dull ache tightened in her chest. Was she really so terrible a person? Had her experience with Bradley changed her so drastically?

She had not thought so, but recent events seemed to point to the contrary.

She did not want to be the bitter spinster living on her sister's generosity, nor the sharp-tongued woman asked to play the role of the wicked fairy because no one could credit her as the heroine. She wanted her old self back, the happy, trusting young woman she had once been. She was only eighteen years old; she did not want to live a life of regret and resentment.

She wanted to marry. She wanted a family. That Cilla, who had been disowned by their father for four years, could be welcomed back into the fold so easily both warmed and stung. That her sister had found such bliss in her second marriage should have pleased her. Instead she wanted to lash out, to demand why she, too, could not have such happiness.

Dear God, perhaps she really was the evil fairy, jealous of her sister. The realization weighed like a stone in her heart.

She neared the top of the flight of stairs. As her head came level with the floor above, a movement caught her eye.

John Ready stood in front of the bedchamber at the far end of the hall. He glanced around, his manner furtive as he clutched his coat closed with one hand, his arm bent close to his chest. She ducked down so he would not see her, then cautiously peered back over the edge of the landing as he let himself into his room and closed the door.

What did he have wrapped in his coat? A lump above his curled arm gave a clear indication that he was hiding something. Dear God, was he stealing from the Baileys?

She had believed his protests of innocence this afternoon. Had taken his word that he had no designs on Annabelle's fortune. Annabelle herself had appeared to trust him completely. What if both of them had been duped?

She narrowed her eyes, her mouth thinning. The Baileys had shown her nothing but kindness, and she would not stand by while this fortune hunter robbed them blind. Gathering her skirts, she hurried up the stairs and headed straight for the former coachman's chamber.

Chapter 4

Genny burst into John's room, taking great satisfaction as he jerked in surprise. Standing on the far side of the bed, he dropped whatever it was he held, then swore softly and glared at her as she remained in the doorway.

"Blast it, woman! Close the door!"

She flinched at his tone. He definitely seemed angry, which said to her that he was probably guilty as well. Ignoring both his demand and her own twinge of disappointment, she took a step into the room, folding her arms across her bosom as she blocked the doorway. "What are you doing, John Ready?"

He strode over to her, yanked her out of the way by her arm, then shut the door. "What part of 'close the door' did you not understand, Miss Wallington-Willis?"

She shook off his hold. "Open that door immediately! Have you no sense of propriety?"

"This from the woman who just burst into a man's bedchamber?"

"We need to leave that door open. What if someone sees?" She turned toward it, and he stepped between her and the portal.

"No, we do not," he said.

He prevented her escape with the sheer bulk of his tall, muscled form, his dark gaze implacable and communicating what she already knew. He would not move, and he could not *be* moved—not by someone like her, so much smaller and softer than he.

Had the air thickened? Why was it suddenly so hard to breathe?

"Let me go," she said.

He raised his brows. "I am not stopping you from leaving."

"Yes, you are."

"No." He smiled, a flash of startlingly healthy teeth through his dark beard. "I am stopping you from opening the door."

"I cannot leave without opening the door, Mr. Ready."

"I am asking you to wait a few moments. Surely that is not too much to ask?"

"Why?" She backed away a step, watching him with growing wariness. "What do you want from me?"

He shook his head and, taking her arm in a firm yet guiding grip, he steered her farther into the room. "I want you to stay here until I tell you to go. This should not take long."

"What should not take long? What do you want?"
She glanced at the neatly made bed with apprehension
as they moved closer to it. Dear God, what had she been
thinking, charging into his room like that? Would she
now pay the ultimate price for her headstrong impulse?
"I can scream very loudly, Mr. Ready. I suggest you
unhand me immediately."

He chuckled. "I am certain you can, Miss Wallington-Willis, but to do so would bring on the very scandal you seek to avoid." They reached the bed, and he
indicated it with his free hand. "Please sit here and do
exactly what I tell you."

Did he think her so cowed by him that he could do
anything he wanted? Even . . . Her breath caught, a
tingle rippling through her. She suddenly became aware
of how small the room was. "I will not."

He sighed and rolled his eyes heavenward. "Please,
Miss Wallington-Willis."

"I will not," she said again.

He gave a gentle push to her shoulder. She nearly
fell backwards, then landed in a seated position on the
edge of the bed.

He crouched down so they were eye to eye. "You will."

There came that shiver again, that quicksilver burst
like champagne bubbles beneath her skin.

"So you are bigger than I. You have proven that."
She glared and curled her fingers into the coverlet, her

mind racing. She could scream, yes, but he was right—it would bring the entire house running. "Let me leave, and I will not report this disreputable behavior to the Baileys."

"Indeed?" He rose, then stripped off his coat.

She swallowed hard as he tossed the garment beside her on the bed. The muscles of his arms flexed beneath the simple cotton shirt, clinging like a lover's hands to every swell and ripple. Her stomach fluttered. She should scream for help, reputation be hanged. But for all that she found him unpredictable, strangely she did not fear him. She still believed she could reason herself out of this predicament.

He reached up and unfastened his neckcloth.

"Stop! What are you doing?"

He grinned and jerked off the tie. "Calm yourself, Miss Wallington-Willis. As I said, this will only take a few moments."

He handed her the tie, then knelt on the floor.

She gaped at the black slip of cloth hanging from her fingers. "I want to leave now, Mr. Ready."

"We are almost done here." He got on his hands and knees and peered under the bed.

"I do not like this one bit!" She dropped the tie as if it burned. The instant it hit the floor, it was yanked under the bed by an unseen force. She squealed and lifted her feet, staring at the spot where the tie had been.

"Blast it!" John flattened himself down on his stomach and stretched his arm as far as he could under the bed.

Genny peered down at him, mesmerized by the play of his muscles beneath his shirt. "What happened? Where did it go?"

"Got it." John's hand reappeared, one end of the tie clutched in his fingers. Slowly he dragged it out from under the bed, making it wriggle like a snake against the wood floor.

"What is under there?" Genny whispered.

He suddenly gave a hard yank. The tie shot out from under the bed, nearly hitting him in the face, then crumpled into a heap in front of him. A second later a fat, fluffy gray kitten darted out and pounced on the end of the strip of cloth. John scooped up the tiny animal by the scruff, then shifted to a sitting position right there on the floor, holding up the kitten to look into its face. "You have been most troublesome, madam."

"That is what you smuggled into the house? A kitten?" Slowly, Genny lowered her feet to the floor. As she looked more closely, she could tell the small cat had gotten into a fight recently. "What happened to it?"

"Precious here had a disagreement with the other barn cats. I brought her inside the house to give her a chance to heal."

"Precious?" Her heart melted.

He shrugged and cradled the kitten in his big palm,

stroking beneath her jaw with the finger of his other hand. "What did you think I was doing?"

Remembering how she had boldly stormed into his room, Genny flushed. "I was not certain. It looked like you were trying to sneak something into your room."

"Oh, I was. The housekeeper, Mrs. Morris, believes that pets might carry vermin and does not allow any in the house. So I had to wrap her in my jacket to avoid discovery." He raised a brow at her. "Given your poor opinion of me, I wager you thought I was up to something reprehensible."

"I thought . . . that is . . . you had . . ." She flushed beet red. "I apologize, Mr. Ready. I believed you might be stealing something from the Baileys."

"Stealing from them?" His expression darkening, he got to his feet, holding the kitten against his chest. "Do you make a habit of maligning a man's character every time you speak?"

"Of course not! I did apologize."

"Yet that does not stop you from looking at me as if I would attack you at any moment."

"I know you will not."

"Do you?" He eyed her with that hot, dark gaze. "From your reactions to my simple request to wait a few moments before attempting to open the door, I believe that is *exactly* what you were thinking."

"Do you think yourself so irresistible?" She stood

up, uncomfortably aware that her slighter height did not gain her any advantage. But at least she was on her feet and not cowering like a frightened girl.

"I am simply reacting to your own behavior. What am I to think about a young woman who charges into a man's bedchamber? You know you should not be here. It could be very dangerous for you."

His voice had deepened, vibrating straight to her belly. She moved away from her precarious position between the bed and the man, hating that he was right. "Come now, John Ready. You and I both know I am perfectly safe in your company."

"Now that is a switch. Just this afternoon you accused me of trying to romance Annabelle to further my social position. Either I am socially ambitious or I am not. You need to make up your mind, Miss Wallington-Willis."

"You make a lot of demands for a . . . a . . ."

"A what?"

She licked her suddenly dry lips. "A . . . coachman."

"You forget, I am no longer a coachman." He set the kitten down on the bed. "I am a man, and I have some years of experience compared to yours. When I see someone like you, I simply cannot walk away."

"What do you mean, someone like me?" When he remained silent, she prodded, "Prickly? Stiff-rumped?" Her voice caught on the last word.

He regarded her with a regret that soothed her shredding composure. "I should not have said those things."

"Why not? They were the truth." She shrugged and turned away. "I am sorry to have disturbed you."

"Wait." He reached out and caught her arm, his touch warm and fleeting before he dropped his hand away. "Please accept my apologies."

"Not for telling the truth." She hesitated, struggling to hide the misery that even now welled inside her.

"It was cruel of me. I was angry." He gave her a self-deprecating grin that made her heart melt in her chest. "You were only looking out for Annabelle. You had no idea I was teaching her to defend herself."

"Your secret is safe with me." Once more, she turned to leave. Suddenly something flew into her skirts. She squealed and spun around, trying to see what had snagged her clothing.

John burst out laughing and came toward her. "Stop, stop. I will get her."

Genny craned her head to see over her shoulder. The little kitten hung by its front paws from the dangling end of the large bow on the back of her skirt. "Oh, no! John, get her before she falls."

"She will not fall, will you, Precious?" He snagged the kitten by the scruff of her neck and tried to pick her up. Genny's bow came with her, still hooked by her tiny claws. "Oops. Wait a moment. She's caught."

Genny watched his lean fingers as he tried to disentangle the cat. "Do not hurt her."

"I will be as gentle as possible."

Watching the care with which he handled the animal, she did not doubt it.

"I think I have . . . ah, blast it." In trying to pull the kitten loose, he had instead tugged her bow free of its knot. "If I can get her to release the sash, we can tie the bow again, and you can be on your way." He gingerly began to peel the kitten's claws from the end of the bow, one at a time.

She turned to face him now that the bow had become completely untied. "Let me hold her, so you can use two hands." She held out her cupped palms.

He hesitated, then plunked the animal into her hands. "She is very quick," he said. "Hold her fast."

"I have her." Genny grinned up at him. "She is purring."

"I guess she likes you." One by one, he freed the cat's claws from the dark pink satin.

"At least someone does." The moment the words left her lips, she wished she could call them back.

Without taking his attention from his task, he said, "Shall I ask what you mean by that?"

"Oh, come now, John. Even you commented on your dislike of me."

"I never said I disliked you." Having freed one paw,

John moved to the other. "I said if you did not forget about the bounder who hurt you, you would turn bitter in your later years."

"Oh, I see. It must have been *him* you called 'stiff-rumped.'"

"That must have hurt. I apologize."

"If that does not indicate dislike, then what does?"

"It seems to me," he said, finally untangling the kitten's last claw, "that it means I care."

She could not stop the cynical smile that twisted her lips. "You barely know me. Why would you care about me?"

"Because you are a good person. You came charging after me with a stick today when you thought I was trying to abduct Annabelle. That takes courage." He took the kitten and stroked its head, his gaze steady on hers.

"What was I supposed to do? Stand there and watch?" She kept her eyes on his fingers as he stroked the cat's fur. That tantalizing tingle swept into her belly again.

"Other people would have. Other women would have run to find a man to protect them, or screamed, not grabbed a stick and tried to pummel me into releasing her."

"There was no time. I did not want Annabelle to get hurt."

"You did what needed doing. So do it again, Genny.

Do what needs doing. Forget the blackguard who clearly broke your heart and get back to living your life."

She opened her mouth to scold him for his familiarity, but instead said, "I thought I had."

"You are so suspicious of everyone. While it is good not to be a naïve child, you have forgotten how to give people the benefit of the doubt."

"Maybe it's easier that way."

"Shoot first and ask questions later?" He chuckled. "Your father would probably approve—*if* you were commanding a naval ship."

"Papa does not know what happened with Bradley," she admitted.

He frowned. "Why the devil not? Excuse my language, but Overton needs a good thrashing, and your father is just the man to do it."

"I simply never told him." She shrugged, hoping he could not sense the half-truth. "It is over now."

"Apparently not, if the cad accosts you in your own house!"

"That has never happened before. The last I heard, he was in India."

"But he is back. What is to stop him from continuing his pursuit of you?"

"I will be more vigilant."

"Will that be enough?" John tried to hold her gaze,

but she glanced away. "What is it, Genny? You are not telling me all of it."

"It does not concern you, John." She lifted her chin and made herself look at him. "We barely know each other."

"I know more than you think."

"I doubt it." She turned and headed for the door. "I had best leave. I do not want a lot of talk."

"I know that you flirt with men to keep them at a distance," he said, as she reached for the doorknob.

That truth stopped her, and she braced herself by clenching her fingers around the knob. She glanced back at him. "Nonsense."

He set the kitten on the bed. The furry creature pounced on the tie tossed on the coverlet as John came toward her. His dark eyes gleamed in a way that made her think he saw more than she would have liked. "Is it?"

"That hardly seems productive. Flirting is used to entice a gentleman closer, not keep him away. Clearly, you have been in America for too long."

"I do not think so." He leaned against the door, his gaze steady on hers. "It is easier to be the one who strikes first, don't you think? Then you never get hurt."

"You are making no sense at all." She turned away from the door, flustered.

"Your bow is still untied. I could—"

"No." The word came out more forcefully than she'd intended, and she whirled to face him, reaching behind her, fumbling for the dangling scrap of silk. "I can do it."

"All right." He crossed his arms, leaning one shoulder against the door. That unwavering gaze seemed to see everything she wanted to keep hidden, and his ever-present calm grated against her frazzled nerves like a hand brushing a cat's fur in the wrong direction. "Let me know if you need my help," he said. "With anything."

"Will you stop saying that? I have already told you I do not need your help!"

"I did not mean to upset you."

"I am not upset." To her horror, her voice thickened as emotion swamped her. "You are a very rude man, John. Why can you not let things be?" She let go of the stubborn sash—which refused to tie—and covered her face with her hands.

"Here now." He came to her, tugging her hands away from her face. "Surely it is not all that bad."

"You . . . you keep pushing. And saying things. And . . . and staring." Jerking her hands from his, she glared at him. "Why are you always staring at me?"

"Because you are beautiful."

She squeezed her eyes shut. "Do not seek to flatter your way out of this discussion, John Ready."

"It is not flattery when it is the truth. Look at me." He

took her by the upper arms and gave her a little shake so that she opened her eyes again. "If you let what he did change who you are, then he has won."

"This is not a battle."

"It sounds like one to me. Now." He turned her around and calmly began restoring her bow. "Forget Overton. He was a fool if all he could see was your social connections."

"How did you know that?" she whispered. Heavens, was she wearing a sign for all to see?

"I inferred as much when you accused me of courting Annabelle to further my social agenda."

"Of course. I had forgotten." The silk around her waist tugged and pulled as he finished up the bow.

"Now." With his hands on her upper arms, he guided her around to face him again. "You are all set to rights, and you are free to leave."

"Oh, yes." She glanced at the door, feeling as if she had never seen it before.

"Genny." He paused until she turned her head to look at him. "I do not want Annabelle," he said.

The ripples in her belly surged like a bubbling geyser, but she would not allow herself to revel in it. That avid look in his eyes could not be for her. "Of course you do. All men want Annabelle."

"Not all men. Not I."

"If you say so," she said with a roll of her eyes.

"I do not want Annabelle," he said again, this time with an intensity that startled her.

She propped her hands on her hips. "And why not? She is beautiful, kind, rich—"

"Are you a matchmaker now?"

"No!" She flinched away, startled. "I am just pointing out that I find it hard to believe that you are not attracted to a beautiful American heiress."

"Every man fancies different qualities in a woman. I am simply not interested in Annabelle."

"She is a lovely girl."

"She is."

"Quite sweet for the most part."

"Most definitely."

"Her family is simply delightful."

"Salt of the earth," he agreed.

"And, of course, there is the money."

"If that is the type of thing a man is looking for, then yes."

"What do you mean, the type of thing a man is looking for?" She gave a brittle laugh. "What man would turn his back on a full purse?"

"Wealth is not everything," he said, "though it certainly makes life easier."

"Men select women the way they select their horses— according to breeding ability and value."

"You, Miss Wallington-Willis, are quite the cynic."

"Oh, I am Miss Wallington-Willis again, am I?" He was looking too closely at her, seeing too much. She bit her lower lip. "You were calling me Genny a few moments ago."

"Was I? An oversight." His gaze dropped to her mouth, held.

The breath stilled in her lungs. Heat rushed from deep inside her like hot honey flooding her body. She licked her lips, watched his pupils dilate at the movement. She knew she was playing with fire. "I meant to say, men are less romantic than women."

"Perhaps you have known the wrong men."

"Is there a right one?" Had she leaned closer to him, or had he leaned closer to her?

"Of course. The key is in knowing him when you see him."

"Perhaps he could carry a calling card," she said, "to make it easier to recognize him."

"You will be able to tell in the way he looks at you," John murmured.

"And how would that be? As if I were the most beautiful woman in the world?"

"Not always. Sometimes he will look at you as if you are a tasty morsel he longs to devour."

"Mr. Ready!" Heat swept her face as his intimate

tone sent delicious shivers rippling through her.

"I was John a few moments ago," he said, the corner of his mouth lifting.

"Oh, stop!" She gave a quick push to his chest as a laugh burbled forth. But rather than pulling her hand right back, she let her fingers linger against him for a brief moment. His heartbeat thundered against her palm through his cotton shirt.

"Genny."

The low half growl had her jerking her gaze back to his, and what she saw there both thrilled and unsettled her. She made to drop her hand, but he clapped his over it, holding it firmly against him.

"John . . ." She swallowed hard. "You are looking at me as if I am a tasty morsel."

"Let's find out," he said, and brought his mouth to hers.

Panic flared, then disintegrated into mind-numbing pleasure. Oh, this was a man who knew what he was doing! For just a moment, she allowed herself to surrender, for her lips to part, her body to lean into his. He smelled of leather and horses . . . and soap. In a swift move, he turned both of them, backing her up against the door with his weight as he deepened the kiss, tasting every inch of her mouth in skillful devastation.

She didn't know how her hands got tangled in his hair. Suddenly they were just there, just like her breasts were crushed against his muscled chest, and her mouth had opened to the thrust of his tongue. Her body sang with sensation, flaring to life as if she had finally awakened to the world for the first time.

He gripped her head between his hands, holding her still as he sought and took what he wanted, what they both needed. Then he tore his mouth from hers and stared into her eyes, sucking in air as if he had been drowning.

For just a moment, she could see the man behind the mystery in those dark eyes—aching loneliness and deep pain . . . and such hot, sexual hunger that she was surprised he had not stripped her naked and taken her like a savage.

Part of her thrilled to the image.

But the other part of her retreated as quickly as possible behind the shield of intellect and sarcasm.

He pushed away from her and slowly backed up, his hands fisting at his sides. "I apologize. I should not have mishandled you that way."

She could hear the sincerity in his voice, see the self-loathing in his expression. She knew he meant it. Knew, too, that his passion had not been feigned. He wanted her, in the simple, basic, primal way that males wanted females. And she gloried in it.

But there were too many unanswered questions. Too many huge, frightening feelings. Instincts clamoring inside her that she had never felt before. Was this really her, this burning, ravenous creature who wanted to throw morality aside and give herself over to him? She had explored passion once before and been burned for her choice, and the fact that the intensity of that experience paled in comparison to what she felt now. . .

"I am not nearly as wealthy as Annabelle," she said.

She registered the shock in his eyes before she turned, opened the door, and left.

He did not follow.

Chapter 5

Father Cornelius Holm rose early every morning; he believed in greeting the new day the moment the good Lord raised the sun. Today he made for Evermayne. Perhaps inquiring here was a waste of time; after all, it was the most obvious place to begin, and the solicitors would certainly have looked there already. But then again sometimes people confessed things to a holy man that they did not reveal to others.

John had not gotten much sleep.

Erotic dreams plagued him, utterly realistic ones where Genny came to him in the night, sometimes naked, sometimes clad in diaphanous nightclothes that revealed more than they concealed. She would slowly strip off the flimsy garments, then climb on top of him to ride him like a wild stallion. Or she would climb into his bed naked and beg him to make love to her.

In his mind, he took her a hundred times, a hundred different ways.

By the time the sun rose, he was hard, hot, and irritable. He took care of the immediate physical problem with a few strokes of his hand, but his efforts only took the edge off. Genny had broken through his careful defenses—practices and disciplines that had served him well for years—and brought the roaring beast of his libido back to vigorous, aching life.

He splashed water on his face from the basin on the bureau, the coolness easing the heat of sexual arousal. He dried off with a towel, then ran a hand over his beard and reached for his trimming scissors. As he raised the implement to his face, he met his own gaze in the mirror, then slowly lowered the trimmers.

He had overstepped by kissing her. Not only had he been raised that a man did not touch a lady of her class unless he had a marriage proposal on his lips, but truly, what could he offer her? The life he had been born to had been ripped away from him, and for the past seven years he had been running, accumulating little more than the clothes on his back and his weekly wage. There had been no time for a home or a wife or children. And it had been too dangerous. What if someone had recognized him?

But now . . . Samuel had discovered treasure on the island where Raventhorpe had left him marooned, and he had offered John a share for mounting the rescue.

At first John hadn't wanted the money. But frankly, he was tired of running. He had been in England for some weeks now, and no one had recognized him. He had come within yards of Raventhorpe—hell, he had shot the earl in the arse!—and even that blackguard had not so much as flicked an eye in his direction

It was time to start a life, but not here, and not with this girl. She was linked to his old life by virtue of being a member of upper society. She was born into that world, would eventually marry in that world and would someday die in that world.

A world where he no longer held a place.

He could not pursue her, no matter how forceful the attraction. She was not meant for him, a man who lived on the fringes of society, a man who fled from his past and lived under a false name. No, she deserved balls and presentations at court and the respect of her peers. He would not take that from her.

Would not allow her good name to be tarnished by whispers of murder.

He rubbed his hand over his beard. As much as Genny's parting comment had stung, he decided he would let it lie. To offer explanations might only make things worse. Let her think him a fortune hunter. His job was to watch over Annabelle and make certain Raventhorpe did not crawl out from under his rock to make any more trouble. He would focus on that, and he would keep his distance from Genny Wallington-Willis.

It was the only way he would survive until he could escape to the safety of America.

Genny went down to breakfast the next morning and found everyone gathered in the dining room with the exception of John.

His absence was a relief. She wasn't certain how she would have greeted him, how she would have acted as if nothing were different than yesterday. But things *were* different. He had kissed her.

Not just kissed her, she mused as she smiled and nodded to the greetings of the others. Taking a plate, she began to serve herself from the sideboard as she searched for the right word. *Unleashed.* That was it. He had *unleashed* himself on her, letting loose his passion and taking her to a place with one kiss where her former fiancé had never brought her even with the most intimate of touches.

She served herself some eggs and a hot roll, then reached for the bacon, layering the meat on her plate without really paying attention. What would it be like to give herself completely to a man as passionate as John Ready? If his kiss was anything to go by, they might both incinerate by morning.

The mere thought stole the breath from her lungs,

and she set down the serving fork with a clatter. What was she thinking? Hadn't she learned her lesson with Bradley? She needed to control her impulses around John. She could not do anything to encourage him. He would be returning to America soon enough, then her life could get back to normal.

Though her normal life was far from perfect.

She turned away from the sideboard to find him standing behind her, his own plate piled high with food.

"Good morning, Miss Wallington-Willis." His gaze slid over her with a thoroughness that left her breathless though his smile could not be described as anything except polite. He reached for the bacon.

"Good morning," she murmured, averting her eyes. She slipped around him and took a seat at the table.

"Genny, dear," her mother said, "Sir Harry would like us all to assemble at noon in the gallery for our first rehearsal."

Genny nodded, picked up her roll, and tore it in half.

"Rehearsal for what?" John asked, seating himself next to Annabelle and catty-corner to Genny.

"That's right, you weren't here," Virgil said. "Sir Harry here has written a play for all of us to perform."

"We all have parts," Annabelle said. "Mama thinks we should perform it at the picnic next week."

"I figure the folks around here will really like it," Dolly said.

"Excellent idea," John said. "I shall enjoy watching the performance."

"Watching?" Dolly laughed. "Dear boy, you are *in* the play!"

John set down his silverware and frowned around the table. "I beg your pardon?"

"You are in the play," Sir Harry echoed. "Everyone is."

John fingered the knife beside his plate and eyed Sir Harry. "Even you?"

"Oh, no!" The baronet laughed. "I am the writer, Mr. Ready. I direct the action."

"I play the princess of the fairies," Annabelle said, spreading jam on a piece of toast.

John shot her a sidelong glance. "Of course you do."

"And you are the prince!" Dolly squealed, clapping her hands. "You and Annabelle are star-crossed lovers."

John shook his head and began to cut a slice of ham. "I am no prince, Mrs. Bailey."

Sir Harry chuckled. "You are indeed, Mr. Ready. You play Frederick, a prince in hiding with a farmer's family."

"We're in love," Annabelle informed him, then bit her toast.

John frowned and glanced from one to the other. "You are all serious?"

"Of course we are serious," the admiral said. "The ladies have made up their minds and will not be swayed.

We all walk the boards next week at the picnic. I am your father, by the way."

John shot his narrowed gaze from the admiral to the baronet. "Sir Harry, please explain. Now."

Sir Harry cleared his throat and adjusted his spectacles. "As I said, you play Frederick, a prince in hiding."

"Right."

"And you are in love with the fair Bella, daughter of the queen of the fairies."

"That's me!" Dolly said, waving her hand. "Queen of the fairies!"

"I'm Bella," Annabelle said.

"King of the fairies here," Virgil said. "But a warrior king. Not one of those foppish fellows."

"Bella loves you, and you love Bella, but there is a problem," Sir Harry went on.

"Of course there is," John said, cutting a glance toward Genny.

She ignored the look and continued to rip her roll into small, bite-sized pieces.

"Bella's sister Malevita is also in love with you and wants you to help her take over Fairyland and rule at her side as king," Sir Harry said in a rush.

"And Malevita would be—?" John looked around the table. His gaze settled on Genny just as Sir Harry answered his question.

"Miss Wallington-Willis is playing Malevita."

"Indeed?" John regarded her with such intensity that she fought not to squirm. "So, Miss Wallington-Willis, I hear you are in love with me."

She noted the insinuation behind the words but did not rise to the bait. "I am certain it is a fairy curse of some sort, Mr. Ready, so please do not be alarmed."

"I am hardly alarmed," John said. "Merely curious. Who assigned the roles?"

"I did," Sir Harry said.

"So if I understand this correctly, both Miss Bailey and Miss Wallington-Willis are in love with me?"

"Exactly." Sir Harry beamed like a teacher with a bright pupil. "Malevita is the wicked sister and will stop at nothing to have you."

"Indeed?" He slanted Genny a heated look from those dark eyes. "But I love Bella, correct?"

"Correct," Sir Harry said.

"So there is no hope for Malevita then."

"I am afraid not," Sir Harry said.

"Too bad. It sounds intriguing." John raised an eyebrow. "Unfortunately, I will not be doing the play."

"What!" Annabelle and Dolly exclaimed together.

"Why not?" Genny asked.

"I am not cut out for the stage." He took a bite of his bacon.

"Nonsense," Genny's mother said. "None of us are of a dramatic bent, except perhaps for Dolly."

"Why thank you, Helen." Dolly preened.

"You must be in the play," Sir Harry said. "We do not have anyone else suited to play the prince."

"I cannot do it."

"Why not?" Virgil demanded.

"Stage fright."

"Stage fright!" Genny scoffed. From the way John continued to focus on his plate, she could tell he was lying. Why? What was so terrible about being in a play? "I cannot credit such a thing," she said.

"Oh, John, do you truly suffer from stage fright?" Dolly asked.

"Best way to get past it is to do the thing," the admiral said. "Play the part. Get past your fear."

John shook his head. "I cannot."

"But what are we to do?" Sir Harry asked. "We cannot have a play without a prince!"

"You play the part," John said.

"Me? No, that cannot be. I mean, I am directing the actors," Sir Harry spluttered. "And . . . well . . . my leg. Who ever heard of a prince with a cane?"

"Wounded in battle," John replied.

"Might work," the admiral said.

"Nonsense," Helen scoffed.

"Or not," the admiral recanted. "Test your mettle, Ready, and do the thing. Life will be more pleasant around here for certain."

"John, please be in the play," Dolly pleaded. "We can't do it without you."

"The whole thing will be ruined," Annabelle said with a frown at him. "And I so wanted to play the fairy princess!"

"John, you will disappoint all of us if you do not play the part," Genny said, more to see what he would do than any desire to save the performance.

He flashed her a quick glance charged with annoyance, which told her stage fright was not at the root of his objection to the play. No, something else kept him from participating. "Naturally I have no desire to upset everyone—"

"Good," Dolly said. "Then you will do it. It is settled."

John scowled. "Mrs. Bailey—"

"Dolly," she corrected.

"Oh . . . uh, Dolly then. As I said, I do not want to upset everyone—"

"Then don't," Virgil warned, a hard glint in his eye. "My Dolly wants you to play the prince in the play. So you play the prince. Is that understood?"

Genny could see John's frustration in his glittering eyes and clenching fingers. "I cannot perform in the play."

"Forgive me, Mr. Ready," Sir Harry said, leaning forward, "but is it just performing in the actual play that is the problem? Would you be willing to rehearse with us anyway, and if need be, I can step into the role of the prince at the time of the performance?"

"Why do you not step in now?" John suggested.

"Because I need to direct the action. Once we have all the movements and lines mapped out, I could step in as the prince for the performance . . . *if* it is strictly necessary."

John tapped his fingers on the table as he considered the suggestion. "So I do the rehearsals, but you play the prince in the actual show."

"Yes," Sir Harry said.

John glanced at the ladies, who all regarded him with their best pleading faces. All except for Genny, who could not suppress the skepticism twisting her lips. Their gazes met for one, hot moment, then he looked back at Sir Harry. "Done."

Sir Harry beamed. "Excellent! This will work splendidly. Do you not agree, Mrs. Bailey?"

"I suppose it will," Dolly conceded, clearly unhappy with the decision.

"I am sorry," John said, "but if you want me in the play, these are my terms."

"Hmph," Virgil said with a scowl. "Can't figure why a fellow would be scared of the stage."

"I am shy," John said.

Genny nearly choked on her tea. "Shy?"

"Shy?" Virgil echoed. "I've known you for nearly five

years, my boy, and I don't recall you ever being shy."

"Only on the stage," John clarified. "I am a truly horrible actor."

"As am I," Genny contributed. "After all, I am playing the villainess, and everyone knows I am not of that nature."

"Oh, yes, agreed," Genny's mom said.

"Don't know anything about that," the admiral muttered.

"So you are saying that because you are playing a character that is so dissimilar from yourself, your performance might suffer?" John asked her.

"I suppose I am. After all, I am no more a jealous, evil fairy than you are a prince in disguise."

For an instant he looked startled and opened his mouth as if to correct her. Then he apparently changed his mind. "As I said, I am no prince, Miss Wallington-Willis."

"As I am aware," Genny said, her words carrying more than one meaning.

He knew she referred to his behavior in his room last night. She could tell by the quick flash of guilt across his face. "While not a prince, I do consider myself a gentleman."

"If walking the boards is such a problem for the lad, just let Archer do it," the admiral said. "Ready can stand in for him during rehearsals while the staging is being formulated. It's not Drury Lane, you know."

"But we want the play to be extraordinary," Helen said. "We are performing it in honor of Cilla and Samuel."

"Best we can do," the admiral mumbled.

"Please forgive my husband," the admiral's wife said. "He tends to be out of his depth if there is no battle plan to follow."

"We have a plan now, Helen, or were you not listening?" the admiral asked with a hint of impatience.

"I was." Helen fixed John with The Stare.

Genny squirmed in her seat. As a child she had been the recipient of The Stare more than once. The Stare made a person feel as if she were still in the schoolroom and had been caught coming into the house with her Sunday clothes all muddy.

John blinked, but to Genny's admiration, that was his only reaction to The Stare. "Mrs. Wallington-Willis, please note that I *am* participating. Just not in the final production."

"True," she agreed.

"A concession," Genny said.

"If you choose to see it that way." John shrugged.

"I will take that concession and thank you heartily for your time," Sir Harry said.

"Then let us consider the matter closed." John finished the last of his breakfast, then stood. "If you all will excuse me, I need to check on Melody's poultice before rehearsals begin."

"Of course," Virgil said, waving his hand in dismissal.

"How is the poor thing?" Dolly asked. "Sam was quite worried she might end up lame."

"She will be right as rain soon enough," John replied as he headed for the door.

"You certainly know your horses," Virgil said. "Sam swears that poultice is magic."

"I will let you know how she is doing," John said, then left the dining room.

Genny watched him go, wondering about the real reason he did not want to be seen on the stage.

She did not have a chance to discuss the matter with John until a bit later, only twenty minutes before the rehearsal was to begin. She caught up with him as he was returning from the stables. He stopped short when he saw her, but she continued along the path to meet with him.

"The truth, John Ready," she challenged as she drew closer.

"I have told you the truth, Miss Wallington-Willis, but you still make up your own."

"You frightened me." She stopped right in front of

him and looked around to be certain they were alone since anyone could approach from either direction at any moment.

"I apologize again for my behavior," he said.

"I understand. I deserve it for imposing upon you like I did. You know, when I . . ." She lowered her voice to a whisper. " . . . when I went to your room." She cleared her throat and continued. "I realize that men are not in control of their baser impulses under certain circumstances."

"You do, do you?"

His tone made her fall back a step. "Do not be angry with me, Mr. Ready. I had good reasons for what I did."

"You accused me of stealing."

"You kissed me."

"I apologized."

"So do I," she said. "Apologize, I mean. I should not have jumped to conclusions."

"What sort of conclusions, Genny?" He folded his arms and waited.

"That you were a fortune hunter. That you would steal from the Baileys."

"I was wondering when I would hear those words. And just to set the matter straight," he said, pointing a finger at her, "I am not after Annabelle or her fortune. I have money of my own."

"You do?"

"I do. And kissing you last night . . ."

Her face flooded with heat at the words. "We do not have to talk about that."

"But we do. You all but accused me—again—of pursuing Annabelle for her money." He stepped closer. "I told you, I do not want Annabelle. She does not set my blood on fire."

"And I—"

"You do."

"Oh!" Her face burned. "My goodness."

"That kiss was . . . well, it was ill-advised. I was not thinking, only feeling. And I wanted you." His voice lowered to a near growl. "God help me, but I still want you."

"Why?" she whispered. "Why me and not some other girl?"

"Your fire. Your determination to do what is right. Your stunning beauty. Dear God, woman, I want you more than breath right now. But I am not staying in England. I cannot give you what you deserve."

"Why not stay?" she coaxed.

"Because I cannot. I had reasons for leaving, and those reasons have not changed."

"Reasons that do not allow you to play the lead in a theatrical production?"

"Yes."

"You are a man of secrets, John."

"Aren't we all?"

She thought of the skeleton in her own closet. "I suppose you are right."

"I cannot offer you a future, Genny."

"So you said."

"I plan to start a new life in America, far away from here."

"Why not someplace closer? Scotland or Wales?"

"I need to leave my past behind. In America, I can blend in. Marry. Have children. Here . . . well, there are people looking for me still."

"What do they want?"

"Never mind that." He gave her a smile that softened the severity of his tone. "If you are in agreement, I believe you and I should stay away from each other. There can be no happy conclusion to this."

"How do you propose to do that?" Genny asked. "We are thrown together in this play. I am supposed to pretend to be in love with you!"

"I did not say it would be easy." He sighed and let his gaze roam over her with one, devouring sweep. "I wish things were different, Genny, but they are not. I have no future to offer you. I had no right to touch you like I did last night."

"Even if I wanted you to?" she asked in a small voice.

He clenched his jaw. "You saw what you unleashed yesterday with one smile, woman. Do not play with fire."

She wanted to continue flirting, but she could see the lines of strain about his mouth. "Very well. If you think this is for the best."

"I do." He glanced behind him as a worker trudged along the path toward them. He took Genny's arm and guided her in the opposite direction. "Have a care with your wiles, Genevieve. My control is not as strong as I thought, and you are yet innocent. I do not want to do something we might both regret."

Guilt pierced her. Would he feel the same way if he knew the truth? "I appreciate your candor."

"Then we understand each other." He walked her to the garden entrance and bowed low. "I regret that we cannot explore this thing between us."

"So do I." Genny lingered by the garden gate, curiosity pricking at her like the claws of a cat.

"Go inside, Genny," he said, when she did not enter. "Forget yesterday and move on to tomorrow."

She studied his face, relishing the unabashed need she saw in his eyes. Dear God, it was true. Finally, a man wanted her for herself alone, not for a social agenda or political connections. The urge to step into his arms and wallow in that simmering desire—desire meant only for her—was nearly irresistible. But they both knew they could not be.

But it would not stop her from dreaming about what it would have been like.

"Are you coming with me?" she asked. "Your presence is required at the rehearsal as well."

He grimaced. "I know."

"Then we should go together."

"I do not think that is a wise idea. Better you go without me. I will be there directly."

"If you are certain . . ."

"I am. I need to change my clothes. I have been out with the horses, and I smell like the stable. I would not want to offend anyone."

"Some people find the scent of horses quite pleasant."

He stilled, his fingers curling into fists, one digit at a time. "Please go inside, Genny."

The rough catch in his voice as he said her name told her all she needed to know. She was making this harder for him. With a nod, she stepped through the door into the garden, leaving him standing outside the wall.

Alone.

Chapter 6

John took the opportunity to change his clothing and gather himself at the same time. He had not had any intention of correcting Genny's assumptions about him; it was easier for both of them if she considered him a fortune hunter. But the relief he had seen in her eyes when he confessed that he had his own money had made his confession worth the risk.

Overton had put that lack of confidence in her eyes, he was sure of it. Damn that useless idiot! Clearly Genny did not believe a man could want her for herself and not for her position in society.

If things were different, he might have proven that to her.

Enough. He needed to put aside any notions of what might have happened between him and Genny if things were different. Things were the way they were, and he was taking the best course of action for everyone involved.

He was shrugging into his clean coat when someone pounded on the door.

"Mr. Ready! You must come. Someone tried to kidnap Miss Annabelle!"

John jerked open the door to find one of the new footmen, Andrew, standing in the hall. "What? Tell me quickly." He shut the door behind him and fastened his coat as he started down the hall with the eager young footman trotting beside him.

"Miss Annabelle and Sir Harry went for a drive before the rehearsal, and some blackguard stopped them on the road and tried to abduct her!"

"Was it Black Bill?" John asked, hurrying down the stairs.

"The highwayman? No, sir. At least Miss Annabelle says it wasn't. Says she's met Black Bill before, and this is a different bloke."

They reached the first floor. "Where are they, Andrew? The drawing room?"

"Mr. Bailey's study, sir."

John nodded and shot down the next flight to the ground floor. "Has the magistrate been called?"

"Yes, sir."

"Good. Bring him to the study as soon as he gets here." As the footman nodded and hurried off to obey the order, John strode into Virgil Bailey's study.

Annabelle sat in a chair in front of her father's desk. Her mother sat beside her in her wheeled chair, holding her daughter's hand and sniffling into a handkerchief.

Genny and her mother hovered around Annabelle and Dolly. Behind the desk, Bailey and the admiral conferred in low voices.

"Mr. Ready."

John turned to see who was addressing him and found Sir Harry sitting in a chair near the door. His hair looked as if he had raked his hand through it more than once, and his clothing was askew. There was no sign of the baronet's usual jocularity; in fact, the hazel eyes behind his spectacles held an edge John had never before seen in the humble country gentleman. "Sir Harry, are you all right?"

"The blackguard ambushed us," Sir Harry replied. Even his voice sounded stronger, more commanding. "Are you aware, Mr. Ready, that Miss Bailey has asked me to teach her to drive?"

"I was not."

"It seemed a simple enough request, and she is such an independent spirit. It seemed harmless. I saw no reason to refuse her."

John nodded and made a note to speak to Annabelle. She knew she was not supposed to go anywhere without him. "Miss Bailey can be quite convincing."

"She can indeed. At any rate, we were in my gig with my mare Brownie. She is a most docile animal, Mr. Ready. I've had her for years and felt she was of sufficient temperament for a lady to drive."

"Understood. What happened?"

"Miss Bailey had the reins, and we were laughing over an amusing anecdote I had just told. Suddenly a masked man leaped out of the bushes and pointed a pistol at us. He demanded that Annab—I mean, Miss Bailey—descend and go with him or else he would start shooting."

"Do you carry a pistol, Sir Harry?"

"Not normally, but I shall do so going forward, that is certain." The baronet's mouth thinned. "I am an excellent shot, Mr. Ready. The villain will not catch me unawares again."

"I assume then that he escaped?"

Sir Harry nodded. "He did."

John sighed. "How is it you can live in an area with a notorious highwayman yet drive about the countryside unarmed?"

Sir Harry narrowed his eyes. "I never said I was unarmed, Mr. Ready." He grabbed his cane, twisted the head, and tugged, revealing a gleaming steel blade hidden in the harmless-looking staff. "I said I did not have a pistol."

John gave a half smile. "Very ingenious—and lethal. I assume you know how to use this weapon, and he simply did not come close enough to give you the opportunity."

"You assume correctly, which is another reason why

I shall also bring my pistol from now on." He drove the blade back into its sheath and twisted the head of the cane to lock it into place.

"I doubt Miss Bailey will be taking any more driving lessons for a while," John said.

"Agreed."

"But your lack of opportunity to use your weapon now begs the question—how did you get away?"

"Miss Bailey saved us." Sir Harry smiled with some admiration. "She got out of the carriage like he told her to. Then that fellow tried to grab her and drag her off, but she apparently dug her heels into the ground to make it harder for him. While he was distracted, I charged at him with the gig. He let go of Miss Bailey and aimed the pistol at me. But Miss Bailey grabbed a rock and slammed it onto his gun hand, then kicked him in the back of the knee. He dropped like a stone—excuse the pun—and let go of the pistol. She grabbed the weapon, then jumped into the gig, gave the pistol to me, and took the reins to race back here. Well, as quickly as Brownie can race." Sir Harry sent an approving glance at Annabelle. "She is a remarkable woman."

"I am glad you are both unharmed," John said. "If you will excuse me, I must go speak to Miss Bailey. The magistrate should be here at any moment."

"Old Gunston? I would not count on much help from that quarter."

Sir Harry's words stopped him when he would have walked away. "Why is that?"

"Gunston was a crony of Raventhorpe's father." When John said nothing, Sir Harry gave a little laugh. "Come now, Mr. Ready. Surely Raventhorpe was behind this incident. Even in exile, he can make his presence felt."

John contemplated his next words carefully before speaking them. "Forgive me, Sir Harry, but I was under the impression you and Lord Raventhorpe were friends."

Sir Harry gave a smile that seemed to hint at more secrets than it revealed. " 'Friends' is too strong a word. We were hunting mates for years, which is where I got this." He tapped his bad leg. "Raventhorpe always said it was an accident, but I cannot help but wonder if he simply did not like that I was a better huntsman than he was."

"He shot you? Deliberately?"

Sir Harry shrugged. "The details of that day are murky in my mind."

"If he shot you, why do you continue to socialize with him? You might very well be his last friend in the upper reaches of society."

"Upper reaches? How exalted. No, I am simply a country squire. I am happy here with my fields and my horses and my tenant farmers. That does not threaten him. And there you go using that word 'friend' again. You know, I embrace the philosophy of the Chinese general Sun-Tzu." Sir Harry leaned in, a conspiratorial grin curving his lips. "'Keep your friends close and your enemies closer.'"

"A wise philosophy."

"I thought so—especially when it comes to Raventhorpe. You know as well as I do that he will not simply ignore the slight Miss Bailey dealt him when she jilted him. He will want revenge."

"I know." John glanced over at Annabelle, then noticed Virgil waving him over. "I had best go speak to Mr. Bailey. But thank you for the information on Gunston. I will keep an eye on him when he gets here."

"I am going to stay here and rest my leg. I'm afraid I aggravated it with all the excitement."

"Sounds like a good idea." John turned to leave.

"If you need help," Sir Harry said as he started to walk away, "my sword is ready."

John gave him a nod, then went over to the others.

Dolly caught sight of him first. "Oh, John! At last you are here!" She threw up her hands, her white handkerchief fluttering like a flag of surrender. "Dear Annabelle was set upon by a highwayman!"

"Not Black Bill," Annabelle said with a stern look at her mother.

"I don't know how you can tell one from the other," Dolly said with a huff. "A villain is a villain."

"It wasn't Black Bill," Annabelle said. "I wish he had

been there, though. Considering he saved my life once."

"Yes, yes. When Lord Raventhorpe carried you off to force you to marry him." Dolly covered her eyes with her hand. "Just the memory of it makes me feel faint."

"Black Bill was the one who stopped the coach and knocked Richard unconscious that day," Annabelle said. "Otherwise, Samuel might not have caught up to us in time, and I might have ended up Lady Raventhorpe." She scowled at her mother. "In fact, if Black Bill had been there today, I have no doubt he would have protected me from this horrible man as well."

"From what I hear," John said, "you protected yourself."

Annabelle smiled, pride lingering in her eyes. "I just did what you told me to do."

Curious gazes turned toward him. "I have been teaching Miss Bailey to defend herself," he said. "She is an excellent student."

"Or you are an excellent teacher," Dolly said with a sniff. "Oh, I cannot wait for this darned leg of mine to be healed so we can leave this dreadful country! I cannot endure any more attempts to run off with my daughter!"

"Oh, Mama." Annabelle rolled her eyes.

"The magistrate should be here shortly, so we can report the incident," John said. "A pity the villain got away."

"I did what you taught me. I got free and ran," Annabelle said. "I didn't even see where he went."

"Which is exactly what you should have done." John looked around at the other ladies. "I would strongly suggest that none of you go off alone anywhere. Always take a male escort with you." He glanced at the admiral and Virgil. "It might be a good idea to carry a pistol with you whenever you leave the house, gentlemen."

"Agreed," the admiral said. Virgil nodded.

A footman knocked on the open door of the study. "Sir? The magistrate has arrived."

"Send him in," John said, then caught himself and looked at Virgil. "With your permission, of course, Mr. Bailey."

"Yes, yes," Virgil said, waving a hand.

The footman disappeared for a moment, then returned with two gentlemen. "Lord Gunston and Mr. Timmons," he announced, then stepped aside.

"Timmons?" John repeated, but the men were already entering the room. Could it be . . . ? Bloody hell, it *was*. Eustace Timmons—Tim to his friends—a face from his past that he had never expected to see again.

"I am looking for the master of this household," Gunston said in his booming baritone. "Which of you is Mr. Bailey?"

"I am Virgil Bailey." Virgil stepped forward as the

men swept past the other occupants of the room.

John turned his back so they would not see his face. What the devil was Tim Timmons doing here?

"I am Lord Gunston, the magistrate. This is my friend Mr. Timmons. We were dining together when your summons arrived."

"I wish we were meeting under different circumstances," Virgil said. "Do you know Admiral Wallington-Willis? And this is his wife, Mrs. Wallington-Willis . . ." Virgil continued around the room, introducing everyone to the newcomers. John managed to stay off to the side and out of visual range of the men, arranging it so Virgil skipped him in the introductions. When Virgil got to Sir Harry, it became clear they all knew each other.

"Sir Harry Archer," Virgil said.

"Ah, Sir Harry. You are a guest here?" Gunston boomed.

"I am," the baronet replied. "Good afternoon, Lord Gunston. And to you, too, Mr. Timmons."

Tim gave a nod and murmured a return greeting, but the magistrate just smirked at Sir Harry. "Bad day, eh?"

"Sir Harry was with my daughter when the highwayman attacked them," Virgil said. "He can offer additional details."

"You are certain it was not Black Bill who was behind this mischief?" Gunston demanded.

"Yes," Sir Harry replied.

"I have seen Black Bill," Annabelle said. "This was not the same man, Lord Gunston."

"You are overset, Miss Bailey," the magistrate said with a dismissive wave of his hand. "I am certain Archer here will provide us with the *accurate* details of the incident. I have no doubt it was indeed Black Bill who waylaid you. He is known to haunt these lands."

"Raventhorpe lands," Tim said sagely.

"Bailey lands now, Mr. Timmons," Virgil corrected. "I purchased this estate from Lord Raventhorpe some months ago."

"Of course. You are right, sir." Tim glanced around, no doubt gauging the level of anxiety in the room. "But perhaps Black Bill does not keep up with the local gossip."

This generated a laugh, and Tim smiled. Once more his gaze swept the occupants of the room, but this time it crossed over John, then came back. Held.

John could see the puzzlement in his face. No doubt the other man sensed something recognizable but could not place John's current appearance as familiar. His gut clenched. Would Tim see the stripling lad of seven years ago in the bearded, competent man of today? Or would he look past him with a stranger's stiff politeness?

"And who is this?" Gunston asked, coming toward him. Tim trailed behind more slowly, a frown on his face.

"Lord Gunston, this is Mr. Ready, a friend of the family," Virgil said.

"Mr. Ready," the magistrate repeated. "Odd name, that. Wouldn't you say, Tim?"

"Yes, odd," Timmons agreed. He held out a hand in greeting. "Pleasure to meet you, Mr. Ready."

"Pleasure is mine," John replied, shaking his hand once, then dropping it.

"Were you a witness to the attack?" Gunston demanded.

"I was not," John replied.

Gunston gave a snort and looked around. "Which of you were in the gig when the highwayman attacked?"

Annabelle spoke up. "Just me and Sir Harry. No one else was there."

"Then you are the two people I must interview. Everyone else, please leave the room."

"I insist on staying with my daughter," Dolly said. "Besides, it is quite cumbersome to wheel me about."

Even Gunston was not immune to Dolly's charm. "Absolutely, Mrs. Bailey. I have no objection to you staying as chaperone. But everyone else must leave, even you, Timmons."

"I thought I might help," Tim said.

"No, no. I am obligated as magistrate to do all the questioning in the strictest confidence. You go with the others, keep everyone calm. Mr. Bailey, certainly you have a drawing room where everyone can wait?"

"Of course we do," Virgil said. "Upstairs."

"Accompany them all upstairs, Timmons. I will stay down here with the others."

"I'm staying, too," Virgil said. "It was my daughter who was nearly abducted."

"Very well," Gunston said, pursing his lips in contemplation. "But everyone else must retire to the drawing room."

As John allowed himself to be herded out of the study with Genny and her parents, he noticed Tim casting him covert glances. Would that look of puzzlement on his face soon give way to condemnation when he recognized John? Or would Tim never associate the man before him with the acquaintance from years ago?

And if he did recognize John, what would he do about it? Was seven years of hiding about to be undone by one unexpected guest?

Genny trailed behind her parents and Mr. Timmons so that she fell into step next to John. "Can you believe it?" she murmured. "Just when we thought Annabelle was safe, someone tries to abduct her."

"I never thought she was safe," John said. "That is why I have been teaching her to defend herself."

"And a good thing you did. It seems she put her lessons into play today."

"Anything to keep her out of Raventhorpe's clutches."

"Do you really think this had something to do with Lord Raventhorpe?" Genny asked. "I thought he was in exile in France."

"He may have hired someone to do the deed."

"I had not thought of that. Would he go so far?"

"I believe so." John slid a wary glance at Mr. Timmons. "He was utterly furious that she jilted him to marry Samuel. He is the type to want revenge."

"He would have to get someone to help him," Genny said. "As I recall, you shot him."

"I did. Right in his . . . in the seat of his trousers."

She giggled. "I bet that angered him even more."

"It did."

She fell into silence as they neared the drawing room. The past hour since Annabelle and Sir Harry had come racing back to the house had left her nerves frayed, and she was more than happy to have John there with her. He had taken on a rather commanding role, getting everyone's stories about the incident, giving orders to the staff about how things should be handled. He seemed comfortable in that position of authority, which only sparked her curiosity.

"Were you ever a captain of a ship?" she asked.

"No."

"Why not?"

"I have no desire to be in command of others. I am

content to have a bed and food at the end of the day."

"You wear command very well," she said, slowing. "Almost as if you were born to it."

A flicker of concern crossed his face, and at that, she wondered if she had stumbled onto something.

"Mr. Ready." Timmons lingered outside the drawing room. "A word, if you do not mind."

"Of course." John waved Genny on.

Reluctantly, she obeyed his direction, slipping into the room with her parents and leaving him with Mr. Timmons.

John faced his old acquaintance with some trepidation. Had Timmons recognized him? If so, what would he do?

"Forgive my impertinence, Mr. Ready," Tim said, "but I feel as if we have met before."

"Indeed?" John kept his face a bland mask of polite inquiry. "Where, do you suppose?"

"I cannot quite place it, but you seem very familiar to me."

"I do not see how," John said. "I have only been in England for about a month."

"Where were you before that?"

"America."

"Oh. Well, I have never been there." Tim frowned, scratching his jaw. "You are English, though. You do not have an American accent."

"My parents were English," John said.

"Ah, so you probably speak like they do."

"Undoubtedly."

"This will drive me mad until I get to the bottom of it," Tim said with a little laugh. "Eventually, I will figure it out. You do remind me of someone."

John smiled politely, but his heart thundered in his chest. He had been so careful. Stayed hidden, resisted the temptation to revisit some of the places of his childhood. Had not even seen his parents. Would he now be undone by a chance encounter?

"Shall we join the others?" John asked. "They must be wondering why we are so rude as to ignore them. And the admiral is not a man you want to cross."

"Oh, of course, of course." Tim adjusted his jacket. "Ah, that *is* Admiral Wallington-Willis, correct? *The* Admiral Wallington-Willis?"

"The same."

"My goodness." A hint of excitement flickered across Tim's very ordinary face. "That man is a hero."

"He is indeed."

"He has been decorated by the queen. Twice."

"Has he? How impressive."

"I hope I do not stumble over my words when I greet him. I am a solicitor, and while my clients are often men of means, I do not believe I have ever met an actual hero before." He cleared his throat, straightened his tie.

"I expected only a casual luncheon with Lord Gunston this afternoon. And while he is certainly of the peerage, his holdings are rather small and his consequence somewhat unremarkable. Indeed, that is why he took the position of magistrate, to lend himself prestige, at least locally."

John kept the polite smile on his face with some effort. He had forgotten Tim's tendency to gossip about others like an old woman at a quilting bee.

"The admiral seems to be a man of great tolerance," John said. As relief relaxed the other man's features, he realized this could be an opportunity to distract Timmons from trying to recall his memory. "But the one thing he dislikes intensely is tardiness. I am certain he is wearing a path in the carpet right now, wondering why we are keeping him waiting."

"Oh!" Tim's eyes widened, and he swallowed. "I should not wish to offend him. As a solicitor, I have made it a point of pride always to be on time for appointments with my clients. Punctuality is a virtue."

"I am certain your clients appreciate that."

"Oh, yes. Some of them are very strict about it."

"We should no doubt put that virtue into practice now."

"Indeed." Timmons started forward then stopped, grabbing John's arm. "One more moment while I regain my composure." He gave a nervous laugh. "I thought this would be an afternoon like any other. You know, have lunch with Gunston, visit a client, go home to my wife. I never imagined I might be meeting someone of the admiral's stamp today."

"Allow me formally to introduce you," John said, taking a step towards the door.

"Yes, yes. That would be very fine." He swiped a hand over his mouth, then rubbed his palms against his trousers. "To think, if I had not decided to go to Evermayne today instead of Thursday, I would have missed this opportunity."

John froze, the breath seizing in his lungs. "Evermayne?"

"Yes. Certainly you have heard of the Duke of Evermayne. Oh, but perhaps not, being from America."

"His Grace is your client?"

"Yes, I am handling his estate." Tim smiled at him. "Thank you for distracting me with conversation, Mr. Ready. I feel calm enough to meet the admiral now."

"Of course." John started for the door. "I thought dukes had estate managers to handle their affairs," he said, reaching the doors.

"Oh, they do for the day-to-day. But this is a different kettle of fish. You see the Duke of Evermayne is dead. I am overseeing the execution of his will."

Chapter 7

The Duke of Evermayne is dead.

The words froze John where he stood. Timmons gave him a puzzled look. "Are you all right, Mr. Ready?"

"Yes." John forced himself to answer, even to smile, though his face felt as if it would crack when he did so. His world had just tilted sharply on its axis. The Duke was dead. The unexpected news sent his careful plans into chaos, leaving him floundering. "Come, let me introduce you to the admiral."

The two men entered the drawing room and headed to the chair where the admiral sat. John performed the introductions by rote, then glanced over the shorter Tim's head to find Genny. She watched him with a tiny frown line between her brows, puzzlement in her green eyes. Even worry.

She knew something was wrong.

He gave a small, negative shake of his head. She frowned a bit more, her gaze intent. Her hands lay in her lap, and she curled her fingers into her skirts as the tension rose between them. Beside her, Helen flipped through a ladies' magazine and chattered about fashion, oblivious to the undercurrents in the room. Genny managed to reply to her mother's conversation, but it was obvious the majority of her attention was on him. She tilted her head, her expression clearly asking a question. *Are you all right?*

Her perception surprised him, and her genuine concern warmed his battered heart. This was not the time or the place to examine the riot of emotion ripping through him, especially not in front of others. Perhaps later they could find a moment alone. Later, when his world made sense again.

Tim's conversation with the admiral drew his attention, though he remained aware of Genny's gaze steady upon him.

"As I was telling Mr. Ready," Timmons was saying, "I was in the area to visit the estate of my client, the late Duke of Evermayne. I ran into Lord Gunston this morning, and he asked me to lunch at his residence before I set out for Evermayne."

"So you have not been to Evermayne yet?" John asked.

"No, my appointment is for three o'clock. I hope that Lord Gunston concludes his inquiries in time so I will not be late. We took his lordship's carriage to come here."

"I had heard Evermayne died," the admiral mused, stroking his silver beard. "What was it they said? His heart?"

"Yes, Admiral. It was very sudden. He always seemed in perfect health, considering he was nearly seventy."

John walked over to a chair and slowly sat down. "When did he die?"

Timmons squinted and pursed his lips as he searched his memory. "About a month and a half ago."

"And you are still untangling the will?" The admiral harrumphed and gave Timmons a sour look. "Seems like you should have the right of it by now, with the man in the ground some weeks already."

Timmons tried a placating smile, but John could see the sweat misting on the balding man's forehead. "As you can imagine, Admiral, the estates of a powerful man like His Grace will take a while to sort out."

"Perhaps," the admiral said.

Footsteps sounded in the hall, followed by the appearance of Sir Harry. "Thank heavens that is over." The baronet made his way to the last empty seat in the room and eased himself down into it, resting his cane against the arm of the chair. "Well, everyone, you will all be glad to know that Gunston has solved the case."

"Already?" John asked.

Sir Harry peered at him over his spectacles. "My

dear Mr. Ready, it is clear as day to Lord Gunston that Black Bill is the culprit."

"But that is not true!" Genny said. "Annabelle has seen Black Bill, spoken to him. She says this was a different man."

"And she said the same to Gunston." Sir Harry gave a wry smile. "He was not inclined to believe a female."

"Surely you told him the truth," Helen said. "You were there."

"I was, but Lord Gunston has determined that my eyesight may not be at its best—spectacles, you know."

"So he does not believe Annabelle because she is a woman, and he does not believe you because you wear spectacles?" Genny shook her head. "But he does believe the culprit is Black Bill."

"He does," Sir Harry confirmed.

"Timmons!" The roar echoed up to the drawing room from the floor below.

"I believe Lord Gunston is ready to depart." Timmons shoved his hand toward Genny's father. "Pleasure to meet you, Admiral."

"Timmons." The admiral pumped his hand once, then released it.

Timmons dug into his coat pocket and withdrew a card. "If you are ever in need of legal advice, sir, here is my direction."

"Thank you, but no," the admiral said. "We have been using the same solicitor in London for some years now."

"Oh." Timmons deflated a bit. "Very well. Still, an honor to meet you, sir."

"I will be glad of your card," John said.

"Of course." Smiling, Tim handed it to him.

The roar came again. "*Timmons!*"

"A pleasure to meet you all," the solicitor said in a rush, with a bow just as hasty. He scurried out of the room.

"Good heavens," Helen said, after he had left. "I do not care if Lord Gunston *is* a viscount. That does not give him the right to flout all rules of society and shout through the house like a wild man!"

"Clearly the man has no sense of leadership *or* civility," the admiral said.

"Mr. Timmons seems quite cowed by him." Sir Harry remarked.

"Didn't like *him* either." The admiral scowled at the empty doorway. "All that blathering on about Evermayne's estate. No solicitor worth his salt would spread that kind of gossip about a client! Clearly the man has no sense of discretion."

"What is this about Evermayne?" Sir Harry asked.

"He's dead," the admiral replied.

"Ah, yes." Sir Harry leaned back in his chair and nodded. "I'd heard that . . . maybe a few weeks ago?"

"Something like that. Blathering fool," the admiral grumbled. "Felt like I was at a tea party."

"Hello, everyone!" Annabelle appeared in the doorway. "Sir Harry, Mama's not feeling well. She says her nerves are frazzled from this morning, and she doesn't think she'll be able to rehearse for the play. Pa is taking her to her room."

"I cannot say as I blame her," Sir Harry said. "Her only child was nearly abducted on her own land!"

"I wish everyone would stop fussing," Annabelle grumbled. "We got away. We didn't need anyone to come rescue us."

"That does not negate the fact that there is a real threat," Sir Harry said. "You need to take precautions, Miss Bailey."

"I know, I know. But you saw what I did. You saw how I was able to get away from him." She lifted her chin. "Anyone else who comes after me has a surprise waiting for him."

"You did very well," Sir Harry said. "However, the rest of us are somewhat unnerved by the incident. I believe a quiet afternoon is in order."

"But I was so looking forward to rehearsal." Annabelle worried her lower lip, clearly disappointed.

"Perhaps we can rehearse just the first scene," Sir Harry said. "Where Frederick and Bella speak of their pain in being parted."

"I regret I cannot participate," John said. His emotions pushed and tugged inside him like two cats in a sack. "I must speak to Mr. Bailey about posting more guards on the grounds."

"Oh, that can wait, can't it?" Annabelle wheedled.

"No," John said. "It cannot."

"I, for one, am completely unsettled by the whole thing," Helen said, closing her fashion book.

"Now, pet, calm yourself," the admiral said.

Helen stood. "I am going to walk around the garden to soothe my nerves. Will you come with me, Robert?"

The admiral heaved himself out of his chair. "Of course, my dear. Consider me your private guard."

Helen looked at her daughter. "Are you coming, Genny?"

"No." Genny stood and smoothed her skirts. "I think I will go to my room and rest. This has been a harrowing morning."

Annabelle looked from one to the other, dismay creasing her pretty face. "But who is going to rehearse with me?"

"I will." Sir Harry stood and grasped his cane. "We will read through the scene, and you can help me decide if any of the lines should change."

"Really?" Annabelle clapped her hands. "I would like that. I would be an author!"

Sir Harry shook his head. "*One* of the authors, Miss Bailey. I did pen the first draft, you know."

"*One* of the authors." Annabelle grinned at the others. "You will all be thrilled with the results, I promise you!"

"Undoubtedly," John said.

"Well, we are off to the gardens. We will see you all at luncheon," Helen said, as her husband offered his arm. "Genny, do not leave the house. Not with this brigand running about!"

"I promise," Genny said.

The admiral crooked his free arm at his daughter. "Come, kitten. Allow me to escort you to the staircase."

Genny pinkened a bit at the nickname, and with a swift, sidelong glance at John, she moved to take her father's arm.

"Behold the luckiest man in the world, gentlemen," the admiral said, "to have two such beauties on my arm!"

The admiral left the room, flanked by his two ladies, and Sir Harry turned to Annabelle. "And where do you keep your writing materials, Miss Bailey?"

"Over here in the desk." Annabelle hurried over to a rolltop desk and shoved it open. Sir Harry followed slowly, his limp more pronounced than usual.

"I will see you all later this afternoon," John said,

then headed out the door with a relief that nearly felled him. Finally, he could be alone to absorb the news that might change the very direction of his life.

The Duke was dead. Dear God, he had thought the old bastard would live to be a hundred. That such a powerful figure from his childhood should succumb to the human frailty of death stunned him.

And changed everything.

Even as he grasped the concept in his mind, he noticed Genny waiting for him at the top of the steps.

"I told my parents I would be going to my room," she said in a low voice as he came closer. "I even started walking up the stairs, then came back down once they were gone."

For him. She did not have to say it; it was there in her eyes.

Her concern touched him, yet at the same time, part of him wanted to howl in frustration. He needed to sort through these developments in his head. Instead, he was forced to do the dance of evasiveness around this perceptive young lady—even though his gut urged him to confide in her.

But it was too soon to make such decisions, the shock too fresh. He needed to sort out his own emotions.

"You are quite clever," he said. "Was there something you needed from me?"

She frowned. "You do not have to pretend, John. I

could see that you were affected by Mr. Timmons's news."

"I am not one to be captivated by idle gossip," he said.

"The Duke of Evermayne is hardly idle gossip," she said. "Who was he to you? How did you know him?"

"Know a duke?" He managed a laugh. "Miss Wallington-Willis, you are imagining what is not there."

"Formality will not make me go away." She stepped closer to him, those green eyes of hers way too perceptive for his liking. "I can tell that the Duke of Evermayne means something to you."

"Nonsense."

"It is not nonsense when it puts that look in your eyes."

"What look?"

"The one that says the ship is sinking, and your only lifeboat has a hole in the bottom."

Her accurate metaphor surprised a laugh from him. "You imagine things, Genny girl."

"I do not believe I am imagining anything. I know you have secrets, John, but I truly want to help you." Her sincerity echoed in her voice, her expression, the way she leaned toward him.

His heart clenched. When was the last time anyone had looked at him like that, like she genuinely cared about what happened to him? He was tempted to reach out to her, but matters were too chaotic just then. He needed to make sense of everything on his own.

"Thank you for your concern," he said, "but I do not have time to talk right now. I must speak to Mr. Bailey about the security on the estate. We cannot have Raventhorpe trying such a thing again."

"I have been wondering about that, about Raventhorpe being behind this abduction attempt," she mused. "How would he accomplish such a thing from France?"

"There are ways. He could have hired someone. I just have to find out who it was."

"I have every faith in you, John. People trust you." She rested her hand on his arm. "Maybe I can use my social connections to help you with your own problem, especially if a duke is involved."

"An interesting offer from a lady who first accused me of pursuing Miss Bailey for her fortune and social connections."

She winced. "I apologize if my original estimation of you was less than flattering, but a girl like Annabelle has to be careful. I understand that you are honestly trying to protect her from a very real danger, which was brought home to all of us after today's incident."

"Indeed?" His simmering patience snapped its frayed tether. "What about your suspicion that I was stealing from our hosts? That was only yesterday."

"You proved me wrong. I apologized."

"It seems your opinion of me changes from day to day."

"Well, your behavior is what creates those opinions! You are a man with secrets, John. I cannot help but wonder . . ." She stopped.

"Wonder what? If I am honorable? If I am the rogue you apparently still think me?"

"I do not think you a rogue! But you are secretive . . ." Her tone rose at the end as if she expected him to confide in her. The strange thing was, he wanted to, and he did not know why.

Rather than question his compulsion to trust her, he turned the tables to deflect her. "As someone who keeps secrets yourself, you should understand."

Panic flared in her eyes for a brief second. "I have no secrets."

"You do." He stepped closer, crowding her against the balustrade. "You told me."

"I did not . . . oh." She looked relieved for a second, then raised her chin with a mulish glint in her eye. "Yes, I told you about Bradley only wanting to wed me because of my father. And since I told you, it is not really a secret any longer."

"It is from your father."

"Is that a threat?"

"No." He backed off a step. "I do not tattle the secrets of others. I was proving a point."

"A point?" She took a deep breath. "Is that why you kissed me yesterday? To prove a point? To prove that you have power over me?"

Insulted, he leaned down. "Naturally. A man can want a woman without any emotion involved, and you were ripe for the picking."

Her eyes widened as if he had struck her. "So you felt nothing? It was just a game?" Her voice caught, stark pain evident in her face.

Damn his hot temper! He had not meant the words, just wanted to punish her, to fire back. To hurt her. Well, he had succeeded.

He was a blundering cad.

"What about what you said to me earlier today," she continued in a low voice, "on the path to the stables? About wanting me."

Her obvious vulnerability tore at him.

"I kissed you because I wanted to." He stepped closer. "Because you were in my bedchamber. Sitting on my bed. Looking so soft and sweet and tempting."

"John," she whispered. Her breath came in little pants, and her eyes looked huge in her face.

She wanted him, too. His head spun with the knowledge. With the scent of her. Dear God, he got within two feet of her, and his concentration shattered.

"Maybe that is why he was able to get so close," John murmured, forcing coherent thought through a haze of lust. "You distract me. I am not watching vigilantly enough."

"What?" She jerked back, searching his face.

"It is you," he said. "You are why he was able to get to Annabelle."

"What! Do not blame me for this. I have done nothing wrong."

"We are both to blame." He stepped away from her.

"What are you talking about?"

He knew what he had to do, and it ripped at his heart. He had to distance himself from her, even be cruel. Lives depended on it.

"You ignore what does not please you, Genny. That idiot Overton treated you badly, and you judge every man by that criterion."

"I do not—"

"It has affected everything you think, everything you do and say. It has even started to impact your family."

"What are you talking about? My relationship with my family is fine."

"Is it? Had you not let your jealousy over your sister's happiness estrange the two of you, you might have learned more from her about Raventhorpe and what he has done. What he is capable of."

"Jealousy!" Her voice broke. Moisture gleamed in her big green eyes. "How dare you? Why are you speaking to me like this? To think I was worried about you."

"There is no reason to worry about me. My job is to protect Annabelle until the Baileys return to America. I am doing that job to the best of my ability, and then I am leaving England. I have a new life waiting for me in America, one where I can start again. Where the past does not matter."

"So you keep saying. Well, good riddance to you, John Ready. You *and* your secrets." She spun on her heel and, grasping her skirts, ran up the stairs.

John closed his eyes and sucked in a breath. He was a bastard. He rubbed the back of his neck and exhaled slowly.

"I certainly hope that drama will not interfere with the play," a voice said. "After all, Miss Wallington-Willis is supposed to be in love with you."

John turned his head and saw Sir Harry standing a few yards away. Behind him, Annabelle hovered in the doorway of the sitting room. How much had they heard? "Do you make a habit of eavesdropping, Sir Harry?" John asked.

"I got up to close the sitting room door and heard voices."

John winced. "My apologies."

Sir Harry gave a nod. "Accepted. Do let me know if there is anything I can do."

"No, thank you."

"Well, the offer remains open. Despite this infirmity

of mine, I stand ready to assist you—at any time." Sir Harry's gaze glittered behind his spectacles, reminding John of the intensity he had seen there just after the abduction attempt.

Strangely, the baronet's support calmed him. "I appreciate that, Sir Harry."

"Very well, then. Back to the play. You know, Miss Bailey truly has a gift for writing. She is a young lady of many talents." He turned away and headed down the hall to where Annabelle waited. John lingered where he was a moment longer, looking up the stairs where Genny had fled. Then he very deliberately turned to descend the staircase.

He had people to protect.

Chapter 8

Genny stormed into her bedroom and shut the door—perhaps a tad harder than necessary—then went to her dressing table and sat down to look at her reflection in the mirror. "You will not cry. You *will not* cry. That man is not worth your tears."

A knock came at the door. "Miss Genny? Are you all right?"

Genny covered her face with her hands, pressing her fingertips against her eyes. "I am fine, Lottie. I just want to be alone for a while."

There was a long pause. "All right," the maid said finally, "but call me if you need me."

"Thank you." Genny listened to the soft shuffle of the maid's footsteps as she walked away, then lowered her hands from her face. Her fingertips were wet. She met her own gaze in the mirror, her eyes red and moist. "You are strong," she whispered. "Remember that."

How was it John had brought her to tears so easily? Two days ago, she had thought he was trying to seduce

Annabelle. Yet even then, she had noticed him. Been attracted to him. Now she knew he was trying to keep the girl safe from a madman, which made her feel better about her attraction to him, but she still did not like the way he kept secrets.

But to his point, she had secrets, too.

Had he guessed? She didn't think so. He blamed her suspiciousness on what Bradley had done to her, and she knew he was right. Bradley was at the crux of it. No doubt John thought she should just forget about Bradley and go on her way, thanking Heaven that she had discovered the truth before they had said the vows. And had that been all there was to it, she might well have been able to do that. But matters were worse than John—or anyone—knew.

Yes, her pride had been hurt by the fact that Bradley had lied to her about why he wanted to marry her, but the worst part—the piece for which she could not forgive herself—was that she had given him her most precious gift. Her innocence.

She slumped back in her chair. She had carried that burden for so long that even admitting it to herself was something of a relief. That night . . . dear God, what had she been thinking?

That she was in love, that she was going to marry this man.

She had gone to the theater with her family, but

Bradley had whispered that he needed to speak with her alone about a matter of some import. She had lied to her parents and claimed a headache, and Bradley had gallantly agreed to see her home.

Since they were out with some very influential people, her parents had agreed to let him take her home. In the carriage that night, Bradley vowed his undying love for her, claiming he intended to approach her father the very next day to ask for her hand. He had presented her with a lovely little locket to show the seriousness of his intentions. Then he had kissed her in a way she had never been kissed before, making her head spin. One thing had led to another.

And she had given herself to him, right there in the carriage.

Two weeks later she had overheard him bragging to his cronies that his naval career was assured now that he had landed the admiral's daughter.

Dear God, how stupid and naïve she had been! Luckily, Bradley had never disclosed anything about that night in the carriage to his friends. When she jilted him, he had threatened to tell, but she made certain he understood that his naval career would be at an end if he breathed a word of what had happened between them. She would ask her father to intervene, and he would not be pleased that a man he had trusted had taken advantage of his daughter, especially when that daughter refused to marry to scotch the scandal.

Her gamble had paid off though Bradley continued to press his suit, following the rules of propriety to the letter. Finally, her father had noticed her discomfort and arranged to send her former fiancé on an assignment to India.

She had not seen or heard from him until a few weeks ago, when he had shown up at Cilla's wedding. Yet his legacy had lived on in the untenable position in which she found herself.

How was she to make a proper marriage now? She was ruined goods. Where could she find a man who would understand her momentary lapse in judgment and not consider her a whore? She did not have the wealth or connections that would encourage a man to overlook such a thing. Certainly her father was a well-known military hero, but in the end even that would not be enough to save her.

She was stuck, perhaps even doomed to the future John had predicted for her: favorite aunt to her sister's children, unless she found a man who would both understand and forgive her mistake. Such men were nearly impossible to find. If only she could erase the past. Start again.

Start again. . .

John had said the very same thing. He was leaving

England for America, where he could start over. Where he could have a life his past would not allow if he stayed in his native land.

She had asked him why he could not stay, but perhaps the question she should be asking was, why could she not go, too?

She liked John. Despite his secrets, his motives appeared to be honorable. Just because a person had a past did not mean he—or she—was a bad person. And just because one man had abused her trust did not mean that another would do the same, did it?

Maybe John was right. Perhaps she needed to give him the benefit of the doubt, to have faith that he was doing the right things for the right reasons. To believe that he would not betray her. This man was the first since Bradley who interested her, and the first, to her knowledge, who seemed to return that interest in a way that had nothing to do with her family connections and everything to do with *her*.

What if she were to go with him when he left for America? Helped him build the family he had talked about?

They had passion between them, something many couples of the upper classes could not claim. And she did trust him with her safety. Surely, that was enough to see them through the hard times ahead. Surely John would understand about her situation.

But what if he didn't?

No, she would not think like that. She would have to overcome her own fears and bare her soul to him, take the risk that he might see her differently once she told him her secret.

Of course, he had been horrible to her. She was not even sure how it had happened. One moment she had been offering her assistance, and the next moment he had accused her of distracting him. Dear God, that had made her so angry, that he would accuse her of being responsible for what happened to Annabelle. Clearly that was nonsense, and she had told him so!

Right before she stormed off.

Oh, Lord. She rested her forehead on her hand. He had tricked her, played her emotions like a virtuoso.

John often lingered on the sidelines, watching people. Learning them. Observing their strengths and weaknesses. It would have been child's play for him to poke at her weak spots and get her angry enough to walk away from him. Maybe to avoid him for the remainder of the house party.

He had said she was a distraction. Clearly he had taken the attack on Annabelle personally. He blamed himself. He was probably trying to push her away so he could concentrate on the danger at hand.

She understood that his purpose at Nevarton Chase was very important, but she had only a handful of days left before Samuel and Cilla returned from their honeymoon, and John returned to America. The clock was ticking. She needed to put her plan into action.

He might resist. She imagined that trying to chip through that armor of honor he wore might prove formidable. But she was not without weapons of her own.

She stood up and regarded herself in the mirror, smoothing her dress and turning this way and that, examining her figure. By the time she was finished with John Ready, he would be repeating the vows before he realized what had hit him.

"Lottie! Come help me dress!"

In the taproom of the Hart and Hound, John nursed his ale and listened with half attention as the barmaid flirted with the fellow at the next table. Her mark was obviously a man of some means, as evidenced by his well-tailored clothing and bulging purse. Not one of the upper ten thousand, certainly, else John would have recognized him.

Maybe.

After letting Virgil know that he was leaving the estate, John had taken Sir Harry aside and asked his assistance in watching over Annabelle in his absence. The stalwart baronet had agreed without hesitation. Then he had spoken to Annabelle and obtained a description from her of the man who had tried to abduct her.

The admiral and his wife had returned from their walk, but Genny had remained conspicuously absent. Guilt over the things he had said to her still pricked at him, but he knew it was all for the best. If he was going to keep Annabelle safe, he could not be distracted, not by anything or anyone.

With the written description tucked in his pocket, he had spent the afternoon retracing the route Sir Harry and Annabelle had taken. The site of the ambush had revealed nothing of note, so he had one last option he wanted to try before he called it a day. That option involved the local tavern—a place crawling with gossip, where a fellow who had recently come into some funds might feel the need to show off his good fortune.

He had asked around about the description, but no one could—or would—shed any light on the man's identity. As soon as he had noticed that his questions were causing some unrest among the locals, he retired to a corner table with a tankard and simply observed.

Late afternoon. Some things never changed, and the sights and sounds of an English tavern were some of them. Not to mention the smells. God save him, but he had missed the scents of good English ale spewing from the tap and brown bread baking and fresh mutton roasting in the oven. He drained his tankard and signaled the barmaid for another. If he did not learn anything in the next half hour, he was leaving.

"Mr. Ready! I say, how fortuitous!" Tim Timmons dropped into an empty chair at John's table without waiting for an invitation. He set his hat and a large satchel down on the seat beside him, then signaled for the barmaid and ordered an ale of his own.

"Mr. Timmons." John bit back his annoyance and reminded himself that the man had the loose lips of London's worst gossip. "Fortuitous indeed. I thought you had an appointment this afternoon."

"I did, I did. Went to Evermayne, spoke to St. Giles. I told him there had been no change, but I told him that in a letter before he insisted I come to see him in person."

"St. Giles?" It felt odd to form his lips around the name after so many years.

"Randall St. Giles. His Grace's cousin, . . . well, third cousin. Impatient fellow. Wants miracles." The barmaid set his ale in front of him, and Tim immediately picked it up and took a healthy swig.

"Randall? What is his interest?"

"Ha! That one? He thinks he's the heir." Tim took another drink.

"The heir? But what about . . . . I mean, His Grace had no son?"

"No sons, just two daughters. Young ones, too. The youngest is, oh, seven I believe."

"Seven." The ale turned to dust in his mouth. "A daughter you say."

"Two. The older one is from His Grace's first wife. She's twelve. Or fifteen maybe. I'd have to check my notes."

John cleared his throat and took a drink of ale, though he barely tasted it. "I had heard—years ago, you understand—that His Grace had a son, not a daughter."

"No, no. Two daughters. Would make things easier if he did have a son. Would save all manner of trouble."

John said nothing. The old bastard had lied to him. What other deceptions could be laid at the late Duke's door?

Timmons drank again, licking his lips as he set the tankard on the table. "Though His Grace did have a brother."

John glanced up at that. "Did he?"

"Yes, but they weren't close. Different mothers, some fifteen years between them in age. Of course, he died, some four or five years ago."

John's blood ran cold. "Died?"

"Accident of some sort. Carriage sank in a frozen lake." Timmons shivered.

John stood and put some money on the table. "I have to leave. Allow me to pay for your ale."

"Why, thank you!" The balding man beamed. "Pleasure to see you again, Mr. Ready."

John nodded, uncertain if his tongue could form any words more coherent than that, and left the tavern.

It took long minutes for the groom to bring his horse from the stables. He flipped the lad a coin—he did not even know what kind—and mounted, turning the horse east.

Toward Evermayne.

Chapter 9

Though it had been years, John remembered the way to Evermayne as if it had only been yesterday.

Some of the landmarks had changed, but for the most part everything looked achingly familiar. When he passed the marker that denoted the border of Evermayne lands, he slowed his mount. The green fields inside their stone walls, the wildflowers sprinkled across verdant carpets, the lush trees promising shade in the late-afternoon sun—everything seemed to welcome him back. A lump formed in his throat, and he swallowed hard. Home.

He urged his mount to a faster speed. Quickly the flower-sprinkled meadows gave way to cultivated crop fields or vast grasslands, with livestock milling about in the waning afternoon. The occasional dwelling appeared, usually simple cottages inhabited by the tenant farmers. The closer he got to the village of Evermayne, however, the more sophisticated the architecture became. Farmers' cottages slowly gave way to brick buildings housing shops and offices. More traffic appeared on the road. A gentleman on horseback, a matron in a single-horse gig, a tenant farmer with his simple open wagon loaded with supplies and wide-eyed children. Everyone glanced at him, tipped their hats, waved hello. He nodded back to them, glad he was not expected to speak. He didn't know if he would have been able to with his emotions choking his airway.

He rode through the center of the village, following the main road beyond the shops and workingman's housing that had sprung up. He passed the livery and an inn that had not been there several years earlier. The road took on a series of curves here, leading back out into the fields and forests he had seen coming in. Anyone else would have thought there was nothing more to see.

He knew better.

The drive came up suddenly, simple packed dirt that appeared to bend into the trees. He turned up that drive and followed that well-traveled track, slowing his mount as he rounded the turn. The house stood back from the road, a two-story brick dwelling that clearly indicated its inhabitants were more than simple working folk. No groom came out to meet him, so he dismounted and tied his horse to the post himself. Then he walked up to the door and raised the knocker.

As soon as he heard echo of his knock inside the house, he wanted to call it back. Mount his horse and leave the way he came. This was madness. What had he been thinking? Sunset was imminent, and he had yet to find any clue to Annabelle's attacker. He should not be here. He should be at Nevarton Chase, guarding Annabelle—

The door opened, and a young girl in the dark colors of a servant looked at him expectantly. "Yes?"

"Is . . ." He took a breath. He could do this. "I am looking for Lady Phillip St. Giles. Do I have the correct residence?"

The maid's face gave nothing away. "I will see if Lady Phillip is at home. Your card, please?"

"No card. My name is John Ready."

"One moment." She closed the door in his face.

He fisted his hand, glancing around him at the familiar surroundings. He was a blundering fool. This was the last place he should have come. But after what Tim had told him, he simply had to know where things stood now. What had happened over the past seven years? This was the only place where he might get the truth.

The door opened again, wider this time. "Lady Phillip will see you, sir. Please come in. I will have Bertie take care of your mount."

"Thank you." He stepped through the doorway and was immediately engulfed in the fresh scents of soap and vinegar. He shut his eyes as memories swamped him. Of course. It was Thursday. The day the servants cleaned the floors in the foyer and halls.

The maid held out her hand for his hat. "Just up the stairs, sir. Lady Phillip is waiting for you on the first floor."

"Thank you." Surrendering his hat, he hurried up the curving staircase, his heart pumping.

As the maid said, his hostess stood at the top of the steps, waiting to greet her guest as he reached the first floor. Small in stature, Lily St. Giles wore her age as gracefully as she did her simple lavender dress. She was the picture of elegance, the perfect lady. As he drew closer, he watched her calm, polite expression give way to hope, then shock, then finally joy.

She raised her trembling hands to her lips, then stretched them toward him. "John," she whispered.

He hit the top step and reached her in one long-legged stride. She took his face in her hands, smoothing her thumbs over his beard. Tears glimmered in her soft blue eyes. The scent of jasmine clung to her skin and clothing. Nothing else felt as much like home.

He closed his eyes and rested his face in her hands. "Mama."

For one moment, everything in his world settled into perfect alignment. Then the sound of footsteps in the foyer below made them both jolt.

"Come into the Chinese drawing room," his mother

said, placing a hand over her heart. She sniffled. "I do not want anyone else seeing you."

She turned and hurried down the hallway to a room that had once been known as the Blue drawing room. He followed behind her. She still moved as quickly as ever, but there was a lot more gray in her dark hair than he remembered. And faint lines around her mouth that had not been there before.

Time went on, aging all of them. He looked different, too.

"In here." She stood in the doorway and waved him into the room.

When he stepped in, he saw why it was referred to as the Chinese drawing room. Red, black, and yellow dominated the color scheme, along with gold statues of dragons and a huge blue vase painted with delicate white flowers. "This certainly is a Chinese drawing room."

She shut the door behind them. "What do you mean? Oh, I remember. The last time you were here, it was blue."

"*Very* blue."

"Hmmm." She looked around. "Well, I have outgrown my blue phase. I enjoy the boldness of the Chinese colors. Now come, sit down."

His mother moved to a sofa covered with scarlet and black pillows embroidered with various scenes of China, while John chose an armchair of blazing purple that looked less alarming than some of the other furniture.

Once they were seated, his mother just stared at him, her hand pressed to her mouth. "I cannot believe this," she murmured. "I thought never to see you again."

"I never intended to return to England, but a mission to help a friend brought me back."

"I simply cannot get over it. You look so . . . so different. Then again, you were so young when you left—"

"Twenty-three."

"Twenty-three. And now . . ."

"I'm thirty, Mama."

"Thirty," she whispered, as awed as if he had just revealed the secrets of turning lead into gold. "You have become a man."

"Every boy does." He leaned forward, reaching out to close his fingers around hers. "Mama, I do not have much time. I should not even be here."

"Oh my heavens, you are right. What were you thinking? You came right to the front door!"

"I admit I was not thinking very clearly. We have a little time, but I will have to leave shortly. Mama, I heard some things today . . . What has happened since I have been gone? Today someone told me that Father—"

"Yes." She pressed her lips together and pulled one

hand from his to search her pocket for a handkerchief. "He died four years ago."

"How?" His voice sounded as battered and torn as his stumbling heart.

"It was winter. His phaeton went into a frozen lake." She dabbed at her eyes.

Emotion nearly choked him. "I do not understand. He was an excellent hand at the reins."

"No one could tell me. Ice, perhaps." She shrugged, her damp eyes reflecting the same sense of emptiness that he felt. She crushed the handkerchief in her hand.

He came to kneel before her as he had when he was a little boy, but now he was tall enough to look her in the eye. "I heard other things, too. The Duke . . . ?"

She nodded. "Just over a month ago. He was very ill."

"So the Duke is dead. Father is dead." His voice hitched. Saying it made it all that more real. "And the Duke has no son?"

His mother gave him a puzzled look. "No, dear."

Her innocent confirmation of Tim's story made a mockery of everything he had thought of as truth. Lies. All lies, piled one on the other like bodies on a battle-field. He bowed his head, crushed by the weight of betrayal. "Damn that old bastard. He lied to me. He lied to make me go." His voice broke. Sobs clogged his throat. He fought them. Lost. "I was not here when Father died. Because of him."

His mother gathered him into her arms, rocking him as she had when he was a child. "Now, John-John. It is all right, my dear."

Her voice murmuring his childhood nickname, the scent of her . . . He wrapped his arms around his mother and wept for the father he had lost. The life he had lost.

"Shh. Everything is going to be fine." She stroked his hair. "The Duke did what he thought must be done. He always did."

"Stubborn old goat," John mumbled.

"He was. But he was your father's brother and the head of the family. In his way, he was trying to protect you."

"He knew." John pulled back and searched for his own handkerchief, sniffing as he rubbed it across his eyes. "He knew that if his wife did not birth a son, I would never leave. So he lied and told me she had given him an heir."

"Your loyalty to your family was always something he took pride in."

"Pride? Him?" He gave a disbelieving snort.

"The Duke was a man who conveyed his feelings through actions, not words."

"Actions?" The anger energized him, pushing past the grief. He got to his feet. "He sent me away, Mama."

"He was trying to protect you. You know how it looked. What people thought."

"I know." He moved back to the hideous purple arm-chair and dropped into it. "People were wrong."

"Of course they were. But there was no proof. Your father worked right up to the day he died to exonerate you—"

"What?" John sat straight up. "Father was trying to clear my name when he died?"

"I believe so. He would not give me details, but he worked tirelessly. He wanted you to be able to come home."

"Oh, my God." Leaning his elbows on his knees, he laid his head in his hands. As if the guilt of missing his father's funeral were not enough. . .

"There is something else you may not have realized."

"What else?" he said, not raising his head. "I feel as if my entire world has spun out of control."

"Darling, your uncle had no son. Your father was next in line for the title, but he predeceased the Duke. Which means—"

John slowly lifted his gaze to hers. "Which means I am the next Duke of Evermayne."

His mother nodded.

"This is madness." He jerked to his feet, began to pace. "I cannot claim the title. You know as soon as I make my identity known, the whole mess will start again. I could be hanged."

"Then why did you take the risk of coming here

today?" She leaned forward, clenching her hands together in her lap. "Walking up to the front door as if you are simply another caller. *That* is madness!"

"I had to know the truth. And you were the only one I could trust to tell me."

Her expression softened. "I will allow you that." She tilted her head, pursing her lips as she turned the matter over in her mind. "What if you did come forward? Perhaps accepting the title will help you clear your name. If you had the power of the title behind you—"

"No, it will not help." He scrubbed his hands over his face. "Nothing but the truth will clear me, whether I am the Duke of Evermayne or plain John Ready. It is better if I stay hidden."

"Well, the next in line after you is your cousin Randall." She wrinkled her nose. "I have never liked him. I have heard disturbing reports that he is already acting as if he is the Duke. Borrowing money against his expectations. And he plans to petition the queen to declare you dead."

"Well, that is one way out of this mess."

"John!"

The shock in her voice added to his guilt. "Listen, Mama. If they declare me dead, then they will stop looking for me. I will be able to return to America and live my life as John Ready. Maybe give you grandchildren."

"Whom I will never see!" she snapped, rising. "Because my son will be dead to the world. John, surely you do not intend to walk away without fighting for the truth?"

"It might be easier for everyone involved if I did. It was what the Duke wanted."

"But it was not what your father wanted. He died trying to prove your innocence!"

He took the hit with a flinch. "I know."

They stood looking at each other for a long moment. In the hallway, the clock struck the hour.

"I should go." He started moving toward the door.

"No! Wait." She hurried after him and locked both hands around his arm. "Please think about it, John. I still have your father's notes. There must be something in there to help you."

"Good, then I will have plenty to read while I await the executioner."

"Do not be impertinent, young man!"

Beneath the sharp, parental tone hid the plea of a frightened mother. He stopped before opening the door and laid a hand over one of hers. The fear in her eyes— fear for him—twisted him up like a rope. "I wish things could be different, Mama."

"Take his notes and journals. I absolutely insist. Maybe you will find something to clear your name."

He sighed. "Ever the optimist." He kissed her cheek. "I love you, Mama. I am glad I was able to see you again even if it was a risk to come here."

She blocked the doorway and stopped him cold with her hands on his chest. "You are not leaving this house without your father's work."

"I have already been here too long."

"Did you not hear me? You are not leaving without it." She folded her arms and glared.

He recognized that look. Nothing was going to move her, and he did not want to have her last memories of him to be negative ones. "Very well, Mama. I will take his notes with me."

"Good. Now come with me." She left the room and headed for the staircase. Dutifully, he followed her down the stairs, feeling six years old again.

On the ground floor, she went to his father's study and opened the door, then indicated that he should go in first. He stepped inside. Even after four years, the scents of lemon and beeswax could not mask the sweet scent of the pipe tobacco his father had favored. A lump formed in his throat, and his eyes misted. How many times he had stood right there, either to visit with his father or receive his lectures? The room looked exactly the same, as if Lord Phillip St. Giles would return any moment.

"I have allowed the staff to clean in here," his mother said, remaining in the doorway, "but that is all. Nothing has been removed."

"Where—" He had to clear his throat. "Where did he keep the notes?"

"Here." She moved to the desk, pausing for just an instant to touch the spectacles sitting beside the lamp, before she opened a large drawer. "This was his journal. He noted everything in here." She took a thick, leather-bound book from the drawer, the pages dog-eared and ragged in places. "There were also these letters." A stack of correspondence tied with a ribbon came next. "Something in one of these letters or this journal sent him to Elford-by-the-Sea."

John took the stack of letters and turned it over in his hand. "Elford-by-the-Sea? Where is that?"

"Somewhere in Cornwall. It is where he died." She frowned. "Come to think of it, the vicar from Elford-by-the-Sea came by here a few days ago."

"The vicar? That is odd. What did he want?"

"I do not know. I was not at home; the maid informed me. He probably had your father's name and was look-ing for a donation. " She picked up the journal and pushed it into his hands. "Guard this, John. It might be the key to your freedom."

"I will." Gripping the book in one hand, he tucked the packet of letters into his coat pocket with the other. "I should go, Mama, before the servants start specu-lating."

She came and kissed him, then looked into his eyes. "Be careful, John. You are all I have left in this world. Do not give up on the truth."

He forced himself to back away a step, far enough that he could not touch her. "Good-bye."

"Good-bye," she whispered.

He turned and hurried from the room that looked and smelled so much like his father, suddenly eager to get out of this house he had once loved so well. This house where he had *been* loved. A footman saw him coming and fetched his hat, then he was forced to wait at least five interminable minutes outside in the cooling evening air while the young groom brought his gelding to him.

He tucked the book into his saddlebag, then mounted quickly and tapped his horse with his heels, determined not to look back. But as he came up on the bend in the drive, he did indeed stop and look over his shoulder. There she stood, watching him from the window. She waved, but he did not return the gesture. Instead, he turned his back and urged his horse to a trot down the drive, around the bend, and out of sight.

Perhaps it was cruel to leave her like this. Perhaps he should have allowed her some hope that he might someday be vindicated. But despite his father's research, was there any hope for a miracle that would restore his life to him? He doubted it. And he preferred that she remember him leaving under his own power, alive and healthy and well.

Because the alternative was watching him hang for the murder of his wife.

Chapter 10

"**T**his play is going to be a disaster unless someone can locate Mr. Ready," Sir Harry said. "We simply cannot rehearse without him. Has anyone seen him today?"

Genny looked around at the others, hoping someone would admit to seeing the elusive man. But no one raised a hand or said a word. And that worried her.

Last night, she had waited for John to come back from chasing Annabelle's attacker, but dinner came and went without him, rendering her extra efforts on her appearance wasted. By the time the evening came to an end—after Genny's adequate performance at the pianoforte and Annabelle's overly dramatic recitation of poetry—Genny had begun to worry. Had he found the brigand only to be done in by him? The possibility grew more plausible as the big grandfather clock in the hallway struck midnight.

Then, in the wee hours, she heard footsteps in the

hallway. Slipping from her bed, she went to the door and opened it a crack—just in time to see John slip into his room at the end of the hall.

So, based on last night, she knew he was alive. But why was he not at the rehearsal?

"I know he came in last night," Virgil finally said. "I checked with the stables, and his gelding, Veritas, is there. Perhaps he simply got back so late that he is still abed?"

"Oh, do you suppose he caught the horrible man who tried to capture Annabelle?" Dolly asked.

"That would certainly be a relief," Sir Harry said.

"I'd like that," Annabelle said. "I hate being stuck in the house."

"But darling," Dolly said. "You haven't been stuck inside the whole time. Just this morning, we went to the village to see the new shipment of silk that came in from London."

"And we had four footmen with pistols," Annabelle complained. "People were staring."

"If people were staring, that makes it less likely our villain will try again," Sir Harry said. "All the better."

"I just hate being trapped."

Sir Harry gave Annabelle a tender smile. "That is because you are a free spirit, Miss Bailey."

Annabelle blushed and lowered her gaze.

"I would hate to wake the man if he was chasing bandits all night," Virgil said.

"But we cannot rehearse without him," Helen said.

"Send a servant to see if he is awake," the admiral suggested. "Perhaps we can postpone rehearsing until later this evening."

"I hate the idea of putting off the rehearsal again," Dolly said. "I just have my heart set on performing the play at the picnic! And we only have two days left."

"The admiral is right. Perhaps it would be a good idea to send a servant to look in on him," Virgil said.

"Look in on whom?" John asked, entering the gallery.

"There you are, John!" Annabelle cried, clapping her hands together.

"Look in on you, John Ready," Virgil said. "We were worried about you. Did you catch that bandit who tried to steal my Annabelle?"

"Unfortunately, no. No one I spoke to could identify someone who even resembled the fellow Miss Bailey described."

"Now what do we do?" Dolly asked. "Keep Annabelle locked in her room?"

Annabelle folded her arms. "I refuse to be a prisoner."

"It's for your own good, sweet pea," Virgil said.

"I won't do it. Think of something else."

"John," Virgil said, "I would appreciate it if you would

come to my study after we're finished here so we can talk about the best way to handle security and the traveling arrangements for the Statons' dinner party this evening."

"Of course."

"Excellent!" Sir Harry said. He clapped his hands rapidly three times. "Attention, everyone! We are going to start with the scene where Bella tells her parents of her love for Frederick. So Mr. and Mrs. Bailey, over here. Miss Bailey, right here, please. Excellent. Ready? Everyone have their pages? And . . . begin!"

As the Baileys began to read through their scene, Genny edged closer to John. "Are you all right?" she whispered.

John turned toward her, surprise on his face. "Why would I not be?"

"You were gone so long last night. I was worried."

His gaze lingered on her for a long moment. She took a deep breath, deliberately thrusting forth her bosom so it strained against the bodice of her morning dress. He glanced down, hesitated, then jerked his gaze away, clenching his jaw.

She smothered a smile. Trimmed with green ribbon, the white cambric morning dress was one of her favorites. Her father had often told her it looked stunning on her in contrast with her dark hair and green eyes, but most gentlemen admired the way the material clung to her female form.

Apparently, so did John.

She leaned closer as if to hear the performers better, tilting slightly, clutching her pages of the script. Her elbow brushed his, and she pulled away with a little "oh" as if it had happened accidentally.

He whipped his head around again. The look in his eyes made it hard to breathe.

"Have a care, Miss Wallington-Willis," he murmured. He swept his gaze over her, once more pausing on her bosom before turning away.

How could he remain so calm? She practically shook with the heat that was rising between them. If someone were to speak to her right now, she did not think she would be able to answer coherently. Her limbs tingled, especially where she had touched him. Didn't he feel the same? Or were men different?

She frowned. She had not considered that men might be different from women in these matters. Perhaps they had more control over themselves.

"Miss Wallington-Willis."

She startled as Sir Harry called her name. "Yes, Sir Harry?"

"I would like you and Mr. Ready to read the scene where Malevita is watching Frederick secretly and confessing her love aloud to the audience."

"Of course." She flipped through her pages, looking for the scene.

"Mr. Ready, there are no words for you in this scene. Malevita has come upon you asleep in the forest."

"I see."

"So if you would consider lying down on this blanket I took the liberty of setting out?"

John stared at the blanket for a moment as if it were the enemy, but then he nodded and lay down right there on the gallery floor.

"Miss Wallington-Willis, whenever you are ready," Sir Harry said.

Genny moistened her suddenly dry lips and stepped forward.

"Perhaps Malevita should enter from the right," Sir Harry suggested.

Genny nodded and moved to the right of the make-shift stage area. John lay "sleeping" on the floor of the imaginary wood, and as "Malevita" came upon him there, Genny could not resist the chance to let her eyes roam over him in a way she had not been able to do overtly at any other time.

"O handsome warrior. O noble prince. My blood burns for thee," she recited. "Look upon him, all you sun and moon and stars, and know he is my love. My mate. My future king."

"Excellent," Sir Harry murmured.

"O love that lives as a flame inside me," she continued, walking around him, her skirts brushing his legs, his arms. She pretended not to notice when the edge of her skirt swept over his face, but his eyes popped open, and he gave her one, searing look that made her toes curl in her shoes. "Thou art my only reason for living. My heart beats for thee." She laid her hand on her bosom and tapped three times to signify her heartbeat. Then she dropped her hand, letting her fingers slide swiftly over the curve of her breast as she did so, a movement so smooth that the other players did not catch the wicked flirtation.

Only John saw.

She slid her gaze over his tense body, his fisted fingers, his clenched jaw—and smiled.

"Excellent!" Sir Harry said, applauding.

The others applauded. too, and Genny gave a curtsy, her cheeks warm with pleasure.

John got to his feet, turned away from her, and said, "What is next, Sir Harry?"

"The scene where you and Bella meet by the stream, and you tell her of your undying devotion."

John nodded. "Very good." He glanced at Genny. "Please step aside, Miss Wallington-Willis."

His dismissive tone rankled, but she was not fooled. She had taken control of the situation, aroused him, and he did not like it.

Her plan was working perfectly.

* * *

What had gotten into that clever minx? He knew when a woman was deliberately flirting with him, and Genny had come after him with her full arsenal loaded and ready. The searing glances, the "accidental" touches, even the clothing she wore . . . All of it sent one unmistakable message.

Take me.

His body heard that message loud and clear and wanted to respond in the most decisive of ways. Hunger hummed throughout his body, held in check only by his will—a will that was rapidly giving way to the bombardment of subtle invitations sent in his direction. By the time they finished the rehearsal—where Genny appeared with him in scene after scene as Malevita, declaring her love for Frederick in the most passionate of verses—she had him so stirred up that the slightest glance from her might push him over the edge.

But he would not let her get to him. He had seen these tricks before; Elizabeth had been a master at the art of seduction. He would not be ruled by his own lusts, no matter how difficult it was to resist.

And it was bloody difficult. Genny was nothing like Elizabeth, and that made her all the more enticing.

"Good work today," Sir Harry said, as they finished the last scene. "This production will be ready for the picnic in no time at all."

"Thank you so much for writing the play, Sir Harry, and for acting as our stage manager," Dolly said.

"My pleasure, I assure you. Mr. Ready, you did quite well at your role. Are you certain you do not want to be in the final performance?" Sir Harry adjusted his spectacles and looked at him with expectation.

"I do not," John said.

"Very well." Sir Harry looked a bit disappointed, but John was not about to take the chance of someone recognizing him. "Then I will see you all tomorrow at the same time to go through the play once again. Admiral, I trust you will remember your lines this time?"

Genny's father bristled. Silver-haired and bearded, the admiral was built like a bull but was also considered one of the greatest logistical minds of their time. "It was one line, Sir Harry. On my honor, I will not forget it tomorrow."

"See that you do not," Sir Harry said, and looked down at his notes.

The admiral's eyes widened at the chiding tone. Then his lips curled into a sneer that, had Sir Harry been the ship of one of England's enemies, would have seen the scholarly baronet scuttled to kindling.

Helen must have sensed the danger, for she patted her husband's arm. "We should get changed for dinner now," she said, then murmured something in her husband's ear. The admiral seemed to calm at that, but he still sent a baleful look at the baronet as his wife turned him away. "Genny, dear, are you coming?"

"Yes, Mama." Genny lowered her gaze in ladylike modesty and followed her parents at a slower pace. The snowy cambric of her skirts moved with the sway of her hips in a manner John found both hypnotic and erotic.

"Are you certain you won't come with us, Sir Harry?" Dolly asked, as Virgil came over and took the handles of her wheeled chair. "They invited you, too."

"I have already conveyed my regrets to the Statons," Sir Harry said. "Unfortunately, I had a prior engagement that cannot be rescheduled."

"What kind of engagement?" Annabelle asked.

"Annabelle!" Dolly exclaimed. "That's none of your business!"

"I was just asking," Annabelle said with a slump to her shoulders.

"Do not scold her, Mrs. Bailey," Sir Harry said with a smile. "Her natural ebullience is part of what makes your daughter so charming."

"You're way too kind," Dolly said.

"Takes me less time to get ready for these things," Virgil said to the men with a grin. "I'll meet you in my study in an hour, John."

"Agreed."

"Good, that's all settled," Dolly said, as Virgil started

to wheel her away. "Come along, Annabelle. Time to get dressed for the dinner party."

"At least I'm getting out of this house," Annabelle said, her lower lip poking out in sulky rebellion as she fell into step behind her parents.

"And if you don't stop acting like an infant, you may never get out again," Dolly scolded. "Land sakes, child!"

Their voices muted as they left the gallery, but Sir Harry remained where he was, looking at the door where they had departed. When he turned back to John, there was a softness in his eyes that disappeared almost immediately.

Sir Harry and Annabelle? John noted the information and set it aside for later.

"I wanted to thank you for watching over Annabelle while I was gone last night," John said.

"No thanks are necessary. I like to do my part." Sir Harry gathered together the pages of his script and collected the blanket from the floor. "So you found nothing?"

He'd found more than he bargained for, but not about Annabelle's attacker. "That is correct."

"My old friend Raventhorpe is a crafty one. He was fond of finding simpletons to carry out his orders." Sir Harry flashed a grin. "Must be why he chose my company so often."

John laughed and fell into step as the baronet started

for the door. "You, Sir Harry, are much more clever than most, I would wager."

Sir Harry gave him a sidelong glance and a smirk. "I never wager."

"A good policy."

"However," Sir Harry said, bringing the conversation back on topic, "I would imagine that if Raventhorpe did hire someone to kidnap Annabelle, that person would not be the sharpest sword in the armory. That should make it easier to find him."

"Because he will make a mistake?"

"Exactly!"

"I do not suppose you know the names of any of Raventhorpe's former cohorts?" John asked, as they traversed the hallway and reached the stairs.

"Alas, no. He did not take me into his confidence. In fact, I do believe he thought me something of a feather-brain." He started up the staircase.

John stopped short, his hand on the rail. "You? Featherbrained?"

Sir Harry laughed. "You flatter me, Mr. Ready."

John bounded up the stairs and caught up with the baronet. "It seems Raventhorpe is the dull-witted one."

"Not at all. Egocentric, perhaps. Believes he is more clever than everyone else. But he is crafty, have no doubt of that."

They reached the landing of the second floor, and Sir

Harry paused, looking John in the eye. "Watch yourself while you pursue Raventhorpe and anyone who works for him. He does not value other people. Thinks they are expendable. And that makes him dangerous."

John's mouth twisted. "I know."

Sir Harry nodded. "Very well, then. I am off to my engagement. Enjoy yourself at the Statons' tonight. Their cook is quite exceptional."

"Thank you, Sir Harry." John waited a moment as Sir Harry turned and headed down the hallway, then he turned and went in the opposite direction, toward his own room.

Sir Harry's lecture on Raventhorpe was almost amusing. John knew the baronet intended to be helpful, but he had no idea how well John knew Raventhorpe—and how well he knew what Raventhorpe was capable of.

The earl was a conniving, greedy bastard. This was a man who kidnapped innocent women and sold them into slavery overseas to become the sexual playthings of wealthy men, simply to line his own pockets. A man who had tried to kill Samuel Breedlove and left him marooned on a deserted island while Raventhorpe attempted to steal Samuel's wealthy fiancée, Annabelle. The same man who, nearly eight years ago, had been John's rival for the hand of Elizabeth Colling, the beautiful, socially ambitious daughter of a wealthy merchant. In the end, John had married Elizabeth.

But Raventhorpe had killed her.

Fury flared, red-hot, nearly blinding him. Somehow, he reached his room. Rested his clenching hand against the doorframe as he struggled with the rage that roared to be released. He knew Raventhorpe had killed his wife, but he could not prove it. And the bastard had arranged things so it looked like John was guilty.

To this day, he had no clear memory of that night. He and Elizabeth had attended Lady Canthrope's ball. Elizabeth had gone missing. No surprise there, as their marriage had already started to crumble. His wife was frequently to be found gambling or flirting with other men—including her former suitor, Raventhorpe. Hopeful, optimistic fool that he was, John had searched for her all over the house. He was determined to make their marriage work.

One of the servants said he had seen her in the gardens, but as soon as John went out to look for her, he'd felt a prick on the back of his neck. The world had gone fuzzy. He fell. And he remembered the servant begging for his forgiveness, something about Raventhorpe threatening his daughter, before he lost consciousness.

When he came to a few hours later, the ball was winding down, Elizabeth was still missing, and his head felt as if he had downed an entire cask of whisky on his own. Unfortunately, his staggering steps and slurring speech were all anyone remembered the next morning, when his wife's lifeless body was discovered beneath the shrubbery in the back of the garden of Canthrope's London town house.

That very day, his uncle, the Duke of Evermayne, had told John that the duchess had just birthed a son, pushing John even further down the list in line to inherit, and that John would be leaving England—forcibly if necessary—to preserve the dignity of the St. Giles name and escape the scandal.

The one saving grace to the whole sordid mess was that never once had Uncle indicated that he thought John was guilty. So John had fled England, while Raventhorpe had continued his dirty deeds unchecked.

But Raventhorpe had not counted on John saving Samuel from that deserted island. Or Samuel coming to England to demand his bride. The earl had tried to have them killed more than once, but they had escaped. Then Annabelle had chosen to jilt the earl. Cornered, Raventhorpe had kidnapped Annabelle and run off with her in a desperate attempt to force her to wed him.

Samuel and John had foiled the scheme with the help of the local highwayman, Black Bill. And John had taken considerable personal satisfaction in stopping Raventhorpe's escape by shooting him in the arse. Afterwards, the bastard had slipped off to France to avoid the gossip about his failed elopement, but he had lost

Annabelle and her fortune—a point to the side of those he had wronged.

So yes, John knew Raventhorpe. Knew how slippery the man could be, how clever. Which was also why he dared not step forward and claim his title. Raventhorpe had gone through a lot of trouble to get rid of John.

And despite his mother's hopes, he was beginning to think that John St. Giles should stay gone. It might be the best thing for everyone.

Richard, Lord Raventhorpe, watched from the rail of the ship as the outline of the English shore became sharper through the lingering fog. Though he had only been in France a few weeks, his sources told him that the scandal surrounding his attempt to elope with Annabelle was beginning to die down. There were other tidbits more appetizing, such as the marriage of the admiral's daughter to that American bastard, Samuel Breedlove.

And the failed kidnapping of Annabelle Bailey.

That fool Green had certainly mucked up what should have been a simple job. Grab the girl, hand her over to Raventhorpe's contacts in Dover, then have her shipped off to his partner in Morocco. The haughty blonde would soon have fetched a tidy price in the slave market. The scheme should have been child's play.

Yet somehow Peter Green had failed. Perhaps he *should* have employed a child!

Ever since he had met Annabelle Bailey, his luck had changed for the worse. Breedlove had stumbled onto Raventhorpe's slave-trading interests in the Caribbean, so the earl had had no alternative but to leave him for dead on an abandoned island. Who knew the bastard would not only live but would somehow get rescued just in time to prevent Raventhorpe from marrying the very wealthy Annabelle?

Then Raventhorpe's plan to run off with Annabelle to his Scottish estate had been foiled by the highwayman Black Bill—who was already a thorn in his side with his penchant for robbing only those who traveled Raventhorpe lands.

And as if to add insult to injury, Breedlove's coachman had shot the earl in the arse. He still had some stiffness walking, never mind sitting.

He strained to recall the shooter's face. Dark hair, beard. He could be any of a hundred men of similar builds and features. But there was something about him that haunted Raventhorpe. Something almost familiar. What was his name? Something ridiculous.

John. That was it. John Ready.

Raventhorpe clenched his fingers around the railing. He only hoped that when all this was said and done, this John Ready was in his sights. He owed him for the bullet in his buttock.

And he always collected what was owed him.

Chapter 11

John Ready was proving the most maddening, elusive man ever created.

Genny took extra care with her appearance for the Statons' dinner party. She wore a sea-green silk that brought out her eyes. The bodice of the dress dipped low enough to reveal a tantalizing amount of bosom that might have been scandalous except for discreet white lace tucked into important places. She wore a cameo on a black ribbon around her neck, and small black bows adorned the top of her bodice and her sleeves. She had asked Lottie to fix her hair so that it looked as though the lush curls might come undone with one tug of the ribbon that held them in place, then completed her toilette with white gloves and her favorite honeysuckle scent. Tossing her cashmere shawl over her arm, she went to meet the others downstairs.

She knew she looked good. Everyone except Annabelle was present in the foyer, including John. He glanced up as she reached the bottom of the staircase, and his eyes widened ever so slightly, his gaze lingering on her bosom. She took a deep breath, enhancing the abundant curves nature had given her, and still he did not look away.

His fascination with her charms made her wonder what he would do if they were alone. Would he kiss her? Slip his hands beneath her skirts?

Heat streaked straight to her center at just the thought of it. She could feel her nipples hardening beneath the layers of cotton and silk. Could he see?

Even as the thought entered her mind, he looked up. His gaze held a hunger that all at once made her glad they were not alone and yet wish they were. Then he very deliberately looked away.

Very slowly, she let out the breath she had been holding. To help regain her composure, she unfurled the shawl from her arm and wrapped it around her, hiding the evidence of her own arousal. She did not want to answer any uncomfortable questions, especially from her parents. Luckily, everyone present seemed to be too much engaged with the debate of who should ride in which of the two carriages that would convey them to the dinner party to pay much attention to what she was doing.

"My Dolly has to go in the landau," Virgil was saying. "And I will go with her, so that leaves seats for three in that carriage and two in the brougham."

Ah, a perfect opportunity. Which carriage would hold John Ready? And how could she manage to get herself into that vehicle with him?

"I will be riding alongside whichever carriage holds Miss Bailey," John said.

She frowned. "Riding?"

"Of course." His tone remained undeniably respectful, but she could see the gleam of victory in his eyes. "My function this evening is as a guard for Miss Bailey. Should the attacker make another attempt, I will be able to move more swiftly to pursue him on horseback."

"A sound plan," the admiral said with a nod.

"Besides, I am not a guest at the dinner party. I feel I will be of more use if I have freedom of movement rather than tied to the etiquette of a dinner table."

"But you were invited," Dolly said.

"Mr. Bailey conveyed my regrets," John said. "Your daughter will be safe enough in the dining room of an elegant house with all of you around her. The danger lies more during the time of transportation, when we are all more vulnerable."

"Don't fret, sugarplum," Virgil said, patting his wife's shoulder. "John knows what he's doing. He's going to keep our little girl safe."

"I do trust John," Dolly said, laying her hand over her husband's. She took a deep breath, shot John a smile that tried to be reassuring but did not quite succeed, then looked around at the group. "Where is Annabelle anyway?"

"Probably still fussing over which dress to wear," Virgil grumbled. "I love our daughter, Dolly, but that gal sure can't tell time worth a nickel."

"She just wants to look her best," Dolly said.

"I'm sending a maid up there to get her if she's not here in five minutes," Virgil said. "We're going to be late to the dinner party, and that won't set well with old Staton."

"Perhaps the admiral and Mrs. Wallington-Willis should leave now in the brougham," John suggested. "Since it only seats two, Miss Wallington-Willis can ride with the Baileys in the landau."

"Good idea," the admiral said.

"Oh, but then they will know we were the ones who were late, and I don't want them to think badly of us," Dolly said. "Especially Mr. Staton."

"Robert and I will tell the Statons that your injury is the reason for the delay," Helen said with a smile.

"Staton will not dare impugn any of your party if he thinks your tardiness is due to your injury, Mrs. Bailey," the admiral said. "I will see to it."

"Oh, thank you, Admiral." Dolly beamed.

"Come, Helen. We should leave immediately if we are to get there at the appointed hour," the admiral said, offering his arm.

"Of course, you are right." Helen took her husband's arm, then glanced at her daughter as the admiral led her toward the door. "We will see you there, Genny dear."

Genny nodded, then smiled at John as her parents left. Through no machinations of her own, she had ended up in the carriage with Annabelle, and where there was Annabelle, there was John Ready. She saw the consternation flash across his face as he realized the same thing.

They were going to the dinner party together, and there was nothing he could do about it.

"I'm ready!" Annabelle's voice came from somewhere above them.

Virgil looked at his watch, then scowled up at her as she rounded the first-floor landing and started down the stairs. "'Bout time. I was just getting ready to send someone up there to get you." He turned to John. "Looks like we're finally ready. Let's get this circus on the road."

"Oh, good," Dolly said, as Virgil turned her chair toward the front door. "Perhaps we will not be too late after all."

Annabelle reached the bottom of the stairs and hurried over to them. "I'm here! We can go now."

John gave Annabelle a stern look. "You remember our talk."

"Yes, yes." She rolled her eyes and shrugged her

blue, ermine-trimmed mantelet closer. "Do not leave the house, even for a walk in the gardens. Do not go anywhere without a member of my family or Genny's—"

"Come along, girls!" Dolly called, as Virgil wheeled her out the door.

"Your mother is concerned with not arriving on time," John said.

"She's always worried about something. Come on, Genny." Annabelle started forward. Genny followed behind her, with John pulling up the rear. Annabelle stepped outside, where the footmen were busy loading Dolly and her wheeled chair into the landau.

Genny paused in the doorway and let one side of her cape slip off. "Oh, no!"

John had stopped short behind her. She glanced over her shoulder at him. His gaze was on her bosom, as she had hoped. She took a deep breath and let it out again, giving him a much better view—since he was behind her—than he had had before. John raised his eyes to hers. A sharp pang squeezed her loins as she saw her own longings reflected in those dark eyes.

She had a sudden image of him pushing her against the doorframe, lifting her skirts, and taking her right there in the doorway.

He must have had the same vision. Grim-faced, he retrieved the trailing end of her shawl and pressed it into her palm. "It is cool this evening. Cover up."

His tone brooked no disobedience. Confident that she had stirred him up enough, at least for now, Genny wrapped her shawl around her, hiding her bosom from view. She heard his long exhale, then he touched her arm, indicating she should walk.

The entire incident had taken two, maybe three minutes, but she knew the heat from those minutes would linger well into the night.

He walked an odd path, John mused as he sat in the servants' hall with the visiting coachmen, footmen, and maids of the Statons' dinner guests. They dined on a meal cobbled together from the scraps of the more elaborate feast being served in the main dining room. He had introduced himself belowstairs as Annabelle's bodyguard.

He knew Annabelle would be fine sitting upstairs surrounded by some of the local elite, and a quiet word with both the admiral and Mr. Bailey made John feel confident that neither gentleman would allow her to wander off on her own or with anyone who was not of their party. Which meant John was free to search out information from the fastest, most accurate source in England—the servants' network.

The upper class tended to ignore their staff, treating them like furniture rather than living creatures who had eyes and ears. Many servants were privy to the secrets of their employers—more so than those employers would find comfortable—and John often used that to his advantage when seeking out information about Raventhorpe.

The table was full, and though he wore his oldest coat, John still appeared a bit higher in the social structure than the other diners since he was not a domestic. To combat the natural suspicion, he smiled a lot, stayed quiet, and acted neither rude nor superior to anyone around him. He simply applied himself with gusto to the soup he was given. After a few minutes of wary looks, the others eventually forgot about him and began talking to one another as they normally would.

" . . . he's buying her jewels, but his wife has no idea she's his mistress . . ."

" . . . and the baby cried all night, but still Mrs. Oreton would not let me feed her . . ."

" . . . he was completely sotted. Owes the baron fifty quid now after he couldn't balance the bottle on his head like he said he could . . ."

" . . . the grays he bought last spring were supposed to be Arabian stock, but he just found out the papers were forged . . ."

" . . . and the magistrate says he's going to set a trap for Black Bill for trying to snatch the Bailey girl. Vows to see the bloke hang for it . . ."

This snippet of conversation caught his attention. The

speaker looked to be a coachman, given his clothing.

"That doesn't sound like Black Bill," said the liveried footman to whom the coachman spoke.

"Are you mates with the highwayman, John Footman?" mocked the coachman. "How would you know what he will and will not do?"

"He's been riding these lands for years now, and while he's quick to nip your purse, he's never tried to snatch a lady before."

"Maybe his reputation is so well-known now that people don't travel these roads as much, so the pickings aren't what they used to be."

"I just think Gunston is wrong. You know how he is—lazy old windbag! He couldn't catch a thief if we tied him up and delivered him to the front door!"

John nearly grinned at the way the footman's summation of the magistrate echoed his own. He kept an ear cocked toward the two men as he reached for a piece of day-old bread. But then another conversation snagged his interest.

" . . . I surely hope that one doesn't become the new Duke of Evermayne. My sister says he's already giving orders and talking of redecorating like Evermayne is already his . . ."

Evermayne.

He glanced around the table, searching for the owner of the female voice. There she was, to his left, a young girl dressed in what must be her mistress's castoffs. A lady's maid, perhaps. Another girl, somewhat older but not as well dressed, scooped soup into her mouth as she listened to the other's conversation.

"Brigands like Black Bill make traveling by coach dangerous for all of us. Good riddance if Gunston captures him," the coachman said from one end of the table.

"Lady Felicity and Lady Marianne have taken Mr. St. Giles in complete dislike," the little maid said from John's side.

"He's never stopped any of us," the footman said. "He only goes for the nobs."

"I even heard a rumor that he's arranged marriages for them," the maid whispered, revulsion heavy in her voice.

"We work for the nobs!" the coachman cried, throwing up a hand to emphasize his point. "If they don't travel anywhere, I lose my place."

"Marriages!" The other maid stared at the lady's maid in horror. "Heavens, Ellie, they're too young, aren't they?"

The lady's maid called Ellie nodded. "Only twelve and seven. But I heard he is trying to get the most money he can in the marriage settlements. And, Katie, one of them is old Crowley!"

Crowley?

John's gut curdled. With all he had learned about his

own family in the past twenty-four hours, he had not considered how this situation would affect the Duke's daughters. His cousins. They *were* young, newly orphaned, and he had only ever considered how the situation concerned him. Who was caring for these little girls? What was Randall thinking to be talking of betrothals when these innocent children were not even out of the schoolroom, when they were grieving for their father? And marriage to old Crowley? Just the thought made his blood boil.

Even as a young man living in London, he had heard of Crowley. The old bastard had a penchant for young girls, and John had heard stories of how Crowley had patronized certain brothels that specialized in children. How he had purchased the children of poor families to sate his perverted lusts.

The old debaucher had even been engaged once. John vaguely remembered Crowley's betrothed, a timid creature of barely fifteen years old, and how she had been found dead below the balcony of her bedchamber at her parents' country estate. An accident, some had ruled it. Suicide, others had said, to avoid marriage to Crowley.

"Didn't he kill his first wife?" the maid Katie asked, echoing John's thoughts.

"She wasn't even married to him yet." Ellie lowered her voice. "They say she killed herself to keep from marrying him."

"Poor thing," Katie whispered. "Which one of His Grace's daughters is going to Crowley?"

"Lady Marianne, the younger one. And there's talk that she might go live at Crowley's estate *now,* with his aunt as chaperone."

Katie dropped her spoon. "Isn't Crowley's aunt a bit cracked in the noggin?"

Ellie nodded, her face the picture of misery. "The old bat is so mad, she wouldn't notice any wicked goings-on. That little girl is going to be living a nightmare, and there's nothing anyone can do about it."

There's nothing anyone can do about it.

The food turned to ash in his mouth, and he took a gulp of the water by his plate, wishing for something stronger.

Twelve and seven, Timmons had said. Two little girls whose father had just died, whose mothers—they had each had different ones—had died before their father, leaving them orphans now. Their fates would be at the whim of their new guardian, and from the sound of things, Uncle had left their guardianship to whomever inherited the title.

Which, as things stood right now, would be Randall.

Could John, in good conscience, leave two innocent children to such a fate?

There's nothing anyone can do about it.

There was something *he* could do about it.

He stood up from the table, ignoring the stares as his chair scraped against the floor, and headed for the exit, silence following him.

Seven years ago, he had allowed his uncle to talk him into running from a false accusation. He had been young and impressionable and completely cowed by his uncle's power. But now that power was his, should he choose to claim it. Had Randall been inclined to treat the title with some respect rather than as his personal gold mine, John would have been content to let his cousin declare him dead and to disappear quietly in America.

But now, knowing how Randall planned to abuse his position and put at risk the well-being of a couple of orphaned girls. . .

He could not allow that to happen.

He knew as soon as he came forward and announced his true identity, the speculation would begin again. The investigation would begin again. But the authorities would move more cautiously before accusing a duke of murder—much more so than if he had still been plain Mr. John St. Giles—which would allow him enough time to scuttle any betrothals that might have been made and assign a proper guardian to look after his young cousins.

It would also allow him enough time to review his father's notes and perhaps find a way to prove his innocence.

In the end, though, it was about protecting the innocent. He had always taken his place in the family seriously, and while he had never expected to inherit—at least not so soon—he would not shirk his responsibilities. Not when his family needed him.

He *was* Evermayne. And soon, everyone would know it.

Chapter 12

Genny was pleased that they took the same carriages in which they had arrived. It meant that John would be their outrider, that he would be nearby.

She was *not* pleased that he had somehow avoided her the entire evening.

She pondered the situation as the landau pulled out of the Statons' drive and turned toward Nevarton Chase. Annabelle chattered about fashion and social connections with her mother—frequently using words like "free" and "unhindered" and "unfettered"—until Dolly finally snapped, "I understand, Annabelle. You don't like being stuck at the estate. But we have no choice, and that is *the end* of it! Do you understand?"

"Yes, Mama." Annabelle's stunned expression gave Genny the impression that Dolly hardly ever spoke harshly to her daughter. Annabelle's ensuing silence spoke louder than any words about her feelings on the matter.

The silence in the coach was broken only by the rasp of the wheels on the road and the occasional soft snore from Virgil, who had drifted off to sleep.

And the comforting sound of horses' hooves outside the window.

John was out there, riding his gelding Veritas, watching over them. She admired his diligence. With John Ready riding guard, no brigand would dare attack them.

While she did wish he was inside the coach with them—the better to continue her flirtation—she would not let the separate modes of transportation stop her. Twice, she had managed to catch his eye and send him a smile, and twice he had urged his mount to a faster pace.

A thump reached their ears, coming from the back of the carriage.

"What!" Virgil jerked awake. "What was that?"

Scrabbling came from above them, then a much bigger whack followed by a human cry of alarm.

The coach shot down the road for a few more minutes, then jolted to a halt.

Genny peered out the window. The moonlit night looked peaceful enough.

"Why have we stopped?" Virgil asked.

"I don't like this," Dolly whispered.

Annabelle reached across and squeezed her mother's hand. "Don't fret, Mama. John is right outside."

They sat for long moments in total silence.

"Everyone, please get out of the carriage," John called from outside.

"I can't get out," Dolly protested. "My leg!"

There was a pause, followed by the low murmur of voices. Then John opened the door to the carriage. "Everyone except Mrs. Bailey, please step out."

"What is this nonsense?" Virgil demanded. "Did we break a wheel?"

"Something like that. Miss Wallington-Willis, please take my hand."

Genny took John's hand, hearing the strain in his tone. Something was very wrong. He helped her down from the carriage, and once she moved away from the vehicle, she saw the problem.

"Do not look so dismayed, Miss Wallington-Willis" said the masked man seated on top of the collapsible roof of their landau. Moonlight gleamed off two pistols in his hand. "I just want to talk."

"Who was that?" Annabelle asked as John helped her down. She looked around and gasped as she saw the outlaw.

"It is only I," said the brigand. "Good evening, Miss Bailey. You do look stunning this evening."

"Black Bill," she murmured, as her father disembarked.

"Black Bill? Where?" Virgil looked around, then spotted the highwayman.

"Right here," the thief said in his ever-cheerful tone. "I am so flattered you remember me, Miss Bailey."

"How could I not?" she said. "You saved me from being forced into marriage with Richard. You saved my life."

"Well, he shot *me*, in case no one else recalls." John folded his arms, his entire body stiff with what Genny knew had to be fury. How could he remain so calm? Her own hands were shaking, and she twisted them into her shawl, edging closer to John. She refused to show fear to this villain.

"Now, do not be so cross, Mr. Ready. Or shall I call you John? After all, once blood has been shed between men, formality seems rather silly, do you not agree? Besides, you lent me this wonderful pistol." The thief held it up to the moonlight, turning it this way and that.

"How did he steal your pistol?" Genny whispered.

John gave her a tight look of frustration, then called out, "I could shed some of your blood, Billy Boy. Return the favor."

Black Bill laughed, and Dolly cried, "What's happening out there? Are we being robbed?"

"My mother is frightened," Annabelle said, her words ringing with rebuke.

"I apologize," the bandit said, raising his voice. Was that sincerity in his tone? "I am not here to threaten you,

Mrs. Bailey, but to have a discussion with my friend John."

"About what?" Virgil demanded. "About how you tried to kidnap my daughter for that no-good Raventhorpe?"

"Pa, no," Annabelle said, taking her father's arm.

Black Bill aimed the pistol at Virgil with a grace both practiced and deadly. "Do not ever associate me with that piece of filth."

Virgil shook off Annabelle's hand. "Stand aside, Annabelle. This varmint isn't getting you without a fight."

"He doesn't want me," Annabelle said, moving between her father and Black Bill's gun.

John tensed, and Genny curled her fingers around his arm. "What is she doing?" she whispered so only John could hear. "She is going to get killed!"

John silently patted her fingers, as if trying to reassure her. He did not take his gaze from the bandit at any time.

Annabelle stared her father down. "I told you, it wasn't him."

"Don't let him take our baby, Virgil!" Dolly cried from inside the carriage.

Annabelle turned back to the highwayman and crossed her arms. "And you, Mr. Black Bill. You claim you want to talk, yet you have held up our carriage, scared my mother half to death—"

"Got rid of the coachman and the footman," John said. "Jumped on the roof from a tree, punched the footman so he fell off the back, then knocked the coachman on the head and shoved him off the seat."

"And where were you, John Ready?" Virgil demanded. "You're supposed to be protecting my daughter!"

"I was trying to get a bead on him, but he moves like a snake," John protested.

Black Bill laughed. "Snake, is it? Not complimentary, are you, John?"

John ignored him. "Then he got on top of the landau and threatened to shoot through that soft top if I did not hand over my pistol. What was I supposed to do?"

"Shoot the son of a bitch!"

"Virgil!" Dolly cried from the carriage. "Your language!"

"Would you have him shoot into the landau and hit one of the ladies?" John demanded.

"Stop it, the both of you!" Annabelle commanded, surprising both men into silence. She glared up at the bandit. "Say what you need to say. It's far too chilly tonight to stay outside too long."

The highwayman smiled, his teeth gleaming in the moonlight. "Well then, since I have no desire to keep the ladies out in the cold, here is what I came to tell you. I did not try and abduct the lovely Miss Bailey."

"So you claim," John said.

"So I claim," the bandit repeated. "I did not do it, but I know who did."

John narrowed his eyes at the highwayman. "Who?" he challenged.

"His name is Peter Green. Raventhorpe uses him for this type of thing when the pig earl is unavailable to do it himself."

"Why should we trust you?" Virgil demanded. "What's to stop you from robbing us blind and leaving us for dead?"

"Why, nothing," Black Bill replied. "Except my honor."

"Hardly a comfort," John said. "Prove your words. Tell me where I can find this Peter Green."

"He rents a room in a boardinghouse near Nevarton, owned by a widow, Mrs. Tansey."

"I went to Nevarton. Based on Miss Bailey's description, no one had seen him or knew who he was."

"He is a bit of a bully, that one. Not the sharpest sword in the armory," the thief said. "Tends to incapacitate the people who talk about him. Quite a deterrent, don't you agree?"

"Wonderful," John muttered, frowning. Sharpest sword in the armory? Where had he heard that before?

"Do not fear, dear friend John," the highwayman said. "I will find him and point you in the proper direction."

"Why are you helping us?" Virgil demanded.

"To clear my name, of course," the thief replied. "I do hate when other people claim to be me, especially amidst such distasteful business. I have standards, you know. What I do is very specific."

"You only rob those on Raventhorpe lands," John said. "I remember you saying that the first time our paths crossed. Right before you shot me."

"Very good, Mr. Ready! Yes, I do try to make that swine's life as difficult as possible. I have a bone to pick with him if he ever returns from his self-imposed exile in France."

"The earl had no choice but to leave England," Genny said. "The gossip about what he did to Annabelle was quite damaging."

"Lovely to hear," the highwayman said.

"Besides," Annabelle said, "John shot Raventhorpe in his ar—"

"Annabelle Bailey!" Dolly called. "Watch your language!"

"—seat," Annabelle finished.

"I had heard that," Black Bill said. "Excellent shooting, John old man. Perhaps we are in alliance after all!"

John regarded the thief for a long moment. "You did not kill our footman."

"That would be correct," Bill said.

"And you did not kill our coachman."

"Right again."

"And you did not shoot me, though you had the opportunity from that branch where you were perched. I saw you jump."

"Is this a test?" Bill asked with a laugh. "I know what I did and did not do, friend John."

"I am just pointing out what the others might not have noticed. You have not killed anyone to have this conversation."

"I am feeling compassionate this evening," Bill said with a shrug.

"You honestly do want to help us."

"I would not say *that*. I simply do not like others infringing upon my territory."

"You know a lot about what is going on in this area," John said.

"Of course I do."

"Perhaps I could pay you to gather information for us."

"Do I look like I work for Scotland Yard? Do not be preposterous. I make my living by relieving others of their wealth."

"You said you wanted to talk," Annabelle challenged. "Are you a liar as well as a thief?"

The highwayman stiffened. "I am no liar. I have every intention of robbing you this evening." He stood and tucked one revolver away, then leaped lightly to the driver's seat and from there, vaulted down to the ground, never losing his grip on the second weapon.

The horses shuffled in their traces, but otherwise appeared little disturbed by the stunts as Black Bill approached the group. "Come here, Miss Bailey."

Annabelle took a step toward him, but her father grabbed her arm. "Annabelle, are you crazy? Stay away from him!"

"You come to me, Miss Bailey, or else I will have to shoot someone to prove my point. Your father, perhaps? A bullet in the thigh or the knee might have him in a wheeled chair beside your mother."

No," Annabelle whispered. "Don't."

"Or perhaps the stalwart John Ready?" He swung the weapon toward John.

"Once was enough," John said.

"That leaves Miss Wallington-Willis, though I should hate to mar such natural beauty." He shifted the pistol again.

Genny stared at the gleaming barrel of the revolver, her stomach churning. She swallowed past the hard lump in her throat. Was this how her life would end, snuffed out by a brigand in the middle of the road?

Then suddenly John stepped in front of her, shoving her behind him with one arm. He said nothing, just stared in challenge at the highwayman.

"How chivalrous, friend John!" Black Bill grinned. "But the choice is Miss Bailey's, not yours."

"I don't want you to shoot anyone. Rob me if you

must," Annabelle said, "but not the others. I beg you."

Virgil stepped forward. "Now hold on there . . ."

"Pa, stay back," Annabelle said, then slowly approached the highwayman.

"Annabelle, no," John said.

"You come back here, Annabelle May!" her father commanded. He started forward, but the sudden shift of Black Bill's aim from John to him stopped him cold. "Don't you hurt my girl, you bastard!"

From inside the coach, they could hear Dolly sobbing.

Genny trailed her hand down the barrier of John's arm until she found his hand. Slowly she twined her fingers with his. After a moment, he squeezed hers, as if reassuring her.

Annabelle came to a stop just beyond arm's reach of the bandit. "I'm here. Go ahead. Rob me."

"Do you think I will not?" He gave her a half smile, never breaking eye contact with her. "Open your purse."

Annabelle slid her beaded reticule off her wrist, then opened it so he could see inside. He shook his head. "Not exactly what I am looking for. Unfasten your cape."

"Stop right there, you—"

Black Bill turned and fired, knocking Virgil's hat right off his head. "Stop right there, Mr. Bailey."

"Virgil!" Dolly screamed.

"I'm all right, sugarplum!" Keeping his gaze on Black Bill, Virgil slowly bent down and picked up his hat. "Don't you hurt her, you son of a bitch, or I'll hunt you down and feed your innards to the dogs!"

The highwayman grinned, then turned back to Annabelle.

CRACK! She smacked him hard across the face. "Don't you ever shoot at my pa again, you animal!"

"Animal?" Something feral swept across his face. "If I were an animal, every one of you would be dead. Except, perhaps, for you, my sweet." He aimed the pistol at her with one hand and used his other to shove open her ermine-trimmed mantelet. The pale skin of her bosom gleamed in the moonlight.

"If you want my wrap, take it," she said, her tone icy. "I understand the fur is valuable."

He laughed. "That is not what I want." He touched her cheek with one gloved hand, then trailed his finger down to rest at the base of her throat. "Are you frightened? Because this says you are." He traced the pulse point with one finger.

"Of course I am frightened," she snapped. "I am not a ninny."

"You are not, are you?" He drew his finger down lower, edging towards the exposed tops of her breasts. "What do you have of value that a man might want to steal?"

She did not flinch. "You tell me."

"Very well." Quick as a blink, he dipped his fingers

between her breasts and pulled free a handkerchief. He lifted it to his nose and sniffed. "Mmm. Attar of roses. This will do nicely. Since when does a lady keep her handkerchief in such a spot?"

"I always have," she replied stiffly. "Is that all you want? No diamonds or pearls?"

"No, this is quite enough." He tucked the handkerchief away in his pocket. "And now that I have robbed you, I will leave you to your evening. Here." He took John's pistol and slapped it into Annabelle's hand. "Be careful not to shoot yourself."

"Maybe I'll just shoot you instead."

He turned before the words left her lips and sprinted. His black clothing made him instantly disappear into the darkness of the trees at the side of the road. She lifted the revolver and fired anyway.

Only his laughter carried back to them.

Genny sagged against John, closing her eyes as she realized the danger was over for the moment. He turned and wrapped her in a brief embrace. Then he pushed her away.

"We have to get out of here," John said, stepping back a pace.

Genny immediately missed the warmth of his body near hers. "I agree. Thank you for protecting me."

He held her gaze. "I would never have let him harm you. Let's get you back in the carriage."

He crooked his arm, and she had no choice but to properly rest her hand there, a poor substitute for the more intimate embrace they had just shared. As they reached the carriage, the shouting between Virgil and Annabelle grew louder.

"Are you out of your mind, letting him touch you like that?"

"What was I supposed to do about it, Pa? Attack him?"

"Maybe you should've!"

"Don't you care that I was almost killed? That we all were?"

And then Dolly's voice sounded above the strident ruckus of her family.

"Someone had best get in this carriage and tell me what happened, right quick, before I shoot the lot of you myself!"

Chapter 13

When they got back to the house, the admiral closeted himself in the study with Mr. Bailey and John, leaving Genny to the maternal fretting of both her mother and her maid, Lottie. By the time the two women finally left her to her rest, she was bathed, dried and tucked between the covers as if she were still in the schoolroom.

She lay in the dark, listening to the sounds of the others moving about the house. Footsteps in the hallways, low voices, the tapping of servants' feet as they scurried about their duties. As the hours crept by, the noises dwindled until she could hear herself breathing in the silence.

She should be asleep. Tonight's adventure should have worn her out completely. But she could not sleep. Did not want to.

She might have died tonight. The moment Black Bill had pointed that pistol at her, she thought she might expire from the fear alone. And yet in that moment, every small thing around her had seemed huge and precious and meaningful.

The warmth of John's hand in hers. The leathery, male scent of him. The cool breeze gently fluttering the curls at her temples. The rush of her own blood, the way he had instinctively pushed her behind him when Black Bill had turned the revolver her way. The heat of John's embrace as he had cradled her for one, blissful moment. It all spoke volumes. For in those few seconds, she knew the truth—she was falling in love with him.

Why had she spent all these months worrying about the betrayal of one foolish man? Clearly Bradley was of no importance, and neither were his words, his actions, nor his attempt to reconcile. There was so much more to life, so much more she wanted. The sheer scope of it awed her, making her relationship with Bradley seem very, very insignificant.

A smile curved her lips. The idea that she might give herself to a man again no longer seemed so impossible, not if it was John. When she wondered who her future husband might be, it was his face that lingered in her mind. When she imagined her future children, they were his.

She was not so naïve to think he loved her. She knew he wanted her, and that one kiss they shared had nearly singed her clothing right off. But the fact that he stopped also showed her that, though he was attracted, he respected her, too. And tonight, his instinctive impulse to protect her made her feel warm and secure and as if she truly mattered.

Wasn't that the first step to love?

She knew he had secrets, but how terrible could they be? Whatever it was, she could forgive him. Whatever darkness lurked in his past, she would stand by his side. And perhaps if she shared her secret with him, then he might be willing to confide in her about his. After all, she trusted John in a way she had never trusted Bradley. She knew that he would never betray her, that he would lay down his life to protect her. That was the sort of man he was.

She knew what she needed to do. She would bare her soul to John, show him that she trusted him with her deepest secrets. Then he would certainly forgive her, confide in her, and together they would heal.

And maybe they would find something wonderful with each other that would last a lifetime.

John entered his room with a bruised ego and a foul temper. First Black Bill had made him look like a fool, then Virgil Bailey had ripped him soundly about his failure to protect Annabelle. But no matter how virulent the words hurled at him by Annabelle's father, they burned far less than the ones he inflicted on himself.

He had failed tonight. Roundly. Too many times he

had allowed himself to be distracted by Genny's flirtations from the coach window. Had he been paying less attention to her and more to his duties, Black Bill might not have caught them by surprise.

Someone had left a lamp burning on the bureau. He was grateful for the soft glow as he stripped off his coat and tie and tossed them on the bed, then jerked the edges of his shirt from his trousers. Rubbing his hands across his face, he went to the bureau and poured a bit of water from the pitcher into the basin, then splashed his face.

A soft squeak broke the silence, and for a moment he thought it was Precious. Then he remembered he had returned the tiny kitten to the barn this morning. Another sound—the swish of material, then another—the quiet click of the door being shut, alerted him he was not alone.

Blinking against the water dripping from his lashes, he reached for the towel. The cloth was pushed into his hand by one smaller and softer than his own. He scrubbed it across his face, then opened his eyes.

Genny.

"I need to talk to you," she whispered.

"It could not wait until morning?" Dear God, she was dressed for bed. A voluminous nightgown of plain white cotton, her hair in a long braid down her back. She looked like a novice at a nunnery.

He felt like a ravaging beast.

"No, it cannot." She took the towel from his hands. The scent of honeysuckle rising from her skin intoxicated him.

"What are you doing in here?" He yanked the towel from her and threw it atop the bureau. "You know what would happen if someone discovered you here—to both of us. Go back to bed."

"Do not talk to me like I am a child."

"Then stop acting like one." He wanted to shake her, to make her understand. But he knew if he touched her, they would both end up in the bed and there would be no turning back. "You cannot come into a man's room, especially in such deshabille, and . . . and . . ."

"And what?"

"You just cannot. Now please leave."

"Not until I have said what I came here to say." She walked away from him, going over to the bed and running her hand along the coverlet.

His mouth grew dry. "We can talk tomorrow."

"When, John? At breakfast??"

"Yes, yes. At breakfast." He could not tear his gaze away from her hand, innocently stroking the bedclothes.

"We cannot talk about this at breakfast, John. Or anywhere else that is not private." She perched on the edge of the bed, biting her lower lip. "I realize my visit tonight is somewhat improper—"

He tensed, stimulated by the sight of her on his bed, where he had imagined her more times than he could count. "Improper? I can think of a better word. More than one. Insane. Reckless. Utterly mad."

"Oh, John." She laughed.

"You find this amusing? To come into a man's room in your nightdress and flirt with him? I don't think it is very funny."

"I apologize," she said. "I did not expect to embarrass you."

"I am not embarrassed." He clamped his lips shut. Why was he encouraging her?

Because he wanted to stretch her out on the bed, shove that nightdress up to her waist, and take her hard and fast, just like he had imagined.

"You cannot possibly know what you are doing to me," he said. "I know a lady like you is unaware of such things, so I am going to send you back to your own room now, and we can forget this ever happened."

"Perhaps," she said with a little smile, "I am not as unaware as you think."

Lust surged through him, glorious, painful. "What the devil does that mean?"

Her smile faltered. "I do not want you to be cross with me, John. I have something important to tell you. And a proposition."

A proposition? Immediately his male mind jumped

to a hundred impossible propositions he would love to hear from her lips. But she was a lady, the daughter of an admiral. An unmarried, innocent—

"I want to go to America with you."

The breath he had been holding whooshed from his lungs. Not exactly the proposal he had imagined. "Why in God's name would you want to do that?"

"To be with you." She stood, her prim white night-dress ineffectual to hide the high, firm roundness of her breasts, the curve of her hips. "We were almost killed tonight, and I do not want to let another moment pass without telling you how I feel."

"Don't." The word exploded before he realized how harsh it sounded. But the startled hurt on her face told him, and he felt like a cad.

Again.

He took a breath, tried to remember to keep doing that, keep breathing. Get through this torment.

God help him, he had to get her out of here. Because if she said another word . . . if she said what he thought she was going to say. . .

"Why are you upset with me?" Genny asked. "You keep talking about going to America, starting over. I know that you want me . . . and maybe you have some feelings for me as well? I thought we could go together."

A day ago, he might have actually considered her sweet offer. He did want a wife, and he did want a family. But now, he was about to commit the worst sort of social suicide, and if things went badly, he would end up with a noose around his neck. He would not subject her to that.

Because, God help him, he loved her.

The realization stunned him. When had that happened?

"John?" She was waiting for his answer. His little warrior. His heart did a slow turn in his chest. She would stay by his side, battle tooth and nail to uncover the truth, no matter what it cost her.

He could not let her do that. She deserved more than a man with shadows and blood in his past.

"You *do* still want me?" The insecurity in her voice threatened his tenuous control. He wanted to take her in his arms and reassure her that everything was going to be all right.

Which was why he had to get her out of there *immediately,* before he did something stupid.

"Want you? I doubt you even know what that means."

She lifted her chin. "Yes, I do."

He started toward her, certain it was a mistake with every step, but unable to stop himself. "When a man wants a woman, he doesn't want tea parties and witty banter and someone to read poetry with."

She tensed, but held her ground. "I know."

"When a man wants a woman, he wants someone to

get naked with him. Get sweaty. Do *improper* things."
He stopped just short of touching distance. "Things
most ladies don't like. There's a difference between a
lady and a woman, Genny, and I need a woman. Not a
lady."

She threw her shoulders back, thrusting her breasts
at him . . . deliberately? "I know."

"You *don't* know, that's what I am telling you." He
waved a hand toward the door. "If you did, you would
be as far away from here, from me, as you could be."

"Maybe it is you who does not know." She did the
unthinkable, the unimaginable, and took that last step
closer to him. Her scent taunted him, made him clench
his hands against the impulse to grab her. "I have been
trying to tell you something important, John. I trust you.
Trust you enough to tell you this because I think we
have a real chance. I know you will protect me and
. . . well, I am longer a . . . no longer innocent. There,
I said it."

No longer innocent.

Roaring sounded in his ears. She had just thrown
a juicy steak at the snarling beast of his libido and at
the same time handed him the perfect ammunition to
send her away. But dear God, he did not want to use it.
No, what he wanted was to take her to bed and sate the
beast once and for all. "Who was it?" he demanded. "I'll
wring his neck."

"You know who," she snapped, spinning away and stalking across the room to the bureau. She looked at herself in the mirror, tucked a dangling strand behind her ear.

He could see his reflection behind hers, his expression stunned. Angry. Hungry. "Blasted Bradley Overton? I'll see him keelhauled!"

"No, you will not." Mutiny lurked in her eyes as she looked at him through the mirror.

"How in God's name is it that your father did not drag the two of you to the nearest church?"

"Because I did not tell him. I have told no one but you." As she turned to face him, the candlelight shone through her nightdress, innocently presenting him with a silhouette of every delectable curve. He gritted his teeth, then nearly bit his tongue in half as she folded her arms against those succulent breasts. "Once I found out Bradley's real reasons for marrying me," she continued, "I wouldn't have it *or* him."

He blew out a long breath. "What were you thinking?"

"That he loved me. That I was going to marry him. That such . . . intimacy . . . was what he wanted." Her lips twisted in a cynicism that seemed far too harsh for her tender years. "I was a fool." She started pacing, proving there was a God as she finally moved away from the candle. "Now I find myself the daughter of an admiral—"

"The *unmarried* daughter of an admiral."

She scowled. "Do not help me. The *unmarried* daughter of an admiral, who must make a good match or disgrace her family yet who cannot offer chastity to her gentleman husband."

"You do have a problem."

She stopped pacing, but kept her arms folded. "I think you and I are a good match for each other. You know my secret now. You are the only man to whom I could ever imagine confiding such a thing because I know you will not despise me or think me a whore. I could be the woman you need. I could be your wife, John."

"Impossible. You cannot leave England. Your family is here. Your friends."

"You left England. If you can do it, so can I."

"This is not about me. I had no choice. You do."

"And you are my choice," she said. "I know you will not judge me. I think you and I would do well together. I think we could have something special."

"You do not know what you are suggesting. It is difficult to leave everything you know and travel to a foreign place to make your home."

"I am willing to do whatever is necessary to achieve a better future. So tell me, John, will you marry me?" She toyed with the end of the braid hanging over her shoulder.

He watched her play with her hair, looking so innocent and yet so alluring. For one moment, he was tempted to take her up on her offer. She had enough grit to make a man a good wife, and he could imagine some hot, lusty nights with her between the sheets.

But no. He was about to step into a hornet's nest, and he would not drag anyone down with him. He cared too much for her to put her in danger—cared enough that the mere thought made his blood run cold. He had to do this to rescue his nieces from Randall's greed, but he was only willing to sacrifice himself. She could not be any part of this.

But she was right, she had a problem. He just did not think he was the solution.

"John?" she prompted, when he did not answer.

"You should not have come here," he said.

"But I am here." She came right up to him, her face set in determination. "I want you. I want *this* heart"— she flattened her palm against his chest—"and *your* arms around me." She leaned against him, her curves molding to his body as if she were made to fit there.

"Genny . . ."

She stood on tiptoe and kissed him.

All reason flew out of his head. He closed his hands around her upper arms. Push her away. Think. But that sweet mouth . . . that lush, female body . . . He dragged her closer, stumbling backwards. Landed on the bed.

With a cry of alarm, she fell with him, their kiss torn

apart as they landed in a tangle of limbs on the bed, with her sprawled atop him. She squirmed, trying to find purchase. He tried to help. Her nightgown rode up, and his palm landed on the silken skin of her bottom.

They both froze for a long moment. Then she raised her head. The look in her eyes spoke of dawning discovery and desire.

He could not stop himself; he smoothed his palm across the sweet curve beneath his hand, watching her eyes, ready to stop. She hissed in a quick breath, her eyelids drooping halfway in a look of pure sensual enjoyment.

God damn it. He took her mouth in a long, hot kiss.

She tried to kiss him back, her inexperience stoking all kinds of fires she could not know existed. He squeezed her buttock, then splayed his hand across her whole bottom and pressed her against him. She made a little sound of surprise, then rubbed herself against his erection in one slow, tentative movement.

Dear God, he was only human.

The thought burned through his mind as he rolled over, gathering her beneath him. Every inch of her pressed against every inch of him. Delicious torment. He could slide into her right now. Have her.

"Touch me," she begged.

He wrapped her braid around his hand and bent her head back so he could probe her mouth, touching his tongue to hers. Teaching her. She responded—a prize pupil. He slipped his hand beneath her nightgown, found the hot feminine folds. Stroked her. Once. Twice.

She cried out beneath his mouth, arching her hips into his touch. "John."

Her voice moaning his name shattered his tenuous control. He shoved her nightdress to her waist, stroked his hands over her flesh. Belly, thighs. Soft. Female. His.

The scent of her arousal clouded his mind to everything but mating. He jerked her nightdress higher, but it caught beneath her. At the same time, she gripped his shirt with both hands, tugged.

"Off," she gasped, then stole his breath with a wet, openmouthed kiss.

They tangled, hands and arms and clothing. He jerked off his shirt, tossed it aside. She helped him strip the nightdress away, threw it somewhere toward the head of the bed, then stretched out beneath him in a sensual display of the female form.

What she lacked in height, she made up for in curves. Her breasts were larger than most women's, a bit more than a handful for him. Her waist dipped inward, flaring out to generous hips. Those smooth, round thighs cradled a dark thatch of hair that guarded the delicate folds he had caressed only moments before.

His, damn it. All his.

He stretched out over her, pressing her into the mattress, her plump breasts crushed beneath his chest, her hands stroking over his back in silent encouragement. She whispered his name, over and over again. Like a prayer. Like a plea. Arched her hips against him.

He kissed her, lost himself in the taste of her, in the sweet way she tried to kiss him back, how she wrapped her legs around his waist. He fed on those succulent curves, touched, kissed, sucked, nipped. She gasped, she moaned, she whispered his name over and over again. Encouraged him with her hands and her voice until he sensed she was ready.

He slipped his hand downward and stroked the moist treasure he had discovered between her trembling thighs, focusing all his skill on bringing her pleasure, watching her face as he brought her closer and closer. Her eyes had slid closed, and the wonderment on her face as the pressure built held him in rapt attention.

"That's it, sweet girl. Let it take you."

She clenched her fists in the bedclothes, arched her hips, tossed her head from side to side. Keened, whimpered, begged. Finally, she arched and stiffened, coating his hand with the hot rush of her climax.

Watching her take her pleasure destroyed the fragments of his control. As she lay there panting, he got off the bed and stripped off the rest of his clothes. She made a sound of protest when he left her, but it changed to a purr of pleasure as he came back naked, hard, and ready.

"Yes." She arched her hips. "I have been dreaming of this. Please, John . . ."

He took her hips in his hands, pushed inside her, shuddering as her hot, wet female flesh closed around him. Home. His. All rational thought spun away.

She clung to him with her arms and legs, met his thrusts with touching eagerness that spiked his hunger even higher. He kissed her lips, licked her throat, cupped her bottom, and held her steady to take him even deeper inside her. The shocked wonder in her gasp stroked over him like a hand on his cock. He buried his face in her throat as the orgasm roared through him, ripping a hoarse groan from his lips.

The pleasure continued to thrum through him as he slowly came back to himself.

Genny's heart pounded beneath the cheek pillowed against one generous breast. Her hands stroked over his back, his hair. She let out a long, contented sigh. "I never knew it could be like that."

The awe in her tone cut through his sexual satisfaction. He nearly groaned. What the devil had he done?

Yielded to his own desires, taken her when he had no right.

Damn it, what could he offer her? He could not marry her, not with the hangman waiting for him. He had no future to share. Nothing but heartache and widow's weeds awaited her if she stayed with him.

He had to make her walk away.

"Get dressed." He pulled out, rolled away, her little mewl of protest battling his good intentions.

"What?"

The puzzled hurt on her face pricked at him, but he forced himself to think of her, of how he would hurt her if this thing continued. "I said get your clothes." He rose from the bed and grabbed his trousers, yanking them on. "Time to go, Genny."

"Not yet." She grabbed her nightdress and scooted from the bed, clutching it in one fist as she lifted her chin and braced herself as if for battle. "You do not want me to go, John Ready. Admit it."

He studied her face, noted the obstinacy there. The admiral's daughter had braced herself for war.

But he did not want a war. And neither did he want to hurt her.

"This should not have happened," he said gently.

She sucked in a breath at the words, then jerked her nightdress over her head and shoved her arms through the sleeves. "Oh, really."

"I owe you an apology," he said, rubbing the back of his neck. "Nothing can come of this."

"I thought we were talking about marriage. I thought . . ." Her voice died away. "Tell me the truth, John. What happened here?"

"A mistake. I cannot marry you, Genny."

"Cannot? Or will not?"

He shrugged. "Does it matter?"

"Yes." She strode up to him, stared up into his face. "We just made love in your bed, John. I thought that was a promise."

He wanted to touch her. Didn't dare. "I know. I am sorry."

"Sorry? I thought you were different. I thought this"—she flung out her arm to indicate the bed—"meant something to you."

"It did."

"It did." She waited, but he said nothing more. "And now that you have had your pleasure, you escort me to the door like someone you met on the street?"

"Genny, that is not what I mean—"

"Then tell me what you do mean, John. Because I just gave myself to you thinking we were making a promise to each other. Thinking we were going to get married." Her voice thickened. "Tell me I did not make the same mistake twice."

"You should never have come." One tear slipped down her cheek. His chest ached at the sight. "Oh, God, please do not cry."

"I am not crying," she said, ignoring the evidence of tears trickling down her face.

"I never meant for this to happen," John said. "But I cannot marry you, Genny."

She stared at him with green eyes glittering like gemstones through her tears, her mouth set. "I thought you were different. I thought you were honorable."

"I am honorable."

She glanced at the bed, then back at him. "Are you?"

He could not reply. He was a cad. He knew it. But it was for her own good.

At his silence, she sucked in a long, shaky breath, then turned and left the room without looking back, closing the door with a soft click behind her.

He was alone.

He nearly reached out for the doorknob, then clenched his fingers hard enough that his nails gouged his palms. He hung his head, letting out a long, slow breath. He was a bastard. He deserved to be skewered and roasted alive over an open fire for what he had just done to her. But he would not call her back. He would not apologize.

Better she hated him and had a chance at a real life than if she stayed with him and let him destroy her.

The walk back to her room seemed colder than she remembered. Longer. Darker. When finally she slipped into her bedchamber, she closed the door behind her and leaned back against it.

And let the tears fall.

She did not sob. Barely made any sound at all. Was not even certain if she could. Silence ruled the evidence of her pain in her stinging eyes, the trails of moisture flowing down her cheeks in the chill night air, her trembling limbs. And the gaping wound in her chest where her heart used to be.

How could she have been so stupid . . . again?

She opened her mouth, sucked in a shuddering breath. Curled her fingers against the solid wood of the door, sagging as her knees buckled. Grabbed the doorknob, pulled herself up. Made herself walk to the bed with slow, careful steps. The slick dampness between her thighs lingered as a reminder of her misjudgment.

So, so foolish. Naïve. Incredibly obtuse.

She had trusted him. She had gone to him and stripped her soul bare, offered him everything she had, everything she was, confessed her most dangerous secret. And he had taken what he wanted, then discarded her like scraps from the dinner table.

How could she have imagined this would work out well? Had she built a fantasy of what she wanted her relationship with John to be rather than what it actually was? Had she written a fairy tale in her mind and tried to make it come true?

She had been here before. But this was worse than what had happened with Bradley—far worse. Because this time she had truly let herself fall in love.

She crawled into her bed, dragging the covers around her as she curled into a ball. The soft pillow absorbed her weeping as she clutched her blankets close. She could not remember anymore what qualities had attracted her to Bradley. But John. . .

She had taken the risk. Had been so affected by his kindness, his bravery, his sense of honor. The passion they shared. Her defenses had crumbled; her cautious heart had softened. Had she imagined all of it? She had thought she had found something special. Something uniquely hers. But it had proven to be illusion. Fairy dust. His words tonight had torn her heart to shreds.

She had gone to him with the idea that he might accept her proposal. That they might even make love to seal their agreement. But no, "make love" was never a term to be applied to John Ready. He had *taken her body*. Yes, that was more accurate. He had refused her proposal. Had taken her like she was any common female. Nothing special or romantic about it.

At least she had not blurted out that she loved him. That would have truly annihilated any trace of dignity she possessed.

But even that small comfort did not ease the devastation throbbing inside her. Maybe nothing ever would.

"You are strong," she whispered.

But for once, she did not believe it.

Chapter 14

Peter Green awoke that morning with a knife at his throat.

"Good morning, Peter," said the wielder of the weapon.

"Good morning, my lord," said Peter, trying desperately not to wet himself as his heart thundered like a racehorse. "Back from France, I see?"

"Rumors of your poor performance reached me even there." Raventhorpe leaned over him. "I was just trying to decide if I should kill you in your sleep or wait for you to awaken. As you can see, I decided on waiting for you to awaken."

Peter's mouth went dry. "How did you find me?"

"It was not all that hard, *Peter Black*. You might want to be more imaginative in your naming conventions. Then again, you may not have the chance."

Peter swallowed hard. He had thought he would be safe here in this tiny room. It was beneath the eaves of the tavern several towns away from his home. Even the scullery maid did not want these quarters! He had thought he had been clever, that no one could find him, yet here was Lord Raventhorpe perching on the edge of his bed like a raven come to foretell his death.

If he did not convince the earl of his loyalty, the raven might be proven right.

"I wasn't hiding from you, my lord," he hurried to say. "I didn't even know you were back in England. I was hiding from the Baileys. They've been looking for me."

"Again," Raventhorpe said, "proof of your incompetence." He pressed the blade hard enough against Peter's throat that it pricked the skin.

"No, no, no!" Peter tried to shrink back into the bedding, but it was cheaply made and did not yield very much. "I started watching them instead, my lord! I changed my name and took a room here and started watching them!"

"Indeed?" Something like genuine surprise flickered across Raventhorpe's sharp face. "And did you learn anything?"

Peter started to nod, then remembered the blade, and said, "Yes."

Raventhorpe pulled the knife back a hair. "Tell me."

Peter took the opportunity to swallow. Though he outweighed the skinny earl, he did not even attempt to dislodge him or gain the upper hand. Should he miscalculate, Raventhorpe would respond like a poisonous snake and kill him without a second thought. The man was completely cracked in the head, which made him more dangerous than even a big fellow like himself.

"There seems to be one man guarding the lady more than the others, some bloke named John Ready. Well, the other day I was following him and he went somewhere that might be of interest to you."

"Indeed?" Raventhorpe withdrew the knife and sat back, still close enough to strike but far enough away that Peter felt comfortable taking a breath. "And where was that?"

"An estate house on Evermayne lands."

"Evermayne?" Raventhorpe breathed. "Evermayne! By the devil, I thought that bastard looked familiar! John Ready, is it?" He laughed, a truly evil sound that made Peter wonder if he was indeed in the presence of one of Satan's minions. Or perhaps Old Nick himself.

"Do you know him then?" Peter asked.

"I believe I do." The amusement slid from Raventhorpe's face to give way to cunning. "This John Ready may well be John St. Giles. And even if he is not, the man known as John Ready shot me some weeks ago. He owes me for that—and for other things."

"John St. Giles? There was a vicar asking about a fellow named John St. Giles at the pub the other day."

"A vicar? How curious." Raventhorpe gave him a considering look. "Perhaps you did save your life today, Peter. You might yet be useful to me."

"Anything you need, my lord. I'm at your command."

Raventhorpe stood and tucked the blade away beneath his coat. "I know you are. And now you know it, too. I want you to follow John Ready and anyone else associated with him. And find out more about that vicar, such as what parish he comes from."

"Yes, my lord. Should I send word to your estate if I find anything?"

"No. I am not staying there. At the moment no one knows I have returned, and I would like to keep it that way for a while. I will contact you." The earl started to turn away, then paused and glanced back at him. "But I will be watching you, Peter, so do not even think about betraying me. I trust you like your manly parts right where they are, correct?"

Peter swallowed hard and nodded, resisting the urge to slide a protective hand over himself.

"Good. Then we understand each other." Raventhorpe swept out of the tiny room, his black cloak swirling.

Peter stared up at the ceiling and whispered a prayer that he would somehow escape this hellish partnership.

Guilt dogged his steps as John made his way down to breakfast the next day. He had had everything planned out so well. Samuel and Cilla were due back from their honeymoon today, which meant much celebration and excitement, and tomorrow was the picnic the Baileys were throwing, including the infamous play. Then the day after the picnic, he was going to announce the truth of his identity to the assembled guests of Nevarton Chase. It was the least he could do for the people who had shown him such hospitality. Whether or not they forgave him for his deception was another matter.

But what happened with Genny had not been part of his plans. How could he look her in the eye, or her family? He did not doubt she was probably spitting mad at him, and she had every right. But he loved her too much to drag her into danger with him, no matter how much he longed to do the right thing, claim her as his wife.

If somehow he was able to prove his innocence and escape execution, he would come back to her, offer marriage. But for now, he could not have her, plain and simple. Elizabeth had died because he had not been able to protect her; he would burn in hell before he allowed the same thing to happen to Genny.

He itched to start the process of claiming his title, to get it over with, but he did not want to disrupt the Baileys' picnic with such drama. Randall could not act on his despicable plans for the Duke's daughters until he legally inherited the title, which meant he would have to succeed in declaring John dead. That bought John a little time, certainly another day or two. Besides, he wanted to tell Samuel first, privately. They had watched each other's backs enough times that he felt he could count on his friend to forgive him the deception and to believe in his innocence.

He walked into the breakfast room to find the entire household already assembled. Automatically, he sought out Genny. He expected her to be glaring daggers at him this morning. Instead, she kept her eyes on her plate and pushed her food around with her fork.

"Good morning, John. My goodness, but don't you look handsome!" Dolly beamed at him. "You've shaved your beard!"

He rubbed his newly smooth jaw. Now that he was no longer as concerned with being recognized, he had gotten rid of the beard in preparation of claiming the title. "I have."

"I like it," Annabelle said with a flirtatious grin. "I prefer a man to be clean-shaven."

"Annabelle, I'm certain that's not the reason he did it," Dolly scolded.

"I, for one, prefer a man with whiskers," Helen said with an impish grin at her husband. He returned her smile.

"What about you, Genny?" Annabelle asked. "What do you think?"

Genny looked up, her expression indifferent. "What?"

John's heart froze like a chunk of ice in his chest.

Annabelle frowned. "Are you all right, Genny? You don't look very well."

"She did not get much sleep last night," Helen answered, patting her daughter's hand. "I believe the encounter with Black Bill gave her nightmares."

Annabelle waved a hand toward John. "John has shaved his beard, Genny. How do you like it?"

Genny blinked as she raised her gaze to his face. "Very nice," she said before dropping her stare to her plate again.

But it had been enough. John's blood ran cold at the utter lack of spark in her eyes. Where was the bright, sensual Amazon who had come to his room last night and boldly proposed to him? Who had made love with him like a wildcat? He had expected her to be breathing fire at him this morning or perhaps freezing him out with icy disdain. That was consistent with the valiant little fighter who had stolen his heart. The creature before him now might have been a doll from the nursery, so lacking in animation was she.

Good God, what had he done to her?

"Well," said Sir Harry, "I am certainly glad you are all safe despite your harrowing experience last night. Hope you are feeling more the thing soon, Miss Wallington-Willis."

Genny remained silent.

"Thank you, Sir Harry," Helen said, squeezing her daughter's hand.

Genny looked up. "Thank you, Sir Harry," she repeated obediently, then went back to studying the meal she was not eating.

John frowned from the sideboard, scooping food on his plate without really noticing what he was taking. Was she trying to make him feel guilty about what he had done?

It was working.

"Let me tell you, Sir Harry, I've never been so scared in all my life," Dolly said. "That Black Bill is a beast! He accosted my Annabelle!"

"He did?" Sir Harry's hazel eyes widened behind his spectacles as he turned to Annabelle. "Miss Bailey, did that vagabond assault your person?"

"Hardly," Annabelle said. She attempted nonchalance as she picked up her teacup and took a sip, but her face pinkened.

"He stole from her!" Dolly cried.

"She was the only person he did steal from," Mrs. Wallington-Willis said. "If he were anyone but a criminal, one would assume he had formed an attachment to Annabelle."

"Absolutely not!" Dolly exclaimed. "That villain can't have my daughter!"

"I'll hunt him down and roast him over an open pit before I let him near her," Virgil growled.

Annabelle made a dismissive motion, but humor gleamed in her blue eyes. "An attachment? The man's a highwayman!"

"True," Helen said with a small frown. "But he is first and foremost a man."

"Easy enough to avoid him." The admiral took up a piece of toast. "We talked about that, Bailey, Ready and I. Taking precautions for the future."

"I have found that it helps to avoid certain thorough-fares," Sir Harry said. "Especially those going through Raventhorpe lands or whatever used to be Raventhorpe lands. Richard sold off many of his properties over the years, most recently this one to you, Mr. Bailey. Though people are no longer purchasing land from the earl, since Black Bill apparently comes with the package."

"Makes it hard to get ready cash, I'd imagine," said the admiral.

"I like the house," Virgil said, picking up a piece of toast. "Bought it because we expected Annabelle to be marrying an earl, and we'd be coming back to England all the time. Now that she didn't marry him, I haven't decided what to do with it."

"Maybe we should just keep it, Pa," Annabelle said. "We might want to come back here and see Cilla and her family."

"I believe Samuel intends to live at least part of the year in America," John said, seating himself at the table. He flicked a glance at Genny a few seats down, but she kept her gaze lowered. "So you would have ample opportunity to see her there without the inconvenience of a long sea voyage."

"Oh." Looking disconcerted, Annabelle sipped her tea again.

"I don't know if we should keep it," Dolly said. "Too many bad memories for me. I broke my leg right on the stairs there after Lord Raventhorpe kidnapped my baby. I was running too fast."

"That's not the house's fault," Annabelle said. "That was Richard's fault, and he's somewhere in France, thank goodness."

"Yet his influence lingers," John said. Still, Genny would not look up. He tried to focus on the conversation while at the same time keeping an eye on her. "Last night, Black Bill gave us the name of the man he thinks is behind the attempted kidnapping, a fellow who supposedly works for Raventhorpe."

"You don't intend to take that seriously!" Dolly exclaimed. "Black Bill is a thief and probably a liar."

"He's not a liar," Annabelle said. "He doesn't like being called that."

"I'll call him more than that before I send him to h—

to purgatory," Virgil muttered, apparently recalling the presence of the ladies at the last moment.

Dolly frowned at her daughter. "I don't like the way you're defending him, sweetheart. He held us all at gunpoint and could have killed us!"

"But he didn't," Annabelle said. "He let us go. He gave John the information he needed, and he didn't take anyone's purse."

"No," Helen said. "Just your handkerchief, correct?"

Annabelle reddened. "Just that," she agreed.

"Why did he do that?" the admiral demanded. "The gal was wearing diamonds and pearls last night. He could have made away with a fortune from that alone."

"Hardly seems like an intelligent sort of brigand," Sir Harry said. "Why take a handkerchief instead of gems? Unless, of course, Mrs. Wallington-Willis is correct, and the highwayman has taken a fancy to you, Miss Bailey."

"I can't figure what he was thinking," Annabelle said. "I was there, same as the rest of you. I saw and heard what you did."

"But you had encountered him before," John said, setting down his silverware. He dragged his wandering attention from Genny and focused on Annabelle. "The day Raventhorpe drugged you and tried to escape with you to Scotland. You said he rescued you."

"He did. He stopped the coach and held a gun on Richard so I could tie him up. Then he knocked Richard out with his own ring."

"The one with the sleeping drug in it that Raventhorpe had used on her," John clarified for the others. He flicked another glance down the table. Genny still was not looking at him. He had forgotten about her vulnerability. How fragile she was beneath that deceptive complacence. How he wished she would use her barbed tongue to put him in his place.

"Astounding," Sir Harry commented. "Either Black Bill is the most foolish dolt who ever walked the earth, or he is stunningly brilliant."

"He has an agenda," John said. "He hates Raventhorpe."

"I would expect that would put him and us on the same side," Sir Harry said. "Do you agree, Miss Wallington-Willis?"

John stilled, every sense alert as Genny slowly looked up, met John's gaze for one long, agonizing moment. The wretchedness shadowing her eyes shamed him, made him want to howl in denial. He had done that to her. He had broken her.

Genny looked over at Sir Harry. "If you will all excuse me, I do not feel well. I am going to lie down." She set her napkin beside her plate.

"Of course, of course," Sir Harry said, rising with

the rest of the gentlemen as she got up from the table.

"Do you want me to come up with you?" Helen asked.

Genny's lips curved in a bare hint of a smile though no such emotion lit her deadened eyes. "No, thank you, Mama. You enjoy your breakfast."

"I hope you feel better, dear," Dolly said. "Samuel and your sister are due back this afternoon, and I know you'll want to see them."

"That would be nice." With a nod to those assembled, she left the room.

John watched her go, disturbed, agonized. He knew what he had done was for the best, but he had not counted on how his heart would ache at seeing the results of his handiwork.

"Is she going to be all right?" Annabelle asked. "I don't think I've ever seen Genny so quiet."

Helen frowned as she looked after her daughter. "I hope so."

"Bad night," the admiral said. "But she's young. She will be good as new by tomorrow. Now about that highwayman—"

"Robert, surely you care about your daughter's health!" Helen said.

"Of course I do. But she's gone to lie down, hasn't she? Best thing for her." He nodded to himself. "Now as to the highwayman . . . Find your enemy's enemy is what I always said. Good strategic thinking. This Black

Bill hates Raventhorpe. Might get an ally out of that."

John tried not to think about Genny retreating to her room. Genny never retreated. Was she crying? The thought ripped through his heart as if it were paper.

"What do you think, Ready?" the admiral asked.

"Ah . . . about Black Bill?" His every instinct urged him to go after Genny, but he forced himself to focus on the conversation.

"Yes, yes." The admiral reached for his coffee. "Perhaps we could get him to ally with us against Raventhorpe, eh?"

"I do not think that is a possibility, sir."

"You just don't like him because he shot you," Annabelle said.

John sliced a look her way. "You would not feel fondly toward him either, Miss Bailey."

"I don't like that idea at all." Dolly sent an anxious look toward her daughter. "Especially if he fancies my Annabelle."

"But he seems to know a lot about what is going on in the area," Helen said. "He might prove very valuable."

"Probably makes it his business to know," Sir Harry said. "Keep tabs on everyone so he can better move about in secret. I imagine he lives here."

"Perhaps on Raventhorpe lands," the admiral said.

"Maybe you should just ask him if he wants to help us," Annabelle suggested. "Or is that a silly idea?"

"I would not even know how to find him," John said. He thought about Genny, alone in her room. Should he speak to her? Or would that make matters worse?

"Seems to me," Sir Harry said, "that you just have to travel certain roads at night."

"Madness!" Dolly exclaimed.

"Only if you want to be killed!" Genny's mother said with a hand to her heart.

"Might work," the admiral said. His wife glared at him, and he applied himself most assiduously to his breakfast. "I said 'might,'" he muttered.

"Do not even consider it," Helen said. "It is too dangerous."

"He is quite unpredictable," Sir Harry said. "Might quite possibly be a madman in the literal sense of the word. After all, he did shoot you."

"Point taken," John said.

"Enough of this foolish talk," Dolly said. "Samuel and Cilla are coming home today, and I don't want anything ruining their homecoming."

"And we've got our final rehearsal for the play this afternoon," Annabelle said. "I hope Genny's feeling well enough to perform tomorrow."

"I would not worry about that," John said with a quick glance upward. "If I know Miss Wallington-Willis, nothing will keep her from the stage."

He hoped.

* * *

Genny lay on her bed and stared at the ceiling. John had seemed in good spirits this morning. He had shaved his beard, revealing a strong jaw and almost aristocratic profile. Even through her misery, she could not ignore the spark that ignited when she had glimpsed his bare, handsome face.

But then, anytime John was within a foot of her, she could not ignore her body's reaction. She wanted him, no matter what he had done. She loved him, no matter what he had said.

She was a fool.

He had shown her a brief glimpse of Heaven last night, then torn out her heart and cast her away as easily as he had shorn his beard. She had dreaded seeing him this morning at breakfast. How was she supposed to pretend everything was all right? In the end, she had given up trying. Everything was *not* all right. She had given herself to him, and he had soundly rejected her. Crushed her heart with his cruel words. And yet he behaved as if nothing was wrong.

She squeezed her eyes shut. Lord in Heaven, how could she possibly act in rehearsal later today? Sir Harry would be playing the prince in the actual production, but John was still standing in for rehearsals. Her character was supposed to be in love with him. It would be torture. But she would manage. She was certainly not going to permit him to drive her into solitude.

But hadn't she already allowed him to do just that?

She had sat at the breakfast table, her broken heart bleeding openly for anyone who cared to see, and practically sobbed into her chocolate. Then when she could not bear the pressure of hiding her feelings any longer, she had fled to her room like a little girl. Was that the act of a woman who had boldly jilted her suitor after learning of his perfidy? She had trusted Bradley, but when he had betrayed her, she had taken a stand and broken it off with him, spiking his ambition of marrying the admiral's daughter to advance his career.

Now John had used her body, then rejected her. Had she given as good as she had gotten in the face of his insults? No. She had just run away. Actually, she had not even run. She had *slunk* away, as if she were embarrassed about what had happened between them.

She was stronger than that.

Annoyed at herself, she got off the bed, went to the vanity table, and sat down in front of the mirror.

She looked like death. Her skin was pale against her dark hair, and her eyes looked like pools of misery. This would not do.

By the time they gathered for rehearsal, she would be back to her old self, even if it took the magic of the rouge pot to do it.

*   *   *

They gathered for rehearsal in the gallery as always. John had expected Genny to stay in her room—had actually thought the practice would be canceled because of her absence—and was surprised to see her join them right on time. Her color was better, and now when she looked at him, there was emotion in her eyes.

Icy rage, but still, emotion. Anything was better than that glassy-eyed stare.

"Miss Wallington-Willis, let us start with you and Mr. Ready," Sir Harry said. "I want to go over the scene where Malevita comes upon Frederick sleeping in the forest and declares her love. Do you feel well enough to do that?"

"Of course, Sir Harry." She sent John a polite smile that held more sharpness than sweetness.

"Excellent! Take your places."

John went to lie down on the blanket Sir Harry had set out, and Genny took her place. As she moved toward him, reciting her lines, he could not help but remember the last time they had done this scene. How she had flirted with him, teased him. Aroused him.

Not so this time.

"O handsome warrior. O noble prince. My blood . . . my blood burns for thee." She took a deep breath, then smiled at their stage manager. "I apologize, Sir Harry. Something was caught in my throat."

"That is fine, Miss Wallington-Willis. Do continue."

She nodded, coughed, then walked around John. "Malevita" was supposed to be admiring the form of her beloved, Prince Fredrick, but John noticed how Genny looked at the blanket, the floor, his shoes—anything she could to avoid perusing his face or body.

"O handsome warrior," she recited, the words sounding wooden and awkward on her lips. "O noble prince. My blood burns for thee."

She stretched out her hands toward him as they had agreed upon in previous rehearsals, giving the impression she wanted to stroke her palms over his body. Only he noticed her fingers quivering.

"Look upon him, all you sun and moon and stars, and know he is my love." Her voice caught. She met his gaze, held it. "My mate. My future king."

Her stance gave the impression of calm control, but her eyes revealed wild emotion rising and falling like ocean waves. Slowly, she began to circle him, a fairy princess longing for her lover. At the last rehearsal she had teased him by brushing her skirts against him. Now she seemed determined to avoid touching him at all costs.

But even though she was only playing a part, he could not help the way he reacted to the passionate words. Could not help imagining she meant the things she was saying to him. Still lying down, he bent one knee, hoping he would not embarrass himself.

"O love that lives as a flame inside me." Her voice roughened. "Thou art my only reason for living. My heart—" She inhaled a deep breath. "My heart beats for thee."

Her voice broke on the last word. Only he was close enough to see how she trembled, how she bit her lower lip to stop its quivering. How her green eyes revealed a storm of pain and misery.

The sound of clapping broke the strange spell that still held them. Genny ripped her gaze from his, her fingers curling into her palms as she held her hands at her sides and faced their stage manager.

"*Brava*, Miss Wallington-Willis! Such range of emotion. You are truly talented," Sir Harry said, applauding with the script tucked under his arm.

She nodded her head in acknowledgment, then stepped away from John and the makeshift stage. She did not look at him again during the rest of the play, not unless she was required to do so by stage direction.

She had made her feelings clear, not by fiery anger, not by icy disdain, but by sheer painful despair. When he had come to breakfast that morning, he had expected some sulky behavior like any other girl her age, but not this bone-numbing anguish. Why had he expected such a thing, when Genny had proven herself time and time again to be more than just another feather-witted debutante? Perhaps because it might have been easier to rub along with her if she *had* acted like a pouty child. But Genny Wallington-Willis never did anything predictable.

She had given herself to the man she had expected to marry.

She had rejected her suitor when any other girl would have wed him out of fear of scandal, no matter her broken heart and shattered trust.

She had gambled when she demanded Overton's silence by making it clear she was not afraid to put her own reputation on the line against his ambition. And she had won that bet.

She had charged to the rescue when she thought John was out to use Annabelle for his own ends.

She had bravely come to his room last night and revealed her secret, then offered herself in a completely honorable proposal of marriage.

He should be horsewhipped for taking her body, then refusing her marriage proposal, but by the time the passionate haze had cleared, the damage was done. Rejecting her had been the hardest thing he had ever done, but he was protecting her, both from heartache and from Raventhorpe. That bastard might well use Genny if he thought it would get to John. Genny was safer far away from him. He would not allow her to end up like Elizabeth. He had failed his wife; he would not fail Genny.

Her reaction had thrown him, though. He had expected her to be sad for a while, then bounce back. Be that firebrand of a woman who stood up for what was right no matter what the cost. Maybe hate him a little. He had seen a glimmer of that when she had first come to rehearsal.

But now, this empty desolation defeated him. He had rejected her for her own good, lied to her for her own good. But in trying to do the right thing, he might have destroyed one of the most amazing women he had ever met. The one woman he might truly love.

And for that, he would never forgive himself.

Chapter 15

After rehearsal, Genny took solace in the gardens. The house now felt like a prison, the walls closing her in with John. Thank God Cilla and Samuel were coming home today. Their return signaled the beginning of the end. Soon John would leave for America, never to return.

How grand his plans had sounded! Leave the mistakes of the past behind. Run off to America and start all over again. Was she one of those mistakes? Apparently so. His best friend's sister-in-law. She clenched her fists. His dismissal of her still stung. But despite that, she knew it was not the true reason he had refused her.

John had always treated her with the respect due a lady of her class—until he had discovered that she was no longer a virgin.

Why had she expected him to be different from any other man? His acceptance of her body but rejection of her marriage proposal proved he was not. One foolish decision had rendered her used goods, and no man wanted used goods for a wife. Not even one running from his past to start anew in America. And she had no one to blame but herself. She had given herself to Bradley of her own free will, just as she had surrendered to John of her own accord.

Would she never overcome this stigma? What were her choices now? She was too truthful a person to fake innocence in her marriage bed, and if she had to trick a man into wedding her, then he was not the sort of husband she wanted. She would rather become the spinster John had predicted, dandling Cilla's children on her knee, than live a lie.

Which was why she had fallen for John in the first place. She had thought that he, at least, would accept the truth—and her. But he didn't, and he hadn't, and his rejection had torn her heart to shreds. But that cut no less than knowing she had given herself—again—to a man who held her in such low regard. If a man like him—a man with secrets and a past he was fleeing—could not accept her for who she was, then she might well be destined to end up alone.

That was how John found her—alone in the garden, a solitary figure standing amidst the glorious rosebushes, her entire being the picture of dejection: shoulders slumped, mouth curved downward. She twirled the stem of an unopened rosebud between her fingers, her focus apparently somewhere other than here and now.

Just the sight of her made his heart ache.

He could not let this lie continue. She meant too much to him. Maybe she would still hate him after this, but at least he would know he had done the right thing.

He was going to tell her the truth.

She must have heard his approach because she turned before he could call her name. Stiffened. "What are you doing here, John?"

"Genny . . ." He hesitated, uncertain where to begin.

She glared at him, but he knew bravado when he saw it. The caution in her eyes betrayed her. "Have you come to humiliate me some more?" she challenged, tossing the rosebud aside. "Or did you think to amuse yourself with the little whore here in the gardens?"

Fury flared at both the words and tone. "Do not refer to yourself like that again. Ever."

"Why not? We both know what you think of me." She turned her back on him, head bowed. "Go away, John. I want to be alone."

By God, she is going to listen. He came forward, took her by the arm, made her face him. "If you still want to be alone once I have finished, I will let you be."

She shook off his hold. "It seems to me that you did enough speaking last night."

"Damn it, Genny, I do not blame you for hating me."

"Hating you?" She curled her lip. "I would have to feel some emotion to hate you, John. Does disgust count?"

He ignored the obvious lie. "If you are going to hate me, at least hate me for the right reasons."

"Last night's conversation is all the reason I need."

Even through his frustration, part of him warmed to see the return of the firebrand he knew. "At least it is better than the imitation of death that you were doing earlier."

She folded her arms. "Say what you came to say and leave, John."

"You are making this harder than it needs to be, Genny."

"Oh, for heaven's sake." She threw up her hands. "If you cannot even spit out what you came to tell me, I am going inside. My headache has not completely faded."

"No. Don't go." He stepped in her path, forcing her to halt what would have been a spectacularly dramatic exit. "I lied to you, Genny."

"As if I did not know that." She looked down her nose at him, but her palpable pain broke through the attempt at haughty disdain. "The only time you did *not* lie to me was last night."

"No, Genny." He took her by the arms again, held her fast so he knew she was listening. "Last night was the lie." He bent his head, trying to get her to look at him, but she stared with stubborn determination at the shirt buttons above his vest. "You gave yourself to me, and I let you think I did not care for you. But I do care."

She jerked her gaze to his, and the moisture shimmering in her eyes hit him like a fist in the gut. "I am not interested in a quick romp before you leave for America. I do not want *you,* John."

He stiffened. She sounded like she meant it.

She took advantage of his distraction to pull away from his grasp. "I need to go inside and rest before Cilla and Samuel arrive."

"No, wait. You have to hear this." He moved with her as she tried to step around him. "Genny, last night . . . I made a muck of things last night. I said the wrong things, did the wrong things. I did not know it would hurt you like that. I was prepared to deal with your anger, but I cannot bear your pain."

She paused, giving him a moment's hope, then tried to go around him again.

He followed her, blocking her exit with his body. "Please hear me out. I need to tell you the truth. About who I am and most especially about my feelings for you. Last night—"

She lowered her gaze. "I said I do not want to discuss last night."

"Last night I said what I did to push you away."

She stilled, cast him a look of disbelief. "Then perhaps you should have said no, John—to all of it. I would have left you alone."

"I did not want to say no. God help me, Genny, but it

took every ounce of control to make you go last night."

"Why the need to get rid of me at all? I gave you what you wanted." She folded her arms, her expression growing more mutinous than miserable.

"Because I am trying to protect you!"

She sighed. "From what? As you pointed out, I am no innocent."

"But you are, in so many ways." He held out a hand. "Please, come sit with me. There is a bench down the path. Let me tell you everything."

Genny hesitated. He looked sincere. His voice rang with authenticity, and his eyes had that hopeful look that made her heart melt in her chest. She wanted to trust him. But what if she did, and he rejected her again?

Still, he was only asking for her to listen. If she did not like what he had to say, she could leave.

"I will listen," she said, "but it will not change anything."

He nodded. "That is all I ask. Come sit down with me."

She allowed him to guide her down the path with a hand at her back, just the gentlest brush of his fingers against her spine. And still her traitorous body warmed beneath his touch. Would he always have this power over her?

Once they reached the stone bench hidden behind a copse of flowering bushes, Genny sat down, folded her hands in her lap and turned her attention to him. John sat next to her. She shuffled over a bit to allow more space between them. It was bad enough she could feel the heat of him next to her, smell the woodsy, leathery scent of him. If he touched her, even accidentally, she might beg him not to stop. "I am listening."

He nodded. "I am not sure where to begin."

"Start with last night."

He gave a nod. "First of all, I would like to apologize for my behavior last night. I had no right—"

"I was in that bed, too, John. I wanted it, too. Now it is over, so let us move on."

"I cannot move on until I say this. Please believe me when I tell you I only meant to protect you and spoke to prevent you from entangling yourself with me. I had to make you walk away at any cost."

"And you succeeded. May I go now?"

"No."

She turned her head away. Let him make his apologies and be done with it. They had little left to say to each other.

"Genny, my name is not John Ready."

She shrugged and poked at a pebble with the toe of her shoe.

"My name is John St. Giles." He went on. "Do you recognize the name?"

"St. Giles?" She feigned disinterest. Why did he persist in drawing out this heartache? "Perhaps I have heard that name before, but I cannot remember where."

"Maybe it was a few days ago when the magistrate was here. He brought a gentleman with him, Mr. Timmons."

Genny nodded, a small smile curving her lips despite everything else. "I remember Mr. Timmons."

"Then perhaps you will remember the client he had come to the country to visit. St. Giles is the family name of the Duke of Evermayne."

"Evermayne!" Triumph edged her tone. "So I was right. You *are* connected to that family."

"The Duke was my uncle," John confirmed. "He died some weeks ago and left no sons. My father was his brother. Father died a few years ago, which means—"

She gaped at him. "Dear, God! You are now the Duke of Evermayne?"

He nodded.

She absorbed the blow as if kicked in the stomach. A duke. He could never go to America now. Never start over in that land where the past could be left behind. He had responsibilities. Lands to govern. He would be required to marry a lady of gentle birth—a virgin. A proper lady, fit to be a duchess.

Of course he could not marry *her*. She would be the most improper of duchesses, a woman lacking in modesty, one who enjoyed bed sport entirely too much. Once more, she had chosen wrongly, and once more, she paid the price for her foolish fantasies.

She spoke through stiff lips. "Now that you are the Duke of Evermayne, you will finally be able to stop hiding."

He let out a long, slow breath. "That is the dangerous part. I need you to promise me that you will hear me out before you make any judgments."

Fear surged like acid in her throat. "John, you are scaring me. Just tell me."

"All right. Remember I told you I fled England years ago? I never intended to return."

"Yes, I remember. And when you did return, you did so as Samuel's coachman."

"He needed my help, and the position of a servant was a way to stay out of sight. I could not let anyone from upper society recognize me."

"Why? Were you hiding from your uncle? Did he disown you?"

"No, he encouraged me to leave England. Insisted, in fact."

She frowned. "I still do not understand. Were you being punished?"

"Not exactly. He was trying to save me." He took a deep breath then said, "Genny, I am a wanted man."

She blinked. Frowned. "Wanted for what?"

"For murder."

He was serious. The breath left her lungs in a whoosh. There must be some mistake. She could not have fallen in love with a murderer. A cad, apparently, but not a killer. "Who was murdered?"

"My wife."

She shut her eyes, but the truth still rang in his words. "You were married?"

"A long time ago." He closed his hand over one of hers. "I did not kill Elizabeth, Genny. You must believe me." He squeezed her hand until she looked up. "Someone else did and made it look like it was me. I am innocent. I did not even intend to accept the title. I was going to let it pass to my cousin while I disappeared in America."

"But you will not. And I understand why. Evermayne is a huge estate."

"It's not the money. I have money from the treasure Samuel and I found. I could have allowed the queen to declare me dead and lived a comfortable life in America."

"But you decided you wanted to be a duke. Do not worry, John. I completely understand."

"No, you do not." He swiped a hand over his face. "Genny, I did not kill Elizabeth, but I cannot prove my innocence. Which means when I come forward, I might be facing formal charges."

Her heart skipped. "Then do not come forward. Let your cousin have the title."

"You believe me?"

"That you did not kill your wife? Yes. You are not the type of man to harm a woman—at least not physically."

He winced. "Genny, what I said to you last night has haunted me since the words left my mouth. I wish I could call back every moment."

"Pretty apologies will not work this time. You hurt me, John."

He had the grace to look ashamed. "I know. I was trying to save you."

"Save me? From what? Becoming a duchess? Do not try to pretend anymore, John. I know the truth. Clearly I am not fit material for a wife, much less a duchess."

"Genny, I could care less that you have had some . . . experience."

"I do not believe you." She pressed her lips together. "You treated me differently once I told you the truth. That was when you started treating me like a . . . a tart."

"No, oh, no." He took her hands in his. "I was trying to save you from *me*. When I come forward, there is every chance I may be executed for murder. I will not be able to protect you from the ugliness of that."

"Executed?" Dear God, she had not considered that.

"If they find me guilty. As a duke I would be hanged by a silken rope, but a noose is still a noose."

"But you are not guilty! Surely there must be some way to prove it. And if not—run, John. Run to America. Leave tonight."

He gave her a tender smile. "And there she is, my fierce little warrior." He bowed his head, brushing a kiss over first one of her hands, then the other. "I knew last night that if I told you the truth, you would want to join the fight."

He was right. If they were together, she would have fought for him. With him.

As her anger faltered, she forced herself to think of the matter at hand. "Surely you are not just going to accept this. I respect your loyalty to the title, but if it is going to cost you your life—"

"It is not just about me, Genny. The Duke had two daughters, just children, and my cousin does not care what happens to them, only about how his connection to them can make him richer. He wants to arrange their marriages to men who will make their lives a nightmare. I cannot allow him to do that."

"So you are coming forward for these children."

"Correct."

"Not for the title or the power it holds."

"I was perfectly happy as a coachman. I do not need power."

"But you will take it to avert disaster for His Grace's daughters."

"Yes."

"This sounds like something from one of Sir Harry's plays," Genny said.

John laughed. "You are correct." His expression softened, and he trailed his fingers along her cheek. "If things were different . . ." He stopped, dropped his hand.

She sighed, glancing down. The rosebud she had discarded lay bruised and beautiful on the stone path. "But things are not different. You have this duty to fulfill. The lives of children hanging in the balance. And even if you did not have those things . . ." She fell silent.

He waited, but she did not continue. "Genny? Even if I did not have those things . . . what?"

When she looked at him, she wished she could say the things he probably wanted to hear. But truth deserved truth. "It comes down to this. You were not honest with me about your true identity, nor last night about your feelings for me."

"Genny, surely—"

She held up a hand, and he fell silent. "Please listen. I believe that you did what you did last night because you were trying to protect me from the unpleasantness that may await you. I understand that. But I would have appreciated being given a choice. I have already suffered the punishment for one man's lies. I thought you at least would respect me enough to allow me to choose for myself."

"Damn it, Genny, you would have stuck by me no matter what the cost. I could not let you do that. Not when everything points to Raventhorpe being Elizabeth's killer."

"Raventhorpe!"

"We were rivals. They were having an affair. The short version is, I am in no position to be anyone's husband."

"Well, you do not have to worry about any more marriage proposals from me, John," she said, cold fury driving her words. "Because you have destroyed any trust we had between us by not telling me the truth when it mattered."

He clenched his jaw, gave a short nod. "I understand. I wish things could be different. But with Raventhorpe involved and the uncertainty of the future—"

"We go our separate ways."

Slowly, he nodded. "Perhaps it is better that way."

"This is how it must be," she whispered.

"This is how it must be," he agreed.

They sat in silence for long moments, as if neither wanted to be the first to leave. Genny glanced at him from the corner of her eye, but he stared at the ground, his hands clasped loosely between his knees. He would not be returning to America now. No grand adventure awaited them. Only the unknown future.

A future apart.

"There you are!" Genny's mother appeared on the garden path outside the clearing. She glanced from one to the other with a hint of concern, but her tone gave nothing away. "Genny, dear, your sister's carriage is coming down the drive. Dolly wants us to meet the newlyweds in the foyer."

"Of course." Genny nodded. John got to his feet as she did.

"You should come too, Mr. Ready." Her mother pursed her lips and gave John a hard look. "I am certain Samuel will want to speak with you."

John nodded and gestured for Genny to precede him. "I would be honored to escort you both back to the house."

"That would be lovely." Helen waited until they reached the path, then, with a smooth move, her mother hooked one arm through John's and the other through her daughter's, inserting herself neatly between them. "How lovely to be a family again. I am very excited to see my daughter, Mr. Ready. My children are every-thing to me. You are aware of that, are you not?"

The implication was clear, but John met her mother's gaze without flinching. "Yes, ma'am."

"I am glad we understand each other. Come, my dears. I am anxious to see my Cilla again."

The confrontation with John had left Genny on edge. She hoped that someday her feelings for him would lessen, perhaps become little more than a nostalgic memory. But she did not think so. She did not believe she would ever be able to relegate him to the attic of her mind, though common sense dictated she should try and forget about him.

But she knew she would not. A woman did not forget a man with whom she had been intimate, much less the man to whom she had proposed marriage. Especially when her heart throbbed in time with his every breath.

As she, her mother and John joined the other guests in the foyer, she caught sight of Cilla. Her heart squeezed as she noticed the way the new bride's face glowed with happiness. Perhaps now was the ideal time to set things to rights with her sister. The strain in their relationship had gone on too long.

And it would be nice to have someone to talk to again.

But was it too late to seek forgiveness? As she thought back to her behavior in the weeks before Cilla's wedding, she wanted to cringe. Dear Lord, she had acted like a child, so angry at her older sister for eloping to America with her first husband that she had nursed the resentment like a flourishing poison. But now, as the newlyweds crowded into the foyer, she realized the true cause of her antagonism toward her sister. When Cilla had returned to England, widowed and independent, Genny had tried to tell herself that she was angry with

Cilla for breaking tradition, for hurting their parents and causing some scandal. But now she could admit the truth to herself.

She felt as if Cilla had abandoned her.

Genny had been only fourteen, not even out of the schoolroom, when Cilla had eloped. But what if Cilla had never left? What if she had remained in London, married a suitable gentleman, and had been there for Genny when Bradley had arrived on the scene? Genny could never have confided her feelings about Bradley to her mother, but she would have felt comfortable telling Cilla. And maybe Cilla could have stopped the disaster before it happened.

But now she realized that, Cilla or not, things might still have gone the same way. Had *anyone* tried to tell her that Bradley was deceiving her, she never would have believed it. At the time her passion for Bradley had swamped her like an ocean tide, sweeping her along the path she had chosen to take. It was only her own frustration at having ruined her chances at a respectable marriage that prompted her outright rudeness in the presence of her sister. Somehow, it had seemed easier to blame Cilla for everything.

Yet now she accepted her own part in her situation. Now she realized that Cilla had only done what she felt was right by following her heart—in essence, nearly the same thing as Genny—and she could not fault her for it.

She was happy to see Cilla. She had missed her sister.

Samuel and Cilla were greeting everyone, shaking hands, kissing cheeks. Cilla hugged their mother, then faced Genny.

"Hello, Genny."

Genny recognized the wariness—and the hope—in the face so like her own. Her sister. Blood of her blood, heart of her heart. She threw her arms around Cilla, pulled her close as tears stung her eyes. "Welcome home."

Chapter 16

After the celebration of the newlyweds' return home had finally died down, the ladies retired upstairs, and John managed to get Samuel alone for a private conversation. They met outside in the gardens, though in a different section from where he had sat with Genny. Even with the distance, though, John could not escape the scent of roses.

To his dying day, he would always associate roses with Genny.

"John, why the hasty meeting?" Samuel joined him in the grotto he had selected. "I've barely been able to change out of my traveling clothes. Is there news of Raventhorpe?"

"There is, but that is not why I wanted to talk to you." John paced, searching for the words to explain.

"What news?" Samuel asked.

"He sent a man to kidnap Annabelle, but she escaped him. Again, that is not why I asked you here."

Samuel frowned. "How did she escape?"

John stopped his pacing and glared at his friend. "I taught her some tricks to defend herself. She got away from him."

Samuel propped his hands on his hips. "And where were you?"

John winced. "I was not there."

"Why in hell not?"

"I was working in the stables. She sneaked off with Sir Harry without telling me. But that—"

"—is not why you asked me here. You said that already. But if Raventhorpe is back, I need to know."

"I have not heard anything to indicate he is back in England," John said. "Annabelle is fine, and we know the name of the man who tried to take her."

"Why haven't you sent the law after him?"

"Because he has gone to ground somewhere. We cannot find him." John folded his arms. "I am trying to tell you something important, Samuel."

"Well, have you tried—"

"I am the Duke of Evermayne."

"—the local taverns and . . . what do you mean, you're a duke?" Samuel frowned. "That's what you said, right?"

"Yes." John took a deep breath. Samuel was as honest a man as the day was long. He was not certain how his friend would handle the facts he was about to unveil. "My name is John St. Giles. Since my uncle the Duke recently died, I am his heir."

"By God, are you serious?"

"Very."

"Is that what you've been hiding?"

John shook his head. "I only recently found out myself."

"Ah. I take it there is more, then?"

John let out a long breath. "Yes, there is more."

"All right." Samuel folded his arms in an identical stance. "Tell me."

"Seven years ago, someone murdered my wife and made it look like I did it."

Samuel's eyes widened. "And that's why you left England?"

"Yes, my uncle insisted." John rubbed a hand over the back of his neck. "I was just a stripling, barely twenty-three. I was drugged and unconscious in the gardens when my wife was murdered."

"Surely you told someone."

"I did not have time. As soon as the news hit, my uncle had me on the first ship out of England. Besides, I had no proof of my innocence."

"Do you know who did it?"

The simple question immediately relieved the tension that gripped him. Despite their friendship, John had been concerned that Samuel might have doubts. "Can't you guess?"

"Who . . . Raventhorpe?"

"The same. My wife was having an affair with him."

"He murdered her and made it look like you were the one who did it? The depraved bastard." Samuel rubbed his chin. "Of course you realize that your uncle forcing you to flee has made you look even more guilty."

"Easy to realize now, but at that time I was young and gullible. My uncle ruled the family, and no one ever disobeyed him."

Samuel rocked back on his heels. "I suppose you rule the family now, since you are the new duke."

"I suppose I do. I only found out about all of this a couple of days ago, so I have not yet had a chance to absorb it."

"What next?"

"I have not told anyone else," John said. "Well, except for Genny."

Samuel raised his brows. "Genny, is it?"

He would not betray Genny's secret. Samuel did not need to know how far their relationship had progressed. "Yes, we have spent some time in each other's company, but no, nothing can come of it. My life is in shambles right now."

"Understood."

John glanced away from the compassion in his friend's eyes. There were times he wished Samuel were not quite so observant. "Tomorrow, the Baileys are throwing a picnic in honor of your homecoming, and

I do not want to disrupt the festivities with this news. I intend to tell Genny's parents and the Baileys after the picnic is over."

"You know if there is anything you need, you have only to say the word."

"I know." John clasped Samuel on the shoulder. "I have a hornet's nest waiting for me, Samuel, and I would rather no one else got stung. But I appreciate the sentiment."

"I'm pretty good with hornets," Samuel said with a grin. "Amazing what some kerosene and a match will do."

"I will keep that in mind."

"You do that." The humor faded from Samuel's face. "You came back to get me, John, when everyone else assumed I was dead. I will never forget that. If you need any assistance from me for anything at all, you have only to say the word."

John swallowed past the lump that had formed in his throat. "Thank you."

"Come along now." Samuel swatted John in the chest with the back of his hand. "We should go back inside, rejoin the others."

John fell into step as his friend started down the path. "I think you just want to get back to your wife. How are those leg shackles fitting you?"

"Like a glove."

"You sound awfully happy about your captivity."

Samuel flashed him a grin. "Jealous, are you?"

John laughed, but a pang of regret pieced his heart. *Ah, Samuel, if you only knew.*

Genny hesitated outside Cilla's bedchamber. She had seen Samuel go outside with John and knew her mother had met Dolly in the drawing room to discuss costumes and props needed for the play. She was supposed to join them, as was Cilla, once her sister changed out of her traveling clothes.

She blew out a quick breath and knocked before her courage deserted her. The door opened a moment later to reveal Lucy, Cilla's maid.

"I need to speak to my sister," Genny said.

Lucy nodded. "One moment." She closed the door, then opened it again a few minutes later. "Please come in."

Genny entered the room. As Lucy closed the door behind her, Cilla came out from behind the screen, clad in her bloomers, chemise, and corset. "Genny, what is it? Has something happened?"

"No." Genny bit her lip and twisted her fingers together. "Might I speak to you alone? Please?"

"Certainly." Cilla nodded at Lucy, who nodded back and quietly left the room. "Forgive me for entertaining in my undergarments, but you caught me in the middle of changing out of my traveling dress." She wrinkled her nose. "After so many hours on the train, I could not wait to get that thing off."

Genny chuckled. "I understand."

"So tell me, what's wrong?" Cilla came to her and took her by the hands. Her sister topped her in height only by an inch or two, but otherwise they looked enough alike that people sometimes mistook them for twins.

"Why does anything have to be wrong?" Genny shrugged.

"Because you were a beast to me before the wedding, and now suddenly you are hugging me and asking to speak privately." Cilla arched her brows. "Something has happened, despite what you say."

Genny pulled her hands from Cilla's. "I came to welcome you home."

"You did that downstairs."

"And to apologize for my treatment of you since you have returned. I was angry, and I blamed you."

"Come, let us sit while we talk." Cilla indicated two chairs by the window of the spacious room. "Why did you blame me? What did I do?"

"You left."

Cilla sighed and nodded as the two of them sat down. "When I ran off with Edward. You were so young—"

"Fourteen."

"Only fourteen. You could not understand. I was in love with Edward. Charmed by him. Completely bedazzled—enough that I stood up to Papa and ran off with Edward anyway."

"And left all of us behind."

"Well, Papa disowned me." Cilla gave her a crooked smile. "He was trying to make me come to my senses. He never expected me to call his bluff."

Genny laughed. "Has it escaped his notice that we are his daughters? Certainly we must have inherited something from him."

"I do not know which is worse, his bullheadedness or Mama's sweet, calm stubbornness. How they stayed married all these years without fighting like cats and dogs is a miracle."

"No, it is not," Genny said. "Mama always wins."

"Only because Papa lets her. At any rate, I left to marry Edward and go live with him in America, and in all the drama around my elopement, I did not take the time to explain to you. To say good-bye."

"I was angry at you for a long time," Genny said. "I kept waiting for you to come home, but you never did."

Cilla leaned forward and grasped her sister's hand. "I am sorry if I hurt you, Genny. I would have written, but I did not think Papa would let you read my letters. Then after Edward died and left me in such dire straits . . . well, I vowed to come back to England only when

I could support myself. To show Papa that I had *not* ruined my life."

"I understand that now. Truly, I do, Cilla. And I am sorry for being such a horrible wretch to you when you did finally come home."

"I understand—"

"No, you do not. I did not even comprehend it myself until I saw you again just today." She lowered her gaze, pulled her hand out of Cilla's. "Things have happened to me since you left England, Cilla. Things I longed to talk to you about. I needed my sister, but you were not here, and that made me even angrier. And then when I made the wrong decisions, I blamed you as well. Because maybe you could have stopped me."

Cilla gave a disbelieving laugh. "As if anyone could stop you once you have set your mind to something. You are definitely the admiral's daughter."

"But you would have tried. You would have talked to me, maybe made me see things differently."

"Heavens, sweetie, what happened?" She lowered her voice. "Was it a man?"

Genny rolled her eyes. "When is it *not* a man that makes a woman act like a fool?"

"Oh, dear. Tell me."

"A year ago. Bradley Overton. He was a naval officer and wanted to marry me. Papa was ecstatic."

Cilla frowned. "What happened?"

"I overheard him talking to his cronies, bragging about landing the admiral's daughter."

"Oh, Genny, no! What did Papa do?"

"He did not know. I broke it off myself."

"Oh, I am so sorry. The man was a fool."

"No more than I was. It had nothing to do with you, but I blamed you anyway. It was easier." She bit her lip. "I was just so ashamed."

Cilla leaned forward. "Genny, did you . . . were you intimate with him?"

Genny nodded.

"You . . . and then you *jilted* him?"

"He lied to me, Cilla. Swore he loved me when it was Papa's connections that he loved. I would not have a man like that, no matter what happened between us."

"I understand. But sweetie, how was it the scandal did not get all over London?"

"I advised him that if he told anyone, I would make sure Papa stopped his naval career in its tracks."

"Huh. Clever."

"It worked."

"Apparently so." Cilla sat back in her chair and regarded her sister. "But now you have a problem."

"I know." Genny buried her face in her hands, then looked up again, hoping for some wisdom from her older sister. "I thought I had found a solution, but everything is complicated now."

"You might as well tell me all of it."

Genny hesitated. "I expected you to rail at me for what happened with Bradley."

"Oh, I think you have been punishing yourself enough for both of us. And as long as you learned your lesson—"

Guilty, Genny glanced away.

Cilla caught the expression. "Oh, no. Tell me you did not—"

"I have fallen in love with someone else," Genny said. "I proposed marriage to him."

"*You* proposed marriage to *him*? What did he say?"

"I assumed he accepted because he . . . we . . . that is . . ." She gave Cilla a look that pleaded for understanding. "I thought it would be all right. That we would be together forever."

"Oh, no. When was this?"

"Just last night."

"What!" Cilla sat straight up in her chair. "This man is *here*? And this happened right under the nose of our parents?"

Miserable, Genny nodded.

"Who?" Cilla demanded. "That Sir Harry fellow?"

Genny shook her head. "John."

"John *Ready*?" Cilla leaped to her feet. "John Ready seduced my sister and will not marry her?"

"Cilla, wait, calm down." Genny rose, tried to take

her sister's hands, but Cilla jerked away from her to stalk the room.

"I cannot believe this. That my husband's best friend would act so dishonorably . . . Well, Samuel will need to hear of this. He will make things right."

"No, please do not interfere." Genny held out her hands. "John spoke to me today. He has very real reasons for not marrying me."

"Ha! Every man does, sweetie. They rarely do it of their own volition."

"No, he truly does have valid reasons."

"Oh?" Cilla folded her arms. "Is he dying of a dreadful illness? A *contagious* illness?"

"Ah . . . no. But—"

"Is he already married?"

"Not anymore." When Cilla raised her brows, Genny added, "She died."

"Is he wanted by the law?"

"Yes."

"Is he . . . what did you say?"

"I said yes." Emotion clogged her throat. "Cilla, he has been running away all these years because they think he killed his wife."

Cilla stared at her with mouth agape for a full minute before she shook her head. "Impossible. I know John. He would never do such a thing."

"I agree. He says it was Raventhorpe, but it was made to look like John did it."

"Raventhorpe? Well, that makes more sense." Cilla gave a decisive nod. "I know John, probably better than you do. And what I know of that man tells me that he is most likely trying to protect you or some such nonsense."

Genny blinked. "Yes. That is exactly what he said. If he cannot prove his innocence, he might well be hanged for murder. Even if he is a duke."

"Which just tells you . . ." Cilla paused. "A duke?"

Genny tilted her head. "I did not mention that?"

"No. Heavens, this sounds like some lurid novel."

"I know." Genny sank down into her chair. "Try living it."

"So John is a duke. Which one?"

"Evermayne."

"Really? I always knew that fellow was far too well-read to be a mere coachman."

"He must come forward to claim the title in order to save His Grace's young daughters from being married off to lechers by the presumptive heir. When he does that, the law will come looking for him."

"True." Cilla came back to her chair, then sat down, tapping her chin with her fingers. "But he is a duke. So they may take their time before accusing him of anything."

"I suppose."

"This is going to be a difficult time for him. I have no doubt there are people who believe he truly did kill his wife." She met Genny's gaze. "Seems to me he is going to need someone on his side."

Genny scoffed. "He does not want me anywhere near him. Clearly I am not fit to be a duchess. Not with my history."

"Nonsense! You get that out of your head right now." Anger tightened her sister's features. "He is trying to be *noble,* silly. He thinks he is going to die, and he is trying to keep you out of it."

"He said something along those lines, but—"

"You told me that you love him?"

Genny nodded.

"Then why are you letting him face this thing alone? Why are you not at his side?"

"He told me to leave."

"And you obeyed?" Cilla shook her head. "Sweetie, I thought you had more gumption than that."

Genny stiffened. "The man basically threw me out of his room. I will not go where I am not wanted." When Cilla continued to stare at her, silent, Genny frowned, thinking back. "Unless . . . do you think he was trying to push me away? Make me hate him?"

"What do you think?"

The truth staggered her. "Yes. That is exactly what he

did. Because he knew that the only way I would leave him is if I hated him."

"Typical male logic." Cilla rose and pulled her sister up out of her chair. "I have had the experience of a bad marriage, and I would not wish it on my worst enemy. I have also had the experience of falling in love and marrying a man who loves me right back. And that, little sister, is worth fighting for."

"But . . . he might be executed. If he fails to prove his innocence, they will hang him." Just the thought brought hot emotion clogging her throat. "We might not have enough time to be together."

"How much time is enough? There is no way to measure it, not when it comes to love. Don't you think you should steal the time you have, however long or short that might be, and enjoy each other while you can?" Cilla gave her a little shake. "Love him. Be by his side, through good and bad."

"If I marry him, I would be the duchess," Genny said, the idea taking hold. "I would be able to raise His Grace's daughters, even if the worst happened."

"Yes. *Now* you are thinking like the sister I knew!"

"Would there be the possibility of a child, do you think? Even in so short a time?"

Cilla laughed and hugged her sister. "Of course. It only takes once."

"Oh! So I might even now be—"

Cilla's smile faded. "Yes, there is a chance, depending on what actually happened between you two . . ." Her sentence ended more like a question, and Genny confirmed with a short nod. "All right, then."

"The possibility of a child might be what I need to make him see reason. Perhaps if I go back to him. Propose again . . ." Genny set her jaw, bracing for battle. "I will not let him push me away this time. Not now that I know he is trying to protect me."

Cilla leaned forward. "That is the spirit, Genny! You never know how much time you have, even under the best circumstances. Life is too short for regrets."

Life is too short for regrets.

Genny took those words with her as she went to bed that night. Her time with her sister had helped her step away from the situation, to think it through logically. Would she regret letting John go, especially if he ended up being convicted of murder? *Yes.*

She could not let him face this alone. Even if he walked to meet the hangman's noose, he would know that she was there with him, praying for him, loving him.

But she refused to let it come to that. Raventhorpe could not win this time. She would marry John, stand by his side, defend him against detractors, take care of those little girls, and help him prove his innocence. Nothing would stop her.

Not even the man himself.

Chapter 17

The Bailey picnic had gone off without a hitch. Hundreds of guests flooded the grounds, eating, drinking, playing games. In the afternoon, the Nevarton Players, as the group called themselves, launched their production of Sir Harry's epic play, *The Improper Princess*. The guests had loved the performance and given a standing ovation at its conclusion. Genny had shone on the stage as the wicked Malevita. She had seemed better today. More herself.

It made it slightly easier to leave.

After all the guests had departed and all the props and tents had been hauled back to the house, after all the Nevarton Players had sought their beds, John finally got a moment alone.

He pulled his clothing from the bureau and began folding it in a neat stack. He would start packing tonight. Tomorrow, after he explained himself to Genny's parents and the Baileys, he would be leaving for London to present himself to Mr. Timmons as the eighth Duke of Evermayne.

Then they would see what came next.

Inquiries probably. Scotland Yard would certainly still look into a murder, even an old one. He had fled England before they had ever questioned him, so perhaps they would not throw him in prison right away. He should have enough time to set up arrangements for the Duke's daughters before they hauled him away in chains. And enough time to go through his father's notes, searching for clues to his innocence.

He picked up his father's battered journal and flipped it open, running a finger over his sire's familiar, cramped script. Father had never given up on him, had always believed in him. Had intended to prove his innocence, so his son could come home. His faith had never wavered.

John cleared his throat, swiped the heel of his hand over his dampening eyes. The loss still throbbed, a fresh wound. Though Father had been gone these four years, to John it had only happened yesterday.

He paged through the book, looked at the last entry. *Jack Norman, Elford-by-the-Sea.* That was where he would start. Tomorrow, after he visited Tim Timmons's office and proved his identity, he would pick up where Father left off. Who was Jack Norman, and what did he know about Elizabeth's death?

The door clicked open behind him. He whirled,

closing the journal with a snap. His mouth fell open as Genny slipped into the room, clad in a nightdress and wrapper, her hair loose around her shoulders.

"What the devil are you doing here?"

She closed the door and glanced at his bag on the bed. "You are packing already?"

"Yes. I am leaving in the morning." He tossed the journal on the bed and took her arm, reaching for the doorknob. "And you are leaving right now."

She flattened her back against the door. "I am not going anywhere."

Determination shone in her eyes. He could make her leave, drag her away from the door, open it, and shove her into the hall. But he could feel the warmth of her flesh beneath his grip. Her scent made his head spin, that sweet honeysuckle. Now that he knew what delectable body hid beneath her clothes, he found it even harder to resist her. "What are you doing here?"

"I want to talk to you."

He sighed. "I thought we already talked."

"I have more to say." She pushed away from the door, sliding her arm from his grasp and wandering over to the bed. "I thought about everything you said, John. And I think you are making a mistake."

"Is that so?" He folded his arms and leaned back against the door. Clearly she was nòt leaving. He would have to wait her out.

"Absolutely. Tomorrow you are going to see Mr. Timmons, are you not?" She picked up the journal off his bed, flipped through the pages.

"I am." He yanked the book from her hands and placed it on the bureau.

She raised her brows at his defensive reaction, but continued, "You are going to step out into view of all the world, attract the attention of the authorities and remind people of the old rumors. And you intend to face this all alone."

"That is the way it has to be. Things might turn ugly. Better it is only I who suffers."

"Why would you do that, when I can be there to help you?" Her coaxing smile urged him to be reasonable.

"You cannot come with me, Genny. We already discussed this."

"Why? Because of heartbreak? How is that different from what I feel right now?" She came toward him, her hips swaying in a way that every male understood. "Let me tell you something, John Ready . . . John St. Giles. If your intent was to spare me pain, you have failed."

"I know." That honeysuckle scent teased his senses again, reminding him of their night together. Making his head spin. "I apologized."

"You need to look at this practically." She stopped in front of him and propped her hands on her hips. "I can help you."

"No. I will not have you ask your father—"

She laid a finger on his lips, making him forget what words were and how to form them. "I said nothing about my father. We should get married."

He shook his head, and her finger fell away. "No. I will not leave you a widow."

"As your wife," she charged on as if he had not spoken, "I can help you raise His Grace's daughters. Both of their mothers both passed away some years ago. They have no one, John, and if you . . ." She cleared her throat. "If things turn out for the worse, then they will be alone again."

"I will appoint a guardian."

"Who will you appoint? Not Randall, certainly. And who is to stop the girls' guardian from taking advantage of their wealth? If I am your wife, I would be their mother. I could look out for them, no matter who controls the financial matters. They would not feel like orphans if you were suddenly . . . gone."

She paused, cleared her throat. Was she upset at the prospect of his execution?

He had been ready to dismiss her idea out of hand, but the more he thought about it, the more it made sense. Whom could he really trust to watch over his cousins? He had been gone from England for years and so had no close friends he could trust except Samuel. But the Breedloves would be returning to America in a few weeks.

"In addition," she said, pacing back over to the bed again, "I would like to point out that by marrying you, I become the Duchess of Evermayne. This grants me tremendous security. You would be taking care of the girls and me at the same time—assuming such a thing matters to you."

"You know it does."

"Actually, John, I do not know. I have no idea how you feel about me." She paused, but when he remained silent, she returned to pacing. "There is another reason marriage might be a good idea. You might get me with child—an heir for Evermayne—which would assure that Randall never inherits."

"An heir?" The thought had not occurred to him, not this way. "This would be a real marriage then."

"Of course. Did you think we would marry for convenience?"

He shrugged. "I did not know your intentions."

She gave him a slow smile that raised his blood pressure. "I would be pleased to provide you with an heir."

If she had not already begun the process.

The thought popped into his mind and would not let go. Damn it. Why hadn't he thought of that? "You might already be with child."

She shrugged. "I might. But that is not why I am proposing this marriage. I think we can help each other."

"It does not alarm you that you might even now be expecting? Genny, you would be ruined."

She narrowed her eyes at him. "John, you had better not even consider wedding me out of guilt. We have good, solid reasons for entering this marriage."

"I still do not want you anywhere near this mess."

"And I do not want you to face your accusers alone. I believe in your innocence, John. I will stand by you, no matter what happens." She took a deep breath, then looked him straight in the eye. "I am in love with you."

She waited for his response, barely breathing. She did not expect him to love her, maybe not yet. But if they had a chance at a lifetime together, love could come.

He stood stock-still for a few moments, then reached for her, pulling her into his arms. He caressed her cheek. "My little warrior." He rested his forehead against hers, looked deeply into her eyes. "I love you, too."

Her heart leaped. Had she heard aright? Then he cupped the back of her head and dragged her closer for a deep, hungry kiss that conveyed beyond mere words how he felt about her. She clung to him, reveling in the heat sweeping through her body as he crushed her against him.

Her pulse stuttered in her veins, her mind fogging with urgent, demanding desire. She pushed against his chest, freed her mouth. "John. What about—"

"Yes, I will marry you." He swept her hair behind her ear, his gaze intent on her face. "I do not know how long we will have. Maybe weeks. Maybe days."

"It does not matter." She relaxed in his arms, laying her palm against his chest. "I will be grateful for any time we have."

"I will need a special license."

She grinned up at him. "I expect the Duke of Evermayne can procure one with little effort."

He chuckled, the sound rumbling through his chest. "I expect you are right."

She stroked her hand down his shirt, listening to the thud of his heart beneath her ear, content, for now, simply to rest in his arms. "You will need to speak to my father."

He gave a huge sigh. "You had to mention that."

She lifted her head from his chest. "He can be a great ally."

"So can you, love." He tilted her chin with one finger and pressed a tender kiss to her lips.

She closed her eyes as her body responded. "Make love to me, John."

He tensed. "We should wait. We will be getting married . . ."

"We do not have time to wait. No moments should be wasted." She opened her eyes, hoping he would see the arousal coursing through her. "Now is the only certainty; it is all we have. We cannot count on tomorrow."

He stroked her hair. "I do not want to think about anything coming between us. What if we cannot get the special license in time? What if we cannot wed?"

"Now is all we have," she repeated. "Tomorrow will take care of itself." She untied her robe and shrugged it off, letting it pool on the floor. Beneath it she wore a silky nightdress with lace trim.

He raised his brows. "Where did you get this?"

"It was part of Cilla's wedding trousseau. She let me borrow it."

"She knows?"

"Yes, she is my sister." She cupped his face. "Tomorrow everything will be out in the open."

"True." He took one of her hands, pressed a kiss to the palm. Her pulse fluttered. Holding her gaze, he slipped her finger into his mouth, tickled the sensitive pad with his tongue, sending tingles flooding up her arm.

"Oh, my." She had not realized she had spoken aloud until he chuckled.

"If you like that, I have more I can show you."

Her insides melted. "I am yours."

With a pirate's grin, he scooped her into his arms and carried her to the bed. His clothing and traveling bag took up one side, so he set her down on the side that was clear, then scooped up his belongings, shoved them in the bag, and set it on the floor.

Genny stretched out on the mattress, her body humming with anticipation, and extended her arms above her to touch her fingertips to the headboard. John came back to her then, pressing her into the bedding with his warm, muscled body and pinning her hands above her head with his hands on her wrists. The position plumped her breasts toward him, and he took advantage, claiming one nipple between his teeth right through the thin material of her nightdress. The playful nip seared a path of heat straight to her private parts. She gasped, arched closer, gave herself up to whatever he wanted from her.

And it seemed that what he wanted was to tease her into madness.

He toyed with her breasts, nipping, licking, sucking through the provocative nightdress. He dipped his tongue into the valley of her bosom, nibbled a path from her collarbone to her ear and back again, kissed her long enough and deeply enough that she began to wonder if he could bring her to climax with just that alone.

He took his time learning her, playing with her, tormenting her. Priming her for his possession. He kept his weight on her so she could not spread her legs, and soon she was begging him to touch her there, take her, anything to soothe the ache. She arched her hips against him, tugged on her arms to free them. But he held her firm and drove her higher with his lips and teeth and tongue.

"Please, John." She tossed her head. She burned. She wanted. The place between her legs swelled with heat and dampness, preparing for him. Only him sliding inside her would stop this torment.

Finally, he released her hands and took his weight from her, settling beside her rather than on top of her. She barely had a moment to protest before he was sliding her nightdress up her legs, bunching it at her waist. Anticipation stiffened her spine and sent excitement roaring through her body. Eagerly she spread her thighs. After long moments, he stroked the slick folds with gentle fingers. Once. Twice. Driving her insane with need.

"My, my," he murmured. "Look at how wet you are." He slid his fingers inside her, out again, then repeated in a rhythm that left her shaking.

She could not speak, could only whimper, arching into the thrust of his fingers. Every touch left a trail of fire. He toyed with one breast at the same time, cupping it, seeming to enjoy its size, its weight in his hand. He kissed her, nipped at her lips, touched his tongue to hers as he squeezed and fondled the plump flesh.

She jerked at his clothes, wild to feel his skin against hers. He allowed her to indulge herself, and eventually he was naked. She reached down, closed her hand around his hardness. He hissed a sharp breath between his lips, pumped once, twice in her grasp. Then he pulled her hand away and took her face between his hands, holding her head still.

"Look at me," he commanded, his dark gaze boring into hers. "Feel me take you."

She gasped as began to enter her, an inch at a time. She arched her hips, clenched her internal muscles, tried to make him move faster. Harder. Deeper. Still, he kept the same excruciating pace, finally sinking all the way in, his loins locked to hers. Her eyes drifted closed.

"No, look at me, Genny." Slowly, he began to move. "Stay with me. Feel me make you mine."

A choked sound escaped her throat. He felt so good, so deep inside her.

"That's it, my love." He locked his gaze on hers as he slowly, thoroughly made her his woman. He seemed to have all the time in the world, his pace slow and steady.

And driving her wild.

She clawed at his back, wrapped her legs around his waist. Begged. Tension seized her muscles. She gasped his name, clutched his arms. "Please, John. I beg you, please . . ."

"All right, here you go." He slid his hand between their bodies, found her sensitive spot, stroked. Pleasure exploded. She grabbed his shoulders, held on as the climax rocked her into near unconsciousness.

"Say that you are mine." He kissed her lips. "Say it, love."

"Yours." The word came out barely audible.

"Again."

"Yours."

He clenched his fingers in her hair. Thrust home, hard. "Again."

"Yours."

"Mine." He erupted inside her.

Chapter 18

They went down to breakfast separately. Propriety demanded John speak to her father before presuming to make any announcement about their engagement, but it was all Genny could do to maintain decorum. Cilla apparently picked up on her excitement since she kept sending inquiring looks her way.

"Everyone just loved the performance yesterday," Dolly said. "You were all wonderful!."

"I think Sir Harry was perfect as the prince," Annabelle said with a smile. "Especially since he hadn't been rehearsing."

"Now, now," Sir Harry said. "I just stepped in where needed."

"I want to know what Cilla and Samuel thought," Dolly said, leaning across the table and grinning at the newlyweds. "Since the play was in your honor and all."

"It was a lovely surprise," Cilla said. "You and Mr. Bailey were quite believable as the fairy king and queen."

"And a very manly fairy king at that," Samuel added, making Virgil preen.

"Let's not forget the admiral and his ladies," Dolly went on. "Genny dear, I'm so glad you were feeling better. You were such a wicked Malevita!"

"Thank you, Mrs. Bailey," Genny said. She glanced at John, wondering when he was going to make his announcement. The sooner he told everyone his true identity, the sooner he could speak to her father. She could not read anything from his expression.

What if he did not speak up? For an instant, that old distrust flared up. But then she pushed it aside. She either trusted the man, or she did not, and she had already decided to trust him. She had to believe he would not let her down.

"You'll notice no one minded a prince with a cane," Annabelle said with a teasing glance at Sir Harry.

"War injury," the baronet replied. "It was Miss Bailey's idea to write that into the script."

"The admiral suggested it," Annabelle said.

"I have to admit, I feel somewhat badly for taking the role in the actual performance," Sir Harry said, "after all the time Mr. Ready put into rehearsing with us."

"Oh, you shouldn't feel bad," Dolly said with a wave of her hand. "John told us all about his stage fright. What else could be done?"

"About that," John said.

Genny held her breath, closing her fingers more tightly around her fork.

John stood. "There is something I would like to announce . . . confess—" He stopped, took a breath, then straightened and looked around the table with a commanding presence. "There is something I need to tell all of you."

Dolly frowned. "You're not going to tell us you don't have stage fright, are you?"

John nodded his head, a smile curving the corners of his mouth. "I am afraid I am, Mrs. Bailey. I did not want to be in the play because I did not want anyone to recognize me."

"Why not?" demanded the admiral. "Is the Yard after you?" He chuckled at his own wit.

John did not smile. "My real name is John St. Giles, and with my uncle's death, I recently became the Duke of Evermayne."

"Evermayne!" Genny's mother stared. "You are the Duke of Evermayne's nephew?"

"My father was the Duke's brother, yes," John said. "Which means I am Evermayne now."

"John St. Giles," the admiral mused, stroking his beard. "I seem to recall some bit of scandal about you a few years ago."

Genny realized the exact moment when her mother remembered the story because she gasped and grabbed her husband's arm. "Not scandal," Helen murmured. "*Murder.*"

"Murder!" Dolly cried. "Who's a murderer?"

"If I recall correctly," Sir Harry said, steepling his fingers as he regarded John with narrowed eyes, "John St. Giles was suspected of murdering his wife."

"Oh, my heavens!" Dolly fanned her face with her hand. "John, say it isn't so. Tell everyone they've mixed you up with someone else."

"I cannot do that, Mrs. Bailey," John said. "It is the truth."

Dolly gaped, then rounded on Samuel. "You! I'm certain you knew. You endangered my daughter by bringing this killer here among us!"

Samuel shook his head. "Now, Dolly—"

"Don't you try and weasel out of this one, Samuel Breedlove!"

"I don't intend to 'weasel' out of anything. John is no killer. He saved my life—and the lives of others—several times over the years."

Virgil stood, brows lowered. "What's your game, Ready? I mean, St. Giles . . . I mean . . . whoever you are."

"No game, Mr. Bailey. Samuel asked me to watch over Annabelle while he was away. I did so. Now that Samuel and Cilla are back from their trip, I can address my own concerns. I will be leaving tomorrow for London to reveal myself to the solicitor."

"What about *our* concerns?" the admiral demanded, also rising. "You are wanted for murdering your wife, young man. And we put you in charge of our daughters!"

Helen covered her mouth. "Dear God, anything could have happened."

"Just a minute," Samuel said, also standing. "Before you go forming a lynch mob, at least listen to what he has to say."

"Perhaps *you* should have listened a little better," Dolly said. "You asked me to allow him into my home. You put our girls in danger!"

"And he did not harm them, did he?" Samuel shot back. "That should tell you something."

"Just that he didn't get the chance!" Dolly folded her arms across her ample chest.

"Here we were looking for Raventhorpe," Virgil said, "when this fellow was lurking in our midst!"

John narrowed his eyes at Virgil. "Do not associate me with Raventhorpe, Bailey. Ever."

"Why not? Seems to me the both of you are cut from the same cloth. And if that's the way it is, you can just leave my house right now."

"You are mistaken." John fisted his hands.

Sir Harry lurched to his feet, steadying himself with a hand on the table. "Now, gentlemen, let us not speak rashly. I believe the new Duke of Evermayne has more to tell us."

"That so, Ready?" the admiral demanded.

"He'd better start talking fast," Virgil muttered.

"I am wanted for questioning regarding the death of my wife, that is true," John began. "No charges have been brought, to my knowledge."

"Yet," Virgil muttered with a glare.

"He admits it!" Dolly cried.

"But I am innocent. Raventhorpe murdered my wife."

"Raventhorpe!" Sir Harry regarded him with some interest. "How do you know?"

"I was knocked unconscious that night, but whoever drugged me whispered an apology. Said Raventhorpe had threatened his daughter."

"A likely story!" Dolly huffed.

Sir Harry held up a hand. "A moment, Mrs. Bailey. We all know Raventhorpe is fond of such trickery."

"And so does Ready . . . I mean, St. Giles," blustered the admiral.

"I have known John longer than any of you," Samuel said. "He does not lie."

"He might have been fooling you all along, Samuel," Virgil said. "You can only go by what he tells you."

"I can also go by what he does. His actions tell me the truth about the kind of man that he is."

"His actions? He's been calling himself a false name and lying to our faces," Virgil said. "That should tell you something for sure!"

Samuel placed his hands on the table and leaned forward. "He didn't have to come back here, put his life in danger, just to help me save Annabelle from Raventhorpe. He hates him as much as we all do."

"Put his life in danger?" Dolly scoffed. "Seems to me he was living off everyone else's generosity."

"And it seems to me, Mrs. Bailey, that you cannot see what is right in front of you." Genny got to her feet, ignoring her mother's urgent tugs on her sleeve. "Is it so far-fetched to imagine that Lord Raventhorpe might have orchestrated things so that John would take the blame for a murder he did not commit?"

"Not at all," Sir Harry said, pursing his lips.

"Convenient, if you ask me," Dolly said. "John knows we all hate Lord Raventhorpe. Pretty smart to throw him out there as the real murderer."

"Is it pretty smart for John to travel to London tomorrow and reveal himself to Mr. Timmons, knowing that he might be arrested and executed in short order?"

"Executed?" Dolly opened her mouth, then closed it, frowning at John. "That does seem foolish."

"Doesn't seem like a passel of money and a fancy title would be worth risking your neck for," Virgil said.

"He is doing it to save His Grace's daughters." Genny walked around the table until she stood next to John. "They are in danger from an unscrupulous guardian unless John comes forward and claims the title. He is risking his life to save those little girls."

"That true, son?" the admiral asked.

John gave a curt nod.

"Would a murderer put his own life on the line for children he has never met?" Genny asked. "Would Lord Raventhorpe ever do such a thing?"

"He surely wouldn't," Virgil murmured.

"John might die as a result of what he is doing. He is sacrificing his own future to do the right thing. Is that the act of a murderer?" Genny stared down the other occupants of the room. "You are all so quick to believe rumors that you do not even recognize when the truth stares you in the face." Defiantly, she slid her hand into his.

"My little warrior," John murmured. "You court danger with your boldness."

Genny's mother frowned at their clasped hands. "Perhaps we were a little overzealous."

Cilla raised her brows at her mother. "A little?"

"Well, what are we supposed to think?" Virgil asked. "All this talk about killing his wife . . ."

"Just like the talk you heard about me," Samuel said. "You remember how Raventhorpe filled your head with lies about me? How you believed all of it so completely that Annabelle nearly married that murderer?"

Virgil nodded, dropping his gaze. "You're right. I'm sorry, John. I guess we did get a mite excited there."

"I could have told you John was no killer," Annabelle said with a little snort. "I have a feeling about these things. I spent a lot of time with him while he taught me how to defend myself, and he never hurt me in any way."

"Of course, you have a feeling about these things," Samuel said. "That's why you almost married Raven-thorpe."

Cilla placed a hand on his arm. "Not helping, dear."

Annabelle scowled at him. "Everyone was fooled by Richard. It's what he does, make chaos out of every-thing until no one knows what's going on. I don't doubt for a minute that he did kill John's wife and set him up to look guilty. It's just the kind of thing he'd do."

"I must agree with Miss Bailey," Sir Harry said. "I've known Raventhorpe for years, and he does tend to slither away from consequences like a snake in the grass. It would not surprise me at all if events happened exactly as Mr. Ready . . . I mean, the Duke said they did."

"The Duke? My stars, that's right," Dolly said. "You're the Duke!"

John nodded. "As soon as I prove my identity to Mr. Timmons."

"How you going to do that?" Virgil asked.

John smiled. "I have the necessary documents. And my mother will vouch for me."

Genny glanced up in surprise. "Your mother?"

He grinned and lifted their clasped hands to brush a kiss against her fingers. "I did not appear from beneath a cabbage leaf, you know."

The admiral cleared his throat. "Young man, I will thank you to cease fondling my daughter."

John looked at the admiral. "About that . . ."

Genny paced the hallway outside Mr. Bailey's study and strained to hear the conversation happening between John and her father. But the muffled voices reached her ears only as unintelligible rumbles from behind those sturdy wooden doors—sounds, not words.

She worried her thumbnail between her teeth. What if Papa would not let John marry her?

No, she would not think such thoughts. She lowered her hand and stiffened her spine. If Papa proved unreasonable, she would simply have to tell him the truth—that she and John had been intimate.

And then Papa would fetch his dueling pistols and spare the executioner his day's pay.

She shook her head and started nibbling on her thumbnail again. She could not tell her father the truth; it would only lessen his opinion of John, and after they had just convinced everyone he was innocent, too. She needed another idea. Something that would assure they could be together. It had all seemed so simple last night when they had made love, but the law said she needed her parents' approval to wed—a fact that she had easily ignored in the heat of passion.

What if Papa said no?

"Genny." Her mother came down the hall, a frown of disapproval creasing her brow. "What are you doing here? You are supposed to be in your room waiting for your father to summon you."

"I cannot simply sit in my room like a child while my entire future is decided," Genny said. "I am old enough to make decisions for myself."

"Is that so? Then tell me, Miss Old Enough, what about the way you led on poor Bradley Overton, then jilted him? That seemed somewhat childish to me."

Genny lifted her chin even as her cheeks heated. "You do not know the whole story."

"So tell me."

"Bradley said he loved me, but he actually only wanted to marry me to advance his career in the Navy."

Her mother blinked, clearly surprised by her candor. "Why do you think that?"

"I overheard him tell his friends."

"Oh, dear."

"I could not marry a man who lies to me, Mama."

Helen frowned. "Then what about . . ." She waved her hand at the closed doors.

"He told me the truth, even though it was not right

away. He is not hiding anything, and our time together may be very short, once he makes his identity known." The words caught in her throat, and she struggled to maintain her decorum.

"I worry about this situation, sweetheart. Especially since you apparently have feelings for the man. I do not want to see you hurt."

"Feelings? I am in love with him, Mama. And if things do not work out, I might lose him. But I would rather have had some amount of time as his wife than never to have been a part of his life at all."

Her mother's expression softened. "Oh, darling. You never take the easy way." She held out her arms, and Genny stepped into them, grateful for the comfort.

"What if Papa will not give his permission for us to wed?" Genny asked, her voice thick even to her own ears. "I do not know what I would do."

"I will speak to him."

She knew that tone; when Mama decided she would speak with Papa, she usually got what she wanted. Genny closed her eyes and prayed.

"I do not like this situation," the admiral said. He stood behind the desk with his hands folded behind his back.

Seated in the chair in front of the desk, John nodded. "I understand, sir."

"While any father would take pride in his daughter marrying a duke, you have to admit that your circumstances are somewhat unconventional."

"I—"

The admiral held up a hand, and John fell silent. "Whispers of murder hang over your head, young man, and you can certainly understand my hesitation as a father to grant you permission to wed my daughter when those whispers say you may have killed your first wife."

"I understand how it looks, Admiral—"

Genny's father scowled at him. "Stop interrupting. You are not a duke yet."

"My apologies."

The admiral gave a curt nod and began pacing. "I have my concerns. This is an awful situation for a young girl. You and I both know that this whole thing could turn out badly, and Genny would be left with a broken heart."

"I agree, and I did try to discourage her."

The admiral paused. "Huh. How did that work?"

John could not stop the smile that tugged at his mouth. "Your daughter is a very determined lady, sir. My resistance stopped her only long enough for her to regroup with another plan."

"She always was a stubborn girl." The admiral glanced at the ground, but not before John saw the pride flash across his face.

"I know this is not the perfect circumstance," John said. "I did not want to drag anyone else into this mess, but she insisted. She stood beside me even when I tried to tell her not to. How can a man resist a woman like that, Admiral?"

"Hmph. How long did it take her to wear you down?"

"A day, maybe two."

"You have more fortitude than I do, my boy." The admiral rocked on his heels for a moment. "I do not like this mess you are in. I believe your story, but unless you can discover some evidence to point away from you, the hangman may well have his way."

"I know. That is why there is no time to waste." John caught and held the admiral's gaze. "I love your daughter, sir. I plan to love her as long as there is breath in my body. And if the worst happens, and I do meet my Maker, at least I will be leaving her with the comfortable life of a duchess. She will never want for anything."

"If I could, I would spare her this heartache," the older man said. "But I suspect it is far too late for that. Her heart is engaged, whether you wed or not. She will pine for you if she does not have you—and Lord knows what else, knowing that clever girl of mine. She will no doubt be planning some wild rescue attempt if they lock you up! Better, easier, if I give my consent to this marriage." He let out a long sigh. "Apparently, a short time as your wife is preferable to no time with you at all."

John let out the breath he had been holding. "Thank you, sir. I appreciate your understanding more than I can express."

"Ha! Understand this, John St. Giles. If you so much as make her sniffle, the hangman might yet be cheated of his day. Take care of my Genny, John. There are rough days ahead." He held out his hand.

John rose and shook the admiral's hand, a wide grin spreading across his face. "She will be well cared for, Admiral, no matter what happens."

"I know." The admiral stepped back and waved a hand at the door. "I told her to wait in her room, but she is probably lurking in the hall right now, listening at the door. Go to her, son. Tell her the good news."

John did not hesitate. He reached the door in two strides and flung it open. Genny and her mother lingered in the hallway, speaking in low tones, but as he stepped through the doorway, their conversation dropped off.

Genny took a step toward him, stopped. Glanced behind him. Worried her lower lip.

"Go on, son." The admiral gave him a little push.

John hurried to Genny and right there in the hallway, dropped to one knee before her. He reached for her hand.

Genny's eyes widened. Her breath caught, and she sent a wild, hopeful look at her father behind him. Behind Genny, Helen sniffled and pressed her fist to her mouth. John gave a little tug at Genny's hand to bring her attention back to him.

"Genevieve Wallington-Willis," he began.

Genny inhaled a shaky breath as she seemed to realize the import of the moment.

"I have spoken to your father, and he has given his consent," John continued. He cleared his throat as his own emotions threatened to rob him of composure. "Genny, I love you. Will you do me the honor of becoming my wife?"

"Yes, John. Yes!"

He got to his feet, and she flung herself into his arms. Helen's soft sobs reached his ears, followed by the admiral's comforting murmurs. He buried his face in Genny's hair, the sweet scent of honeysuckle filling his lungs and love swelling his heart.

Finally, she was his. He only hoped he could protect her from the challenges to come.

Chapter 19

Evermayne
Two weeks later

The new Duchess of Evermayne glowed as only a bride could as she danced with her father in the ballroom at Evermayne. John watched them from across the room, unable to believe his good fortune. Genny was his.

"Here you are, still hiding in the shadows," Samuel said. He handed John a flute of champagne, then clinked his glass to John's. "Congratulations, my friend. I'm astonished at how quickly you pulled all this together."

"Well, Timmons had everything sorted out." John sipped at the excellent champagne that had come from Evermayne's vast wine cellar. "He had already determined that I was the rightful heir; it was simply a matter of locating me. When I walked into his office with my credentials and my mother, it took no time at all to get everything finalized."

"And the special license?"

John grinned. "That treasure of yours came in handy for that."

Samuel chuckled. "That you took ownership of the title *and* managed to marry your lady love within a fortnight simply commands my admiration, John. Or should I address you as Your Grace now?"

"We've sweated together for too many hours over the years, Captain. I do not want anything to change between us."

"Nice to see you're not letting this duke thing go to your head." Samuel grinned as a diminutive figure darted out of the crowd around the dance floor and stopped in front of John.

"Cousin, Mrs. Hart says I must have my luncheon now, but if I go to the nursery, I will miss *everything*." Lady Marianne St. Giles stomped her tiny foot, then gazed up at John with big blue eyes inherited from her late mother, a renowned beauty. "Please say I may stay longer, Cousin. *Please*."

John looked down into that cherubic face, and his resolve to be stern wilted. Though he had only been their guardian for a matter of days, the duke's daughters, seven-year-old Marianne and twelve-year-old Felicity, had already wound themselves around his heart.

"Your governess knows what is best for you," he said in a halfhearted attempt to appear somewhat parental.

She simply held up her arms, regarding him expectantly. Unable to resist the silent plea, he lifted the little girl and settled her on his hip.

Once their faces were level, Lady Marianne patted his shoulder as if approving the action. "I know I should mind Mrs. Hart, Cousin, but I am getting a new mama today, and that is a special occasion. Do you not agree?" She tilted her head, her light brown curls tumbling with the movement, and gave him a smile that showed her tiny white teeth.

"Of course a new mama is a special occasion." John sent a pleading look at Samuel, who only shook his head and hid his smile behind a sip of champagne.

The little girl propped her elbow on John's shoulder and gestured with her free hand. "If it is a special occasion, I would expect that Felicity and I should not be banished to the nursery."

"Uh . . . perhaps not."

"Marianne!" The horrified hiss came from somewhere near his waist. "What are you doing? We are supposed to go to the nursery for luncheon."

Man and child both glanced down to see Lady Felicity, Marianne's older sister, staring up at them with her arms crossed and worry in her eyes.

"I am attempting to convince Cousin John that we should stay," Marianne said.

"It is not our place." Lady Felicity glanced around,

as if concerned about gossip. Blonder than her sister, Felicity had John's uncle's dark eyes, and, like her sire, she saw much and trusted little. After ascertaining no scandal was imminent, she turned that suspicious gaze back on him. "Cousin, do you think it is appropriate for a bridegroom to be holding a child at his wedding? It makes for a most odd spectacle."

"Oh, do not be such a stickler, Lissy."

"But he is the *Duke* now," Felicity whispered. "It is not done." And lower still, "Father would never have done such a thing."

The pain beneath her words touched him. He set Marianne back on her feet, then crouched down so he was more on a level with both girls. "I am the Duke, true," he said, "but I have not been one for very long, so you must forgive me any missteps. Perhaps you can help guide me."

Felicity hesitated, then gave a short nod. Marianne nodded enthusiastically.

"Excellent. Now, Felicity, while a wedding is a very important occasion, I consider this one to be doubly so because not only do I get a wife, but you get a new mother. Genny and I will be your guardians, and we are very much looking forward to making you a part of our family."

"Do I have to call you Papa?" Felicity asked, her voice wavering.

"Not if you do not want to. I know you loved your father very much, so perhaps you do not feel right addressing anyone else as Papa. If that is the case, you may call me John or Cousin or Evermayne or whatever strikes your fancy."

"I like Cousin," Marianne said, sending her sister a look of challenge.

"I can call you Cousin," Felicity said, her shoulders visibly relaxing.

"Good. Now, Felicity, I am going to ask Mrs. Hart to allow you girls to eat with the rest of the guests. This is your family, too, and you should share in the festivities."

This won him a little smile from Felicity and a huge one from the irrepressible Marianne.

"Ladies! There are you are!" Mrs. Hart arrived, clearly harried by the escape of her charges. "I am so sorry, Your Grace. The children are supposed to return to the nursery for their noon meal."

"Calm yourself, Mrs. Hart. I would like to ask that you deviate from your normal schedule and allow the ladies to remain with the rest of us for their noon meal. This is a very special day, and I should like to have my whole family around me."

Mrs. Hart blinked. "Well . . . of course. If you insist."

"I do. And I also insist that you help yourself to some of the wedding breakfast. This way you may supervise the girls and still share in the joy of the day."

Surprise melted into pleasure on the woman's face. "Of course. Thank you, Your Grace. Come along, ladies."

"Thank you, Cousin," Felicity said, and made her curtsy.

"Yes, thank you, Cousin!" Marianne curtsied and followed the action with an audacious wink before Mrs. Hart shooed them along.

"The little one is going to be a heartbreaker," Samuel said. "They seem to be getting very fond of you."

John heard the concern in his voice. Shared it. "I know."

"If things do not go well—"

"I know. But at least they will have Genny."

"You underestimate your impact, I think."

"What should I do? Be cold to them so they will not miss me if I am hanged?" John clamped his mouth closed, shook his head, sighed. "I apologize for snapping. I am well aware of the pain they may suffer if Scotland Yard decides I am the villain, but I cannot be distant. It is not my way."

"I would no doubt feel the same way. The whole situation is monstrous."

"I beg your pardon, Your Grace."

John looked at the servant who had interrupted them. "Yes, Tristan?"

"A gentleman is here to see you, Your Grace. Ernest explained it was your wedding day, but he is most insistent." He lowered his voice. "He says he is from Scotland Yard."

His blood chilled. Had they come for him already, today, on the day of his wedding?

"I will see him in my study," John said. "Samuel, please make my excuses."

"I will."

John headed out of the ballroom.

The inspector from Scotland Yard stood in the center of the study, perusing the leather-bound volumes contained in the huge floor-to-ceiling bookshelves from his position in the middle of the room. He was a large man, broad in the shoulders with a few extra pounds around the middle. Silver peppered his dark hair, and his nose gave the impression it had been broken more than once. When John entered the room, the man gave him a wide, friendly smile, but his sharp blue-eyed gaze gave the impression that he missed very little.

"Your Grace." The inspector bowed. "I am Inspector Brooks of Scotland Yard. I apologize for disrupting your wedding celebration. Might I extend my congratulations?"

"Thank you, Inspector." John moved behind his desk and gestured toward the chairs on the other side. "Please take a seat."

The big man moved with surprising grace—probably

good in a fight, John thought—and sat down. He pulled a worn notebook and silver mechanical pencil from his pocket, then withdrew a set of spectacles and slipped them on. "I am investigating the death of your late wife, Elizabeth St. Giles."

"Of course," John said, projecting calm while his guts knotted.

Brooks flipped through the pages of his battered book. "According to witnesses, you were last seen attending a ball at the home of Lord and Lady Canthrope on the twelfth of May, 1869. This was the last time your wife was seen alive."

"That is correct."

"It was also the last time you were seen in England until your return approximately a week ago." Brooks regarded him over the top of his spectacles. "Why did you leave England, Your Grace? Certainly you had to know there would be questions about the circumstances of your wife's death."

"At the time, my uncle, the previous Duke, was the head of the family. He decided it would be better if I left the country until the scandal died down."

"So the Duke coerced you to leave?" He made a notation in his book.

" 'Coerced' is a hard word, Inspector." John frowned. "The Duke was the head of the family. He could make life very easy or very difficult." When the inspector raised his brows in inquiry, John added, "Let us say he encouraged me to leave until the scandal died down and leave it at that."

"So the Duke *suggested* you leave England. Did you give no thought to the investigation that would follow?"

"I was young, Inspector, and besides, I had no knowledge of what had happened to Elizabeth until my uncle told me."

"You did not notice when she did not leave the Canthrope home with you?"

The disbelief in the man's voice grated. "I am still not certain what happened to me that night. I . . . blacked out, then awoke later in the gardens when the last of the guests were leaving. When I could not find Elizabeth, I assumed she had gone home without me."

"I see. Had you been drinking that night, Your Grace?"

"Some, but I was far from foxed."

"Hmmm." The inspector made a note in the book.

"I told you, I was *not* foxed." John hesitated. How much should he reveal? Could he trust this man to listen to him? "I think I was drugged."

The inspector lifted his head. "Indeed?"

"I was looking for Elizabeth. She had a habit of wandering off on her own during these sorts of affairs. There was a servant who told me he had seen her in the gardens, led me out there. Then I felt a prick on my neck, and, suddenly, everything went dark." Even now, the memory lingered in his mind like a spider in the corner. "When I woke up, it was hours later, and the ball was nearly over. I could not find Elizabeth, so I went home."

Brooks flipped through the scribbled pages of his notebook. "According to the other guests, you were disoriented, staggering." He raised his gaze to John's. "Sounds like you were indeed foxed that night, Your Grace."

"I told you, I was drugged. I went home and passed out, and I did not hear that Elizabeth had been murdered until the Duke told me the next morning."

"Why would someone go to such lengths to make you look guilty of murder?" The inspector's reasonable tone gave no indication whether he believed John's story or not. "From what witnesses have told us, you had some trouble controlling your wife, Your Grace. Also, you were clearly impaired in some way that evening. What's not to say you drank too much and accidentally killed your wife in a fit of rage?"

John fisted his hands on the desk. "I am no killer, Inspector."

Brooks sat back in his chair as if they were just passing the time in casual conversation. "If you did not kill her, who did?"

"Raventhorpe."

"Raventhorpe? The Earl of Raventhorpe?" Brooks raised his eyebrows.

"That is my guess. Raventhorpe was my rival for her hand. After we married, he began an affair with my wife." He could see the man did not believe him, and he leaned forward, pressing his conviction. "The earl is not all he appears to be, Inspector. You could talk to Samuel Breedlove. The earl tried to kill him. Or Miss Annabelle Bailey. He kidnapped her and tried to force marriage on her."

"Samuel Breedlove." Brooks scribbled in his book. "A friend of yours?"

"Yes, we worked together aboard ship back in America."

"And what about Miss Bailey? What is the connection there?"

"I recently spent several days as a guest at a house party at her parents' home."

"I see."

"Do you? Do you really, Inspector Brooks?" John waited until the investigator met his gaze. "I did not kill Elizabeth. Perhaps if you speak to some of the others I have mentioned, you will see that I am telling the truth."

"Perhaps." The inspector closed his notebook and pocketed both that and his pencil. John could not tell from his impassive expression whether or not he was inclined to believe him. "I will make inquiries of the people you mentioned. In the meantime, I should let you rejoin your wedding celebration."

"Thank you." John stood as the investigator rose, still uncertain about how well his story had been received. "Please let me know if you have any further questions."

"Oh, I will. By the by, where are you and your bride going on your honeymoon?"

"We have postponed our wedding trip. The duke's daughters only recently lost their father, and we did not want to go away together too soon after so many changes in the girls' lives. There will be time for a wedding trip later on." *He hoped.*

"That is indeed good news." Brooks walked to the door. "But I would advise you not to go on any trips until this matter is settled, Your Grace." He paused with his hand on the doorknob and looked back. "It might give the wrong impression."

John gave a tight nod. "Understood. A footman will show you out."

"Please convey my best wishes to your bride," the inspector said, then stepped out into the hallway.

John stood where he was for a long moment, not fooled by the seemingly casual conversation he had just had with the inspector. The man thought he was guilty, but he would investigate everything thoroughly before accusing the Duke of Evermayne of murder.

Tomorrow, he would go through his father's notes

again. There had to be something in there that would point the finger at Raventhorpe, or at least prove John's innocence. If not. . .

If not, his new wife would find herself a widow before she even had time to be a bride.

Pushing the notion to the back of his mind, he left the room to rejoin his wedding celebration.

The guests had left. The sun had set. The girls slept peacefully upstairs in their nursery. And the new Duchess of Evermayne regarded herself in her looking glass as she prepared for her wedding night.

The thin white cotton nightdress she wore clung to the curves of her body in a way that hid nothing, with provocative lace insets to tease at a glimpse of skin and covered with a sheer white pretense of a robe. She had left her hair hanging loose about her shoulders, and even though she had shared her body with John before, she still reveled in the magic of the night.

They had said the words, and now she would become his wife in truth.

As if he had heard her thoughts, the door between the rooms opened, and John stepped through. He had shed his wedding attire and wore a lush robe of dark blue velvet. She rose from her dressing table as he closed the door behind him and turned to face her.

"You look beautiful."

Heat warmed her cheeks. "I want to look beautiful for you."

"You always do." His lips quirked. "Even if you were naked, I would still find you beautiful."

"John!" She laughed.

"I love the way you laugh." He came to her, sweeping her into his arms. The flimsy material of her attire could not block the heat of his flesh, and her own body responded, pulse accelerating, heat curling low in her belly.

"You make me happy," she whispered, then gasped as he peeled down her sheer robe with one firm yank, trapping her hands at her sides when the tie prevented further disrobing.

"Mine," he murmured, then pressed her hard against him, taking her mouth in a kiss that drowned her in hot sensation.

Arousal seared through her, searching, hungry, demanding. She struggled to free her hands, but he held her fast, rubbing her against him. Her breasts swelled at the friction, her nipples surging to hard points that quickly became sensitized to excruciating pleasure. She groaned, surrendered, became pliant in his arms. Anything he wanted was his.

"What do you want, sweetheart?" He whispered the words against her throat as he nipped the flesh there. "Tell me."

"I want to touch you." When he raised his head to look at her, she stood on tiptoe and pressed her mouth to his, tasting him, trying to convey what she felt.

His hands clenched in her clothing, then he ripped his mouth from hers. "Yes. Touch me."

She let out a long breath. "Help me."

He jerked open the tie of her wrapper, peeled it down her arms. The instant the garment was gone, she reached for the belt of his robe, tugged it open. He was naked beneath it, his erection thrusting forward as if eager for her touch.

She reached for him, curious, fascinated. When she closed her fingers around the shaft, his breath hissed from between his lips, and he leaned his head back, closing his eyes. He reached for her blindly, clasping his hand on her shoulder and thrusting his hips forward as she continued to explore him. Energized by his enthusiasm, she stood on tiptoe and kissed him, still running her fingers up and down that hot, hard flesh.

A guttural noise erupted from his throat. He pulled back from her so her hands fell away from him. He shrugged off the robe, let it drop to the floor.

She started to unbutton her nightdress, and he joined in. Once the last button came loose, he grabbed her gown in both hands and tugged it over her head, then threw it across the room. She stood before him, naked, uncertain. She started to cover her bosom, her sex, but he guided her hands so that she cupped her breasts.

"That's right, offer them to me." He bent and took one nipple into his mouth.

She shuddered, whimpered. Wet heat bloomed between her legs. Her head spun, rational thought swirling away. She swayed. He grabbed her hips, steadying her without ceasing his delicious torment.

"My wife." He tongued her nipple, then moved to the other one, stoking the fires within her even higher. "God, I love you."

"I love you. I want to . . . I hardly know what I want," she groaned. She dropped her hand, found his shaft. "I want this." When he looked up at her, his gaze hot and wild and hungry, she added, "I want my husband."

"Aw, sweetheart." He dropped random kisses on her bosom and neck as he straightened, then took her mouth in a carnal, openmouthed kiss that shut down her brain and singed her nerve endings. When he slipped his hand between her legs, stroked her there, her knees nearly buckled.

"Bed," he commanded, bumping her back a step with his body.

"Bed," she agreed, thrusting her hands into his hair and holding on as he fed on her mouth again and guided her backwards. When she felt the edge of the mattress against her bottom, she tried to ease onto it without breaking the kiss. She missed and would have slid to the floor if he had not caught her.

"Easy, love." With a grin, he bent, grabbed her with one arm and stood up with her draped over his shoulder.

"John!" Scandalized, aroused, she laughed and slapped her hands against his back.

"My, my, what is this?" His big hand caressed her bare buttock. "What a lovely bottom you have, wife." He gave her a light slap.

"John!" The light smack fueled her desire, stunning her. When he dumped her on the bed, then came down on top of her, his weight crushing her into the mattress, that desire exploded into aching, maddening need.

His erection rubbed against her thigh, and she spread her legs, arching her hips. "Take me, John. Make me a wife."

He sucked in a breath, his dark eyes ferocious as he looked into hers. He took her wrists, pinned them to either side of her head. "Tell me you love me."

"I love you."

"Tell me you want me." He rocked against her, nudged her with his shaft.

"I do want you." She tugged at her hands, but he held her fast. Inexplicably, this only increased the feral need raging for release. "Make me your wife, John. Please, before I go mad."

"My wife," he whispered, lowering himself between her thighs.

"Your wife," she agreed, then cried out as he eased inside her, so slowly she wanted to scream. He filled her completely, stoking the ache, easing and inflaming the hunger all at once.

"Mine," he murmured.

"Yours."

He grinned like a pirate, then hooked his arms beneath her bent knees and sent her to paradise, claiming her irrevocably as his wife.

Chapter 20

"**L**ady Evermayne."

Genny grunted and buried her face in the pillow.

"Lady Evermayne." The sleep-roughened baritone rumbled near her ear. "Wake up, my love."

Genny frowned and eased one eyelid open. "What?"

John smiled down at her, his jaw darkened by his morning beard, lending him the look of a rogue. "Are you always so out of sorts in the morning, wife? Perhaps I shall have to brighten your mood." He cuddled against her, his erection prodding her hip.

"Heavens, John! How can you be so randy so early in the morning?" Despite her protest, another part of her, that newly discovered sensual side of her, thrilled at his condition.

"'Tis a man's natural state upon waking, love, and more so when I wake up with you." He nuzzled her neck and cupped her breast.

The gentle hum of desire flickered to life in a body

she had thought completely sated. She shifted beneath the covers, winced as her aching muscles protested. "You are quite the enthusiastic lover."

"Is that a complaint?"

"Not at all. Just an observation." She rolled over so she could look at him.

He propped himself up on his elbow, then bent and kissed her with lingering thoroughness. "Good morning, wife."

"Good morning, husband." Curious, she rubbed her hand along his jaw. "Scratchy."

"I will shave this morning." He studied her with concern creasing his brow. "How do you feel? Was I too rough last night?"

"No." She stretched, grimaced as her muscles protested. "I am certain I will become used to it."

"I apologize. I will endeavor to be more gentle."

"I am fine, John. Truly."

He traced his fingers along her cheek. "My little warrior. You need only tell me if I need to move more slowly."

She could not stop the grin that curved her lips. "Well, that worked, too."

He laughed and dropped a kiss on her lips. "I have created a monster."

"No, you have created a wife. I want to be a good wife to you, John." She looked him straight in the eye.

"And as your wife, I do not expect secrets between us. You have not told me about your visitor yesterday."

He sighed, lifted her hand, and pressed a kiss to it. "How did you hear about that?"

"Believe it or not, John Re—John St. Giles, I do notice when my husband leaves his own wedding celebration. Who was he?"

"I was hoping to spare you any worry."

"Too late. I have been worrying since yesterday. Who was he?"

"Inspector Brooks from Scotland Yard."

"What?" She sat up, her playfulness evaporating. "What did he want? You are still here . . . why? What did you tell him?"

"Calm down, love." John sat up, then put his arm around her and leaned back, cuddling with her against the pillows. "He asked some questions. I answered them. I also told him about Raventhorpe."

"Did he believe you?"

"I have no idea. I did give him Samuel's name and Annabelle's. I hope their stories will influence him to believe in my innocence."

"What if it does not? What if he decides you are guilty?"

"He does not seem a man to make snap judgments. He will investigate, and hopefully, in the meantime, I will find clues in my father's journal that will clear my name."

"What if he comes back today and takes you away?"

"Now, now." He tightened his embrace. "We cannot think that way. We only have this moment, and we cannot borrow trouble. I know I am innocent. There must be some proof of it somewhere."

"I am scared, John." She fought back panic choking her. "I only just found you. I cannot lose you already."

He remained silent for a long moment. "Perhaps we should not have wed," he said finally. "The last thing I want is to hurt you."

"Stop right there." She sat up so she could look him in the face. "I chose this of my own free will. I would rather have a short time with you than no time at all. I just . . . we have only been married a day. Is it selfish of me to want more than that?"

"No, sweetheart. Not at all." He caressed her cheek. "I do not deserve you, Genny. Your love humbles me." He leaned in and pressed his lips to hers, his mouth gentle, reverent. As if he tried to communicate with a single kiss the power of his love.

Her own heart slowly turned over in her chest. She took his face in her hands, responded to the kiss with just as much care, as much feeling. Did he know? Could he feel the depth of her love?

"Hey, now." He broke the kiss, then swiped her cheek with his thumb, holding it up so she could see the dampness. "Do not cry, love. Please. It breaks my heart."

"I did not know I was." She sniffled, swiped at the moisture trailing down her face. "I do not want our time together to be one of tears."

"Agreed." He tucked a lock of her hair behind her ear. "No more tears. Smiles and cries of passion only."

He surprised a laugh from her, one that emerged half like a sob. "I never realized how lusty you are, wicked man."

"I hid it well when I thought I could not have you." He made a face. "It was not easy, not with you invading my room in your nightdress all the time."

"Well, I had the most improper dreams about you."

His features sharpened with interest. "Oh?"

"They kept me awake some nights."

"Only some nights? I must have been better at hiding my lust for you than I thought."

"I am fairly new to lust." An impish impulse had her yanking the bedclothes back to display the nearly irresistible erection that had been tenting the sheets. "Though I am willing to learn."

"I thought you were tired. And in pain."

"Is this painful?" She trailed her fingers along the hard shaft.

He narrowed his eyes. "It's getting there."

"Maybe I can help you." She shoved aside her own covers and straddled him. "Will this work?"

"Oh, yeah." He grasped her hips while she gripped his shoulders. "Hold tight, sweetheart." He guided her so she sank down on him, taking him deeply into her body. "Oh, God, yes."

"My goodness." At his urging, she began to move up and down, at first tentatively, but then with more confidence. "This is like riding my gelding."

He barked a laugh. "Hardly, love."

She laughed. "Well, no, you are hardly gelded, are you?"

"Hell, no." He tugged her head down and began kissing her. Slowly. As if he had all the time in the world to learn her taste, to savor her essence. He barely moved inside her, flexing his hips so that they rocked together in an easy, gentle rhythm.

Somehow, his tenderness devastated her more thoroughly than his wild passion. The tension simmered rather than boiled, building steadily, one slick stroke at a time. She grabbed the headboard, clinging as he moved her the way he wanted, teasing her with deep, slow kisses to her mouth and breasts. He unraveled her, one layer at a time, taking her apart, viewing her essence, learning her secrets. Swamped by emotion, stripped bare by sensation, she spoke from her heart.

"Give me your child, John. Give me a piece of you I can hold forever."

His face tensed with a ferocity that should have scared her but only thrilled her. He gripped her hips more tightly, closed his eyes. Thrust once, twice. A guttural cry ripped from him as he surged one last time and held her there while he shuddered.

She watched him, fascination and tenderness and satisfaction curving her lips. She had pleased him, driven him past his famous control. And, just maybe, they had made a child this morning.

He opened his eyes, and the way he looked at her—utter possession, boundless love—set her quivering. He pulled her head down, kissed her. Then he flipped them over so she landed on her back with him on top of her. His smile had her parting her legs even as he slipped his fingers between them.

"Your turn."

Father Holm urged his aging nag faster as it pulled his little cart along the road. Finally, after all these weeks, he knew for certain where he could find John St. Giles! The letter rested in his pocket like a lead brick, the onerous task of finding its owner beginning to weigh on him. But it was his sacred duty, and he took such things very seriously.

John St. Giles had just become the new Duke of Evermayne. All he needed to do was go to the Evermayne estate and hand the letter to the new duke. That had been the stipulation, that he personally deliver the letter to none other than John St. Giles. Then his duty would be discharged.

"Stop!" A brawny masked man emerged from the trees at the side of the road, pointing a revolver at him.

Father Holm slowed the cart. "I am a man of the Church! Do not incur God's wrath today, my good sir. Step back from the temptation of thievery!"

"I said stop." The fellow came closer, his weapon never wavering.

The vicar pulled up on the reins, bringing the cart to a halt. "Think about what you are doing, young man. I have no wealth for you to steal."

"So you say." The brigand signaled with his weapon. "Get down, Father."

"Think about what you are doing, my son!"

"I am. And what I'm doing can get me out of a nasty fix."

The vicar hesitated, then slowly began to climb out of the cart. "You will regret this wickedness, young man," he warned.

Peter watched the vicar climb out of the cart and resisted the urge to wipe the sweat from his brow. Damn Raventhorpe anyway for sending him on this mad quest.

Find the vicar, he had said. Find out what he wants from St. Giles. They had split up to look for the holy man, and only by pure luck had Peter spotted him as the cart started along the road to Evermayne.

This fellow might well know something that would allow Peter to finally escape Raventhorpe's employ. At the very least, perhaps this St. Giles fellow would pay for whatever information the vicar had for him.

"Young man, think about your soul," the vicar said, once his feet were on the ground. "'Thou shall not steal!'"

"Keep your sermons. What do you want with John St. Giles?"

The vicar stiffened. "I do not know what you are talking about."

"Leave off, Father. Everyone knows you have been coming around here looking for the bloke for weeks now. What do you want with him?"

"That is a private matter between me and His Grace."

"His Grace?"

"His Grace the duke."

"What does a duke have to do with this St. Giles fellow?"

The vicar gave him a cautious look. "Surely you have heard? John St. Giles just assumed the title Duke of Evermayne. It was in all the newspapers."

"Oh, sure. Sure. I knew that." He hadn't actually, but that didn't matter now. If this St. Giles fellow was a duke now, he could certainly afford to pay for whatever secrets the vicar harbored.

"My son, stop this madness. Allow me to deliver my message to His Grace. I assure you, I have nothing of value worth stealing."

"Yes, you do, Father. The message is what I want."

The vicar stiffened. "No. I am on a mission to fulfill a sacred promise. I cannot give you the message. It is meant only for the eyes of John St. Giles."

"For his eyes? So it's a written message?"

The vicar gave a little groan. "Yes, a message from a dead man. Surely of no value to you."

"Where is this message?"

"I will not give it to you."

Peter pointed the gun in his face. "Yes, you will."

The vicar raised his chin. "I will not."

"Damn it, Vicar! I don't want to shoot you."

"Then do not shoot. Let us go our separate ways, my son."

"I can't. I need that message."

"No. You will have to shoot me."

"Damn it." He stared at the holy man for a moment. "I don't want to go to hell for killing a vicar, but I *will* get that message."

The shorter man folded his arms. "I refuse."

"Sorry about this." He shoved his revolver in his belt, then swung a fist and clocked the churchman.

The vicar fell to the ground, groaning and rubbing his jaw. Peter grabbed him by the front of his coat, dragged him to his feet, and started pummeling the smaller man. Each time he struck, he said, "Give me the message."

Each time, the vicar refused.

Finally, the older man collapsed, unconscious.

Peter stared down at the beaten pastor, scowling. How the devil was he supposed to find this message if the fellow couldn't tell him where it was? Finally, it occurred to him. He could search the man, the cart, any bags he had. He started with the man and hit gold almost immediately. The vicar carried an envelope in his coat pocket. A name was scrawled across it, though the letters meant little to him since he could not read. He recognized a 'G' though; he had seen that letter when someone wrote his own name. And he knew that St. Giles had a 'G' in it.

"This has to be it," Peter muttered. He stuffed the envelope in his own pocket. He started to stand, then noticed a coin in the road. "Must have fallen out of his coat," he muttered, and bent down to pick it up.

A shot rang over his head and struck the cart.

The old nag screamed, then set off at a run, taking the wagon along with it. And thundering straight at him was a masked man dressed in black, riding a black stallion. On a stretch of road that had once belonged to Raventhorpe's family.

Black Bill.

As the highwayman raised his gun again, Peter jerked his own out of his belt and fired it at the approaching rider, causing him to swerve. Then he ran like the devil himself was after him and plunged into the woods.

Gunshots brought Father Holm out of his stupor. When he opened his eyes, a masked man in black—a different one from the one who had assaulted him—was leaning over him. He should have been afraid, but something in the man's calm demeanor made the vicar believe the man meant him no harm.

"How many fingers, Father?" the masked man asked.

"Three," the vicar answered.

"Good. Let's get you out of here. Can you ride?"

The vicar nodded. "If we go slowly. I am somewhat the worse for wear, I am afraid."

"Where were you headed, Father? Perhaps I can assist."

"Evermayne." His head began to spin again. He patted his coat, shoved his hand in the pocket. Empty. "Gone," he whispered.

"What is gone?" the highwayman asked.

"Letter. Gone."

"You had a letter for Evermayne?"

"Gone. He took it." His throat clogged as he realized he had failed his sacred duty. "May God forgive me."

"Easy now. Let us get you to safety, then we will deal

with the matter of this letter." The highwayman shoved his shoulder beneath the vicar's arm, then helped him to his feet and over to his horse.

The vicar hesitated as they neared the huge black stallion.

"Have no fear of Tarik, Father." The highwayman patted the horse's neck. "He will carry us to safety like the wind he was named for."

With help from the stranger, Father Holm soon found himself seated behind the fellow on the back of the beast.

"Yalla!" the highwayman cried, and they took off like a blazing fire down the road toward Evermayne.

"Be careful, Felicity!" Genny called.

The little girl screeched and ran away just as John would have caught her. Genny and Marianne muffled their giggles as the blindfolded Duke snatched thin air.

"I know she is here somewhere," he said, lowering his voice to an exaggerated growl.

Felicity ran across the patch of lawn where they played, then circled around and crept up behind John. She poked him, then sped away as he whirled to try to catch her. Genny clapped a hand over her mouth to stop her laughter, but Marianne squealed with mirth. John stopped and snapped his head toward them. "I think I hear Marianne!" He lunged across the grass with his arms extended.

Marianne screamed and darted behind Genny just as John reached them. She did not have a chance to escape; he grabbed her arm and held her fast.

"You have to guess who it is!" Marianne shouted, her blue eyes sparkling and her cheeks rosy with exertion.

"And if I guess correctly, this person"—he held up Genny's arm—"becomes the 'blind man?'"

"Yes!" Even the normally reserved Felicity bounced in place as if she would have to dart away any moment.

"Can you guess who it is?" Marianne asked.

"I do not think it is Mrs. Hart," John said, sending the girls into peals of laughter. "Nor do I think it is Ernest, the butler."

"No!" Felicity howled, covering her mouth with her hands.

"Who could it be, then?" He lifted one hand to Genny's face, tracing her cheeks, her lips. "Whoever this is, she certainly is pretty."

Genny tried to keep a straight face but could not stop her lips from curving into a smile.

"Who could this be? Hmmm." He loosened his grip on her arm, slid his hand down to find the plain gold band on her finger. "I think this might be my Genny." He leaned in, kissed her gently. "Yes, that is definitely my Genny."

"You have to be the blind man now, Genny!" Marianne shrieked.

John whipped off the scarf they used as a blindfold and handed it to her, grinning.

She took it. "I think you cheated, Your Grace. I do not recall any rules about kissing in Blind Man's Bluff."

"Exactly. Which means it was not against the rules." He winked at her.

"Oh, no!" Felicity groaned. "Here comes Ernest. I bet Mrs. Hart sent him to fetch us for our lessons."

Marianne scowled. "I do not want lessons! I want to play with Cousin John and Genny!"

"Now, now." John flicked his finger along the little girl's nose. "We all must do what is required of us before we can do what we would like to do."

"Lessons are required of us," Felicity said with a wrinkle of her nose.

"You do not have lessons, Cousin John," Marianne said. "What is required of you?"

John crouched down so they were eye to eye. "Taking care of Evermayne and everyone in it—including you two ladies." He stood up as the butler reached them. "Have you come to fetch the ladies, Ernest?"

The sharp-faced butler glanced at the children. "No, Your Grace." He returned his attention to John. "A . . . visitor has arrived."

"Who is it?"

"A vicar, I believe. He has been injured."

"A vicar? What does he want here?"

"He asked for you, Your Grace. And . . ." The butler paused, frowned as if searching for words. "He was delivered in a most unusual manner."

"Delivered?" Genny asked. "Like a package?"

"He was left at the door by a . . . I believe it was by Black Bill."

"See to the children, Ernest." John took Genny's hand and led her back to the house, leaving the butler to round up the girls for their lessons. "A vicar," he muttered. "Someone said something to me about a vicar. Who was it?"

"What does he want with you?" Genny asked, hurrying to keep up with his long strides.

"I suppose we are about to find out."

The servants had put the vicar in the drawing room. When John and Genny entered, the older man struggled to sit up from his half-lying position on the sofa. He looked to be a fairly short man, his light brown hair balding at the crown, and he looked as if he had been beaten. A bruise shadowed his jaw and his cheekbone, and he moved with the care of someone in great pain.

"I am the Duke of Evermayne," John said. "This is Her Grace, the Duchess of Evermayne. And you are . . . ?"

"Father Cornelius Holm." The holy man got himself settled in what was apparently a comfortable spot on the sofa, then tried to smile. "Your given name is John St. Giles, Your Grace?"

"It is."

"Ahh." He smiled as if relieved. "I am the vicar of the small parish of Elford-by-the-Sea. I have been looking for you for some weeks now."

"Elford-by-the-Sea?" John guided Genny to an armchair, then settled himself into its twin. "That was the village my father visited the day he died. Why have you been looking for me?"

"I was fulfilling a vow." The vicar's voice roughened, and he coughed. John got up to ring for a servant.

"Some water for the vicar," he said, when a footman responded. Turning back to his guest, he came to crouch down in front of him. "Father, what vow were you fulfilling? One for my father?"

The vicar shook his head. "For one of my parishioners. He entrusted me with a letter addressed to you. I was to deliver it personally into your hands."

"A letter?" John stood. "From whom?"

"A man named Jack Norman."

The footman returned with the vicar's water before John could say anything else. He moved aside so the footman could serve their guest, but he could not stand still and prowled back and forth between the sofa and where Genny sat. Jack Norman. He knew that name.

The servant left, and he waited until the holy man

had sipped some water and seemed a bit steadier before he picked up the conversation again. "My father went to Elford-by-the-Sea the day he died . . . to see Jack Norman."

Behind him, Genny sucked in a breath, but Father Holm just nodded. "That he did. 'Tis not my tale to tell, but Jack had regrets in life, as many of us do. He wrote down those regrets in a letter to you and entrusted me with it. In case something happened to him, he said."

John tensed. "And did something happen to him?"

The vicar nodded. "'Twas a black day indeed. First his daughter and her new husband were murdered by brigands on their wedding trip, then poor Jack took his own life the very same night."

"How terrible," Genny breathed.

"At least," the vicar said with a meaningful look at John, "that is what we are led to believe."

"You do not think he killed himself."

"Why would he? His daughter had just married, and the news of the tragedy did not reach our village until the next morning. He had no reason to take his own life." He let out a big sigh and shook his head. "There was evil afoot that night, I tell you. Upon his death, I retrieved the letter and tried to find you, but to no avail."

"When was this?"

"Four years ago. Just a few days after your father died."

John narrowed his eyes. "I do not believe in coincidence, Father."

"Neither do I. 'Tis evil, I tell you."

Or Raventhorpe. "I only just returned to England a few weeks ago, Father. How did you know to come looking for me now?"

"Because the duke died. With Lord Phillip gone, you were the natural heir. I assumed you would claim the title eventually. In the meantime, I went to all the places you might go, hoping to find you. I went to your parents' house, then to see Mr. Timmons, the solicitor for the estate, then to the inns and taverns all around the area. It was not until I saw in the newspaper that you had claimed the title that I knew where to find you."

"You must be exhausted with all that traveling," Genny said.

"I did it a bit at a time. The church cannot run itself, and I am the only vicar in residence. I went looking for you when my schedule allowed. I once had to forgo my search when I had three funerals and a wedding in the same week!"

"And somehow you found me." Was this the miracle he had been searching for? He forced himself to be calm though anticipation churned in his gut. "Where is this letter? I am most eager to read it."

"Ah. And that is where my tale takes its own tragic twist. The letter was stolen."

"Stolen!" Genny cried.

"Who stole it?" John demanded. "Was it Black Bill? They say he brought you here."

"That fellow? No, not at all. It was another thief entirely. A big fellow who stopped me on the road and demanded the letter. When I refused to give it to him, he beat me into unconsciousness and stole it. The other man came afterwards, found me in the road, and brought me here."

"Blast it." John turned away, stared at the insipid watercolor hanging above the mantel. "If it had been Black Bill, we might have had a chance of recovering it. He is something of a . . . gentleman thief."

"How extraordinary," the vicar said.

"But this other man . . . I have no idea who he could be."

"He seemed to know about the letter," Father Holm said. "He did not demand my purse, simply demanded the message. He said it would get him out of a nasty fix."

"If it is not Black Bill, who could it be?" Genny asked. "Raventhorpe?"

"I doubt it," John said. "He rarely handles these tasks himself. He usually has a servant to do it or hires someone."

"Peter Green?" Genny suggested. "If he is trying to get free of Raventhorpe . . ."

John rubbed his chin. "That is certainly a possibility."

"I am so sorry, Your Grace," the vicar said. "I have failed you, and I have failed Jack Norman. Clearly whatever he wanted to tell you in this letter was of great import to him."

John met Genny's gaze, took strength from the love shining there. "Yes. To me as well."

"I suppose," the vicar said, "what we need now is a miracle."

Chapter 21

Raventhorpe lingered in the corner of the tavern, nursing an ale and listening to the chatter around him. With each minute that passed, his temper burned hotter.

Peter was late.

He detested tardiness. He believed in precision, in careful planning and clever execution of those plans. Peter Green was neither careful nor clever, a fact that had begun to chafe. The oaf had fallen into certain bad habits, such as thinking and asking questions. He really should have killed the fool when he'd had the chance.

But he hadn't, and now he smelled mutiny. The more time that passed, the more he suspected that Peter had decided to enact some plans of his own. Some of the men from the livery had been talking earlier of a horse and cart that came back without a driver—the vicar's rig. He suspected Peter had succeeded in robbing the vicar of his secret and now plotted to betray *him*.

It's what *he* would have done.

If he had not been so furious, he might have actually drummed up a little appreciation for the idiot's courage. He would be certain to tell him that.

Right before he killed him.

The miracle arrived in the form of a small boy at the kitchen door early the next morning. John had instructed the staff to alert him to anything odd, and a child demanding a shilling in exchange for delivering a message to the duke definitely fell into the category of odd.

"I know what you're looking for," the child recited. "Bring as much money as you can carry and meet me at the old church on the hill at two o'clock today. Come alone."

"Who gave you the message?" John asked, passing over the shilling.

The lad snatched it away and tucked it into his pocket. "Some bloke. Big fellow."

"You do not know his name?"

"No." The child grinned and ran away.

John went to find his wife and finally located her in the sewing room, reworking a bonnet. "You do realize that a duchess does not need to redo her bonnets? We can afford new."

"It comforts me." She wound a ribbon around the crown of the hat. "Is something wrong? You have that look in your eye."

"What look?"

"The one that tells me something has happened but you have not decided if you are going to confide in me or not."

"We have been married a matter of days, and already you think you can read my expressions?"

Her green eyes held a melancholy that tugged at him. "Since we do not know how much time we have, I have been paying particular attention."

The simple statement touched his heart. "God, Genny."

She shrugged and turned her attention back to her bonnet. "Whatever it is, just tell me, John. We can weather the storm together."

How was it he had found this extraordinary woman only when he might lose her again? "I just received a message from the thief who robbed Father Holm. He wants to meet me at the old church at two o'clock, told me to bring money. I believe he intends to sell the letter to me."

"I do not like it," Genny said. "What if it is some kind of trap? What if Raventhorpe is behind this?"

"He might well be, but what choice do we have? My instincts are telling me that this letter could clear my name. I have to find it, whatever the cost."

"What if the cost is your life? I am not ready to lose you, John." She set down the bonnet and all pretense of mending it. "I doubt I will ever be ready, no matter how close the inevitable looms."

"If I get this letter, and it proves my innocence, we will have our whole lives together."

"Not fair." She tried to smile, but he easily read the concern in her eyes. "You are going to do it, aren't you?"

"Yes. It might be our only hope."

"You should take someone with you. Samuel. Sir Harry. The admiral. They can watch your back."

"Perhaps." He frowned, then shook his head. "No, it is better if I handle this myself. I do not want to endanger anyone else, and it would take too long for them to get here."

"I do not like it, but all right." She nodded, then turned her attention to choosing the color of thread. "But you had better come back to me, John St. Giles."

"Always, my love." He kissed her, savoring the taste of love on her lips.

And wondering how much longer they had before Inspector Brooks hauled him off for his date with the hangman.

John left at half past one, heading for the old church on the back of his gelding. Genny watched him from the window in the drawing room, only turning away when he had disappeared around the bend in the road.

The passage of time haunted her. Only weeks ago, the

years had stretched before her, long and lonely. She had not believed she would ever marry, not after the foolish mistake she had made with Bradley. But then John had come along. He did not care about her past, only about her happiness. He had married her and saved her from having to confess her secret, from having to shame her family. The only downside to her marriage—her husband could be taken away at any time and hanged for murder.

Did this mysterious letter contain information that might clear his name? She wanted to believe it, but she was afraid to hope. What if she built up her expectations only to have them dashed? Better to err on the side of caution.

"Excuse me, Your Grace?" One of the maids came into the drawing room where Genny stood looking out at the empty drive.

"What is it, Martha?"

"Mrs. Hart wanted me to let you know that Lady Marianne seems to be playing her games again. Lady Felicity is in the nursery working on her lessons, but no one can find Lady Marianne."

Genny let out a long sigh. "That young lady will exhaust us all with her high spirits. Tell Mrs. Hart to stay with Lady Felicity in the nursery while I go check Lady Marianne's usual hiding spots."

"Yes, Your Grace."

Genny could tell that the maid had expected her to order the servants to search for Marianne, but she was fairly certain she knew where to find the mischievous child. Ever since John had taken over the title, little Marianne had gotten bolder and bolder in her waywardness. Genny had thought at first it was just her way of coming to terms with a new situation, but now she was beginning to suspect it was simply the child's natural temperament.

She searched the house first but found no sign of the little girl. Then she went outside to look in the garden. Marianne had a favorite place of all, a little alcove in the rose garden that boasted a fish pond. She stepped into the shrub-lined grotto, expecting the little scamp to be dangling her fingers in the water after the fish. And froze.

"Good afternoon, Your Grace," Lord Raventhorpe said. Marianne sat in the grass nearby, sucking on a stick of candy.

"Hello, Genny!" the little girl called, waving her treat in the air. "Look what Lord Raventhorpe brought me."

Genny took one slow step after the other, eyeing the earl as she would a wild boar. "Marianne, sweetheart, Mrs. Hart is looking for you."

The little girl scrunched her face into a scowl. "Do I have to go?"

"Yes."

"All right." Marianne got to her feet, then curtsied to Raventhorpe. "Thank you for the treat, Lord Raventhorpe."

"My pleasure." Raventhorpe watched Genny with a half smile on his face while Marianne trudged toward her. "It seems to me, *Your Grace,* that the child has better manners than her guardians. You have not even greeted me properly."

"My apologies. I am simply wondering what you are doing here." *And how you got on the property with no one seeing you. And what you were doing alone with Marianne.*

"Such a lovely child," the earl said. "You should treasure the young ones while they are about, for you never know when they will be gone forever."

She heard the threat, stiffened. "I cannot fathom why you did not come to the front door, Lord Raventhorpe."

"I saw this darling girl out here alone, and I knew you would want me to watch over her. After all, a child playing alone outside is subject to all sorts of danger." His cultured purr added a menace to the words that chilled her blood.

"Genny, are we going inside?" Marianne tugged at her skirt.

"I believe it is best if the child returns to the house alone, do you not agree, Your Grace?"

Genny opened her mouth to protest—then closed it

when Raventhorpe slid aside the edge of his coat so
she saw the blade nestled there. She met his gaze, that
unfeeling, pale blue stare, and knew with utter certainty
that he would kill Marianne without a blink of remorse
if he thought it would further his own ends.

"Go to the nursery, Marianne," she said. "You are
late for lessons."

"Come with me." Marianne grabbed her hand and
tugged.

"I will come along shortly." Genny held Raventhorpe's stare, as if she could control his actions with
the sheer power of her will. "You go on now."

"But—"

"Go, Marianne!"

The little girl's lower lip trembled. "I am going. But
I do not like you anymore." She stomped out of the
alcove.

"Well done, Your Grace." Raventhorpe stood, his
tall, deceptively slender form as graceful as a serpent.
"I could have killed her, you know."

"I know. What do you want?"

He laughed. "Right to the point, eh? Excellent." He
strolled over to her as casually as if they attended a
picnic on a lovely spring day. "Where is your husband,
Lady Evermayne? I saw him ride out."

"I do not know where he went."

"Now, now." He made a tsking sound as he stopped

before her. "I know the vicar is here, the one from Elford-by-the-Sea. And I know he has been combing the countryside looking for your husband for weeks now. Why?"

"I do not know."

He grabbed her arm, jerked her forward. "Do not lie to me!"

She knew she trembled, could not stop the physical response to fear. But she lifted her chin and met his gaze even as her knees weakened. This man could end her life with one swipe of that evil-looking blade, but he would not find it easy. She was an admiral's daughter, by God, and would not go down without a fight. "Threatening me will not make me more cooperative."

"Tell me where he went. What did the vicar give him? Or tell him?"

"The vicar did not give or tell him anything." At least that much she could say with truthfulness.

"So, the idiot may have indeed been successful." Raventhorpe glanced away and seemed to be speaking to himself.

Genny edged her foot backwards, hoping to put distance between them. But before she could move even an inch, he grabbed her arm and presented the length of cold steel to her throat.

"I have no compunction about killing you, my dear. But think, once you are gone, I will move on to His

Grace's adorable cousins. Your husband will come home to a bloodbath."

"No," she choked. She squeezed her eyes shut as if she could banish the grisly image of death the earl had conjured. Not the children. She had to protect the children.

"Where is he? Tell me!"

She had to lead Raventhorpe away from the house, away from the innocents. "He is meeting someone."

"Who?" He leaned in closer. "Where? And do not attempt to be clever, dear lady. If I suspect any sort of trickery, I will cut my losses and kill you, then return for those children." He bared his teeth in a terrible, stomach-jarring smile. "Perhaps I will take them away with me instead of ending their lives. I know some foreign gentlemen who would pay handsomely for such innocents."

Bile flared in her throat. "No. Leave them alone. I will tell you what I know."

"I am waiting."

She closed her eyes in a moment of prayer, hoping John forgave her for what she was about to do. But she had to keep the children safe. "He is meeting someone. I do not know who. But this person apparently stole something from the vicar yesterday and now has offered to sell it to John."

"What is it?" He twisted her arm in a painful grip.

"He did not say! Just to meet him at the old church at two o'clock. And bring money."

"Ah. So, he is trying to betray me, is he?" Raventhorpe laughed, a sound that made her skin crawl. "I had not thought dear Peter had the stones to even try it." He pursed his lips and considered her before turning and dragging her along behind him. "Come, Your Grace. Let's go find your husband."

John arrived at the old church, a ruined pile that had centuries ago been the family chapel at Evermayne. But a pretentious great-great-uncle had declared the little chapel too plain for a duke's use and had built the current church, a stone masterpiece with a spire reaching toward Heaven itself. The old chapel had been abandoned, left to fall apart under the ravages of the elements and the passage of time.

The four walls still stood, but the door had long rotted off the hinges. The roof had been destroyed by a storm long before John's birth, leaving the stone frame open to the whims of Heaven. Some of the stained-glass windows remained, but many had gotten broken or had panes stolen over the passing years.

John walked through the ruined doorway, braced for anything. Black Bill, Raventhorpe, a gang of thugs. But instead he saw only one man, his face half-covered by a scarf, holding a gun. He stopped. "Did you lure me here to kill me?" he asked.

"In a church? I don't want to go to Hell." The brigand snorted. "It's a precaution. There are thieves about, you know."

John arched his brows and pulled out his own revolver, pointing it at the brigand. "I know."

"What the devil!" The bigger man frowned. "I didn't think you'd bring a pistol, too!"

"You have one," John pointed out.

"Yes, but I'm . . . ah, never mind." The thief focused on John's bag. "Is that the money?"

"It is." John opened the bag and displayed the notes and coins inside. "What will this buy me?"

"This." The fellow pulled a letter from his pocket and waved it. "It says John St. Giles on the front. I know because the blacksmith read the name for me. And you're John St. Giles, right?"

"Yes, I am John St. Giles." He focused on the document that might save his life. "Did the blacksmith read the letter to you, by chance?"

"No. I don't care what's inside, just who might pay me the most to get it." He chuckled.

"I have a sack of money for you. What do you say we make an exchange? You leave the letter there on the pulpit, and I will leave the money here near the baptismal font. Then we both walk around the room—on opposite sides—until we switch places. Then you take the money, and I take the letter."

The thief frowned for a moment, clearly thinking. Then he nodded. "Good idea. And we've both got guns, so there won't be any tricks."

"No tricks," John agreed. "I will count to three—"

"Bugger that! I'll do the counting." The thief set the letter on the pulpit.

John put his bag on the floor, his gaze fixed on the letter. His heart hammered like a piston, anticipation firing his blood. Would this simple piece of paper prove to be the key to his freedom?

"One . . ."

He tensed.

"Two . . ."

He flexed his fingers, already imagining the look on Genny's face when he told her they had forever ahead of them.

"Three!" The thief moved to his right, circling the pews.

John headed down the center aisle, switching his gaze back and forth between his opponent and the pulpit where his future lay. He snatched up the letter just as the other man got to the bag of money.

"Well, now, look at this!" The thief hefted his fortune, his eyes crinkling with what was probably a smile beneath the scarf.

John waved the letter. "We each got what we wanted. What say you we go our separate ways?"

The thief chuckled. "I think I got the better bargain. You just got a letter. I got a whole bag of money." He crushed the bag against his chest with both arms.

A shot rang through the church. The thief's eyes widened, then he crashed forward to the floor, the money spilling from the bag.

"That is what happens to traitors." Raventhorpe stepped into the church, dragging Genny with him, a revolver in his other hand.

John's blood turned to ice. What was Genny doing here? How had Raventhorpe gotten to her?

Her wide, fear-filled gaze seemed to beg his forgiveness.

"What is this about, Raventhorpe?"

"Ah, John. My old rival." Raventhorpe strolled into the church, stepping over the fallen thief and dragging Genny in his wake. "It has been so long since we met face-to-face."

John slipped the letter into his pocket. "Not that long. How is that bullet wound, by the way? Sitting down all right?"

Raventhorpe stopped and glared at him. "I owe you for that and much more, John St. Giles. But no, it is Evermayne now, is it not? You always did have the devil's own luck." He held the revolver to Genny's temple. "Especially with women. First Elizabeth, then the lovely Genny."

"Elizabeth chose me as her husband, Raventhorpe. Just as she later chose you as her lover."

"Ah, yes. She was a wicked little thing. Found you too tame in the bedroom, my boy. Wanted a real man between her thighs." He eyed Genny. "Do you suppose your current bride feels the same?"

"Leave her be. Your quarrel is with me."

"Oh, were you under the impression you were in charge here?" Raventhorpe raised his brows. "I suppose that depends on how much you value your bride. Put down the weapon, John, and show me the letter Peter stole for you."

John held up the gun, keeping his eyes steady on his enemy, then bent and put it on the floor. He knew Raventhorpe would kill without conscience. Had he not learned that lesson when Elizabeth had been murdered? He had not been able to protect her then. Could he protect Genny now?

"Very good. Now show me the letter."

John kept his gaze on Genny as he pulled the letter from his pocket. She watched him steadily, hope and confidence shining in her eyes. Somehow, he would make this work. Somehow, both of them would walk away from this today.

Even if the cost was the proof of his innocence.

"Read it, John. Let us see if this scrap of paper was worth the steep price you paid . . . that you might yet pay."

John opened the letter with trembling fingers.

"Who is it from? Come now, Evermayne, do not dawdle." He leaned close to Genny and stage-whispered, "The suspense is thrilling, would you agree?"

She ignored the earl, brave girl, and kept her gaze steady on John as he began to read.

"Let it be known that this letter serves as the confession of Jack Norman, former footman to Lord Canthrope of London, in the matter of an incident on the twelfth of May, 1869, wherein Jack Norman admits to assisting under duress in the act of murder."

"Duress!" Raventhorpe exclaimed. "I did not hold a knife to the man's throat. He helped of his own free will."

"There is more," John said.

"Go on, then." Raventhorpe waved his gun hand.

"On the evening in question, I was persuaded by threat to the lives of my family to assist a certain gentleman, who shall remain nameless in this

confession, to lure away from the company one John St. Giles. My orders were to guide the young man into the garden under pretense of searching for his wife, at which time I was to render him unconscious by pricking his skin with a ring dipped in a drug, which had been provided to me by the unnamed gentleman. I obeyed these orders, to my everlasting shame, but did so only to save the life of my daughter.

"Let this letter serve as a statement that on the night Elizabeth St. Giles was murdered, her husband, John St. Giles, lay unconscious in the gardens at the Canthrope residence, incapable of doing harm to anyone, and that he was cast in that state by my hand. May God have mercy on my soul."

John's voice broke on the last line. He looked up at Raventhorpe's smug expression, at the tears shimmering in Genny's eyes.

"Jack Norman could not write nearly that well," Raventhorpe said. "He must have had the vicar write it for him. Pity that, as I will now have to eliminate him as well. At least old Jack was wise enough not to name the gentleman who enticed him to such wickedness. Now—" Raventhorpe smiled, and John tensed.

The bastard looked entirely too pleased with himself. "Set the letter back on the pulpit, John, and walk away, or else your wife dies."

"No, John!" Genny surged forward, only to be yanked back by Raventhorpe. "Do not do it. It is your only proof!"

John took a step forward. "What is to prevent you from killing her as soon as I give over the letter?"

"What is to prevent me from killing her right now?" Raventhorpe yanked her closer and pressed the gun harder against her head. "That letter does not implicate me, John. Nowhere does it say I killed Elizabeth."

"Then why do you want it?" Genny cried. "It cannot hurt you."

"No, but its absence can hurt your husband." Raventhorpe switched his reptilian stare to John. "I did not go through all that trouble to make you look guilty just so some fool with a conscience can undo everything."

"John, do not do it," Genny begged. "He will never go away. He will haunt us just like he did Annabelle. Remember what you taught Annabelle to protect herself?" She stared hard at him as if willing him to read her mind. Then she flicked her gaze at the ground and back up at him, clearly trying to communicate something. "Now I am just like Annabelle, John, and must do as she did."

He realized what she was suggesting and gave an imperceptible shake of his head. He would not risk her life on some mad gambit.

She pressed her lips together, clearly frustrated with him.

"Enough of this nonsense. Put the letter back on the pulpit, John, then walk away."

"Let Genny go first."

Raventhorpe laughed. "Do you think you have some power here? I hold all the cards. You will do as I say."

John gazed at Genny, at a love he had never thought he would ever possess, and knew he would do anything to keep her alive. Even if it meant sacrificing his own life to do so. "Very well, Raventhorpe." He started walking back toward the pulpit.

"John!" Genny's shriek ripped through the church.

John dropped to the floor as a bullet whizzed by his head and struck the wooden pulpit. Raventhorpe stood with his weapon still aimed, having clearly tried to shoot John in the back. Rage twisted the earl's features, and he turned the gun on Genny.

She looked at John, gave him a hint of a nod, then went limp in Raventhorpe's grasp, just as John had taught Annabelle to do.

The earl stumbled, his gun hand flying off target as he was dragged off-balance by Genny's dead weight.

John dove for the weapon he had set on the floor,

grabbed it, and rolled onto his side, then aimed at the earl. Fired.

Raventhorpe cried out. His gun fell to the ground, and he cradled his bleeding arm.

Genny grabbed the gun, sat back against the side of the pew, and aimed it at Raventhorpe. "Stay where you are. I would remind you I am an admiral's daughter, and I do know how to shoot."

Raventhorpe's lips peeled back from his teeth. "Why you little—" He lunged for Genny. A shot rang through the church. The earl howled and went down, grabbing his thigh. Genny scrabbled out of his reach.

John raced forward as Inspector Brooks emerged from behind the baptismal font and hurried toward the fallen earl, gun drawn. "Stay right there, Raventhorpe," the inspector said.

"Inspector, where did you come from?" John asked.

"I have been following you," the man said. "I thought you were a murderer, remember."

"Thank goodness you are here," Genny said.

The inspector flashed a smile. "I was here when His Lordship shot that poor fellow. Cold-blooded murder, that's what it was. I saw the whole thing. And I heard the entire conversation—including the letter from the witness clearing you of murdering your wife."

"So John is free?" Genny asked as John helped her to her feet.

"He will have to give statements and present the letter as evidence," Brooks said. "But in the end, yes, he will go free."

She looked up at John, her eyes shining. "Free," she whispered.

"Free," he echoed, and pressed a soft kiss to her lips. "You are a madwoman to be taking such chances with your safety. I would not have been able to go on if I lost you." His voice broke at the end, betraying the stark fear that had turned his insides to jelly.

"I could not simply stand there and let him destroy your chance to clear your name." She laid her head against his chest. "I would do anything to save you, John."

"And I you," he murmured.

Inspector Brooks cleared his throat. "My apologies for interrupting, but Your Grace, would you please hold your pistol on the earl while I get the handcuffs on him?"

"I will do it," Genny said. She pointed the gun she still held at Raventhorpe. "I would remind you again, Lord Raventhorpe, that I am an excellent shot."

"I forget nothing," Raventhorpe snarled.

"I will find something to staunch that bleeding," John said, nodding at the earl's injuries while the inspector bound his hands in the cuffs. "I would not want you to expire before you stand trial, Raventhorpe."

As John walked away, the inspector called out, "Don't forget the letter, Your Grace," and pointed at the document, which lay near the pulpit where John had dropped it during the excitement.

John picked up the letter, turned it over in his hand. So strange to think that something so small could have such importance in his life. He turned, looked at Genny fiercely holding Raventhorpe in her sights.

Then again, maybe not so strange after all.

Chapter 22

G enny lay in her husband's arms, drawing circles in the fur of his chest. Through the curtains she could see the rosy glow of dawn over the garden. They had not slept; they had spent the entire night making love, as if they needed to forge their bond over and over again after nearly losing everything that day.

"Do you think we will be safe?' Genny asked.

John made a gruntlike sound, and she realized he had been dozing. "What?"

She propped herself up with her elbow on his chest and waited until he opened his eyes. "Do you think we will be safe now that Raventhorpe has finally been arrested?"

"I warned Brooks not to turn his back on him." John yawned and stroked his hand over Genny's unbound hair. "As long as he is on his guard, all should be well. But the bastard has always been slippery."

She slapped him lightly on the chest. "There is a lady present, Your Rudeness."

"Really?" He fondled her bottom. "Hmmm, so there is."

"You, sir, are insatiable." She kissed him, lingering as his hand stroked over her buttock and up her back. "Seriously, John, should we worry?"

"About Raventhorpe? Just keep our guards up." He curled his arm around her, pulled her closer. "I lived half my life hiding and worrying about being discovered, my love. I do not want to live that way any longer. We will be vigilant, but I will not live in fear. Not anymore."

"I do not want to live in fear either. But I might have lost you tonight—would have surely lost you if that letter had not come to light. I want to live joyfully."

"That is exactly what you should do." He dragged her more fully on top of him, then smoothed his hands along her back. "I always felt that I should have been able to protect Elizabeth from Raventhorpe. But I could not, and she died. From that point forward, I made it a policy not to let anyone else get close enough to me to put me in that position again. I was a bad bet. And then I met you."

"What did I do?"

"My little warrior. You bullied your way into my heart, slipped right beneath my defenses when I wasn't looking. You taught me what real love is, and how the more you have, the more you have to lose."

She wrinkled her nose. "That does not sound very pleasant."

"You also taught me that there are people in this world who will support others no matter what the cost. You could not know your father would approve of our marriage when you stood up at the breakfast table and threw your lot in with mine. Yet you did it anyway."

"Since meeting you, I have been inspired to do all manner of improper things."

"Oh?" He waggled his eyebrows.

She slapped him on the chest. "I was not talking about *that*."

"Why not? I thought you liked *that*."

"I do. I just meant . . . You make me less afraid. Bolder."

"I like bold."

"I know you do." She frowned, struggling to put the feelings into words. "You make me brave and happy. I feel as if I can do anything as long as you are by my side."

"You know what, my darling Duchess? I feel exactly the same way." John lifted her hand to his lips and kissed her fingers. "And suddenly I have an urge to see how improper we can be . . ."

"John!"

She laughed as he rolled over with her, starting the day—and the rest of their lives—with love and laughter and a sense of coming home.

For both of them.